MISFITS, GEMSTONES, and other SHATTERED MAGIC

Library and Archives Canada
Doidge, Meghan Ciana, 1973—
Champagne, Misfits, and Other Shady Magic/
Meghan Ciana Doidge—PAPERBACK EDITION

Cover design by: Elizabeth Mackey

ISBN 978-1-927850-77-0

— Dowser 8 —

MISFITS, GEMSTONES, and other SHATTERED MAGIC

Meghan Ciana Doidge

Published by Old Man in the CrossWalk Productions
Salt Spring Island, BC, Canada

www.madebymeghan.ca

Author's Note:

Misfits, Gemstones, and Other Shattered Magic is the eighth book in the Dowser series, which is set in the same universe as the Oracle and Reconstructionist series.

While it is not necessary to read all three series, *in order to avoid spoilers* the ideal reading order is as follows:

Other books in the Dowser series to follow.

More information can be found at
www.madebymeghan.ca/novels

For Michael
Misfits. Together. Forever.

*T*wo more elves were at large in Vancouver, but thankfully they'd been keeping a low profile while I faced the most daunting task of my twenty-seven years—planning and executing my wedding. I was dealing with a disgruntled grandmother with an extensive guest wish list of the magically inclined, all of whom didn't particularly like each other. Plus a fiancé whose concept of time was altered whenever he stepped into a dimensional pocket, and a best friend who'd spent months planning what was certain to be an insane bachelorette party. How was I supposed to find time to worry about possible invasions, or the motley crew of magical misfits who had unrepentantly upended my peaceful existence?

Not that I was complaining.

Who didn't love wielding deadly weapons, opening a bakery, and marrying their soul mate in the same week? Or was that just my sort of thing?

Chapter One

An elf stood at the door to my bakery. Well, actually, it was Bryn's and my bakery, but still ... an elf.

In Whistler.

I mean, I expected this sort of thing in Vancouver. But if you weren't into outdoor sports involving snow, then Whistler was a pricey destination in the winter months. Plus, the village and the municipality around it were both seriously lacking in the magical department.

Or at least they had been.

In less than an hour, I was hosting a grand opening for Cake in a Cup Too. And I was pretty damn magical. Also, still not much of a wordsmith when it came to naming things. Plus Bryn, not being magically inclined herself, had unwittingly staffed the bakery with at least one skinwalker—Maia Thomas, an Adept who could cloak herself in the form of a chosen animal. In her case, a raven. And just for good measure, I'd dragged a telepath along to help pass out free mini-cupcakes to potential customers.

The elf caught my eye and smiled.

Smiled.

And despite the rows of sharp, shark-like teeth she displayed, I briefly believed she was genuinely pleased to see me. A dense crowd of shoppers and skiers crossed back and forth through the retail square behind her—all of whom were nonmagicals. I could tell that with utter certainty because the new bakery wasn't warded. Unfortunately, despite the lack of shielding magic between us, I also couldn't taste any power from the elf. That was unnerving.

Her long hair, pale to the point of being practically white, flowed gracefully over her shoulders and halfway down her back. Simple braids twisted back from her temples, exposing ears that were indeed slightly pointed. As with vampires and werewolves, the fantastical depictions of elves in nonmagical culture were obviously rooted to some degree in the truth, perhaps from the earliest encounters between Adepts and humans.

This particular elf had a pale, iridescent complexion with a subtle green undertone. If I'd been closer, I knew that iridescence would have revealed itself as finely scaled skin that was currently picking up light reflected from the bakery's floor-to-ceiling front windows. The elf was easily six feet tall, wearing the cutest baby-blue puffy winter jacket and skinny-legged jeans tucked into calf-hugging polished black boots. She had the same sharp features as the warrior I'd faced in a park in Vancouver three months before. But with her significantly smaller frame—that first elf had been even taller than Warner—she came off as delicate. More feminine, somehow.

Based on my limited experience and the few ancient tomes detailing historic clashes with elves that I'd read since the previous September, I had the distinct feeling that regardless of how graceful, even elegant, she appeared, the elf likely packed a punch. Thankfully, the same went for me. Though standing five foot nine inches and endowed with ample assets, 'delicate' or 'elegant' weren't adjectives that had ever been applied to me.

The elf also had a massive gemstone embedded in her forehead. The gem was a slightly darker tint of her skin tone and appeared to be surrounded by a simple raised design that followed the edges of the stone.

It bothered me that with nothing but twenty feet and some triple-paned glass between us, I couldn't taste her magic. Because that was my thing, my advantage. The thing I was supposed to do better than anyone else. The thing that made me special, made me THE DOWSER in all caps.

Elves, it seemed, were very skilled at masking their power. Either that or I wasn't particularly attuned to their magic because they came from another dimension. But since the elf standing just beyond the bakery door was only the second one I'd ever encountered, I didn't have enough experience to draw a conclusion either way. Still, it was better all around for the very vulnerable humans meandering through the center of Whistler Village that she wasn't doing anything that would have allowed me to taste her power.

Speaking of magic, Peggy Talbot paused a few steps beyond the door that led back into the kitchen, just on the edge of my peripheral vision. The willowy blond was dressed similarly to me in jeans, a brown Cake in a Cup T-shirt, and a white ruffled apron. She was also carrying a large tray of mini *Chill in a Cup*—mint-chocolate cake with mint-chocolate buttercream. The telepath had frozen at the sight of the elf. Her blackberry-jam-infused power swirled around her.

Well, it was always good to know I wasn't seeing things.

The elf's green-eyed gaze flicked to Peggy, then returned to me. Her smile became challenging. Then she beckoned. Her slim fingers were tipped with thick nails that were only slightly too short to be called claws. The gesture was meant to be enticing, but I wasn't that easily fooled. Too many big bad monsters with sharp teeth had a habit of seeing me as a little snack that would tide them over on their way to taking over the universe.

Yeah, I wasn't feeling at all dramatic.

I tugged at the ties to my apron—which was white with chocolate-colored printing, rather than the pink I'd used to brand the Vancouver bakery. I placed it on the counter, then stepped around the glass display case.

Outside, the elf melted back into the crowd. Possibly literally, because I lost sight of her almost at once. Whistler Village on a Saturday morning in December was seriously thronged with people pre- and post-ski, but still.

"Jade?" Peggy set her tray down next to four others on the white granite counter that backed the display case. I had just finished stocking the domed case with cupcakes, but I didn't glance back to admire all the tidily arranged prettiness.

"Stay here," I said, stepping around the deep-brown plush chairs and the low, white-topped tables scattered across the bakery storefront.

Pausing at the glass door to scan the crowd outside, I glanced right, catching sight of Bryn rearranging the large seating area in front of a sleek gas fireplace that ran the length of the far wall. My dark-haired co-owner paused to artfully throw a native-inspired printed wool blanket across a low-backed couch. Then she retrieved it and tossed it again. Nervous, repetitive, soothing behavior. Bryn had sunk all her savings and then some into the new bakery. She was so deep into the zone that I knew she wouldn't even notice me stepping out, as long as I was back before opening.

I unlocked and pushed open the heavy glass door, stepping outside. Smiling cheerfully in response to drawing the interested glances of nearby pedestrians, I made a show of glancing at, then tapping, my bare wrist. "Forty-five minutes! And we're giving away mini-cupcakes and chocolate shots for as long as supplies last!"

A few people murmured agreeably, glancing up at the hand-carved bakery sign above my head. Bryn and I had decided to leave the windows bare of logos, making it appear as if there were no barrier between exhausted skiers, snowboarders, hikers, and Whistler residents seeking the comfort of cupcakes.

Similar to the setup of the original Cake in a Cup in Vancouver, apartments occupied the two upper floors of the cedar-sided, blue-metal-roofed building in which the bakery was housed, along with a bath shop and a clothing store. Specifically, six two-bedroom apartments—one for Bryn and five for crazily expensive short-term rentals. The entire village was filled with similar-sized mixed retail and residential buildings, then edged by million-dollar mountain chalets. The immediate area was considered ski-in and ski-out, hence the price tag.

I scanned the winter-clad, fleece-and-knit-swathed crowd with my eyes and my dowser senses. Unfortunately, I didn't taste even a hint of unfamiliar magic in the immediate vicinity. I was beginning to regret that I'd had to murder the only other elf I'd ever met before I could truly taste his power.

Peggy appeared beside me, pressing my green ski jacket against my arm while awkwardly tugging a rainbow-striped toque with a bright-pink fake-fur pom-pom over her light-blond head.

"What did I say?" I asked without taking my attention from the crowd. Though I accepted the jacket. I was wearing only a T-shirt, jeans, and sneakers, and it was actually cold, even for me.

"Get my coat," Peggy said perkily. "Tell Bryn we're going to go spread word for the opening. Then follow me outside to look for the elf."

I sighed. "I didn't even think anything like that at all."

Peggy laughed quietly as she mimicked my scan of the crowd.

I had hired the telepath and her twin, Gabby, to work at the bakery two and a half months before. I'd needed new staff with Bryn relocating, and had deemed it easier to keep tabs on the Talbot sisters if I saw them practically every day. I had forced them to work mostly opposite shifts, though, discovering early on that they were incapable of getting anything done while together.

Gabby had taken a liking to baking and was proving to be a quick learner, which was good—because she wasn't particularly delightful with customers. That was Peggy's forte. Hence, the decision to bring her with me to Whistler to help Bryn with the grand opening. Todd, Tima, and Gabby would handle the Saturday rush in Vancouver, and I had put up a notice over a month before informing customers that the bakery would be closed on the following Sunday and Monday.

Peggy tugged on arm warmers—also rainbow-striped, but with rows of hearts—that I guessed were a gift from Mory. The young necromancer knit practically every waking moment, to the extent where she couldn't possibly wear everything she made. The telepath lifted her hand, her jaw resolutely set as she pointed to our right.

"You can hear her thoughts?" I asked, already stepping in the direction she'd indicated.

"Nope." She followed at my heels. "But there's a weird feedback coming from that direction."

Feedback.

Delightful.

Preceded by her huckleberry-and-wild-onion magic, Maia Thomas—Cake in a Cup Too's second full-time employee—jogged up behind us, keeping pace with Peggy without a word.

I glanced back, giving the dark-haired skinwalker one of my best narrow-eyed glares. My disapproval slid off her like softened butter on Teflon.

Great. I was following a dimensional inter-loper—who might just be able to manifest knives out of thin air or snap a dragon's neck—with two young Adepts at my back. I could freak out and fret. But unless I actually locked them up somewhere, and possibly lost the elf's trail in the process, I knew I wouldn't be able to stop them from wading in.

Welcome to my life.

"Stay behind me," I said, brushing shoulders with various winter-weather-clad pedestrians as I negotiated the crowd.

The cobblestones underneath my feet were mostly bare of snow, thanks to diligent village maintenance crews, but the mountains soaring above the village were covered with fresh powder. It was currently snowing, but so lightly that the icy crystals were almost mist.

Warner, Kett, and Drake were skiing some crazy-high trails that had required them to be out of the apartment at five A.M., then flown to the mountaintop in a helicopter. Audrey, the beta of the West Coast North American Pack, and Lara, a pack enforcer, were skiing black-diamond runs on Blackcomb with Kandy. The werewolves had flown in from Portland for my pend-ing shower, bachelorette party, and wedding—if the elf

I was following didn't have other nefarious plans for me. Jasmine was doing something tech-related in the apartment she and Kett had rented above the bakery. Or maybe she was gaming. Whatever it was took two laptops and a tablet. Although she could tolerate being outside by day, the newly turned vampire still preferred to stay out of the sun.

Yep, everyone else was playing while I was getting ready for the grand opening of Cake in a Cup Too. And I wouldn't have had it any other way. Especially since the vampires were the only ones who I trusted around cupcakes. What with them only needing blood for sustenance.

An elf following me to Whistler was an added and unexpected complication.

Over the previous three months, we hadn't heard a peep from whoever had occupied the other two prison cells that had been unexpectedly discovered hidden along the shoreline of Kits Beach. Warner and Kandy had expected immediate attacks—or even an attempt by the elves to claim the entire territory. And I couldn't blame them for that strong a reaction, given that the one elf we'd faced had made a serious attempt to murder them both. But it had been so quiet since that attack that I'd begun to think the elves had simply moved on. Or, based on this sudden reappearance, perhaps they'd simply retreated an hour and a half north into the mountains.

And yeah, I was still waiting on the meeting I'd demanded with Pulou, who had apparently stashed powerful beings—not just magical treasure—in hidden caves in the Vancouver shoreline. Despite the fact that he'd previously summoned me himself—and sure, I had pretty much told him to screw off—the treasure keeper had ignored every request I'd sent him through Blossom. Our mutual disdain was possibly about to bite me in the ass. Because all the things I didn't know about the elf that I was presently attempting to track with two fledglings at my heels was ... well, pretty much everything.

At the corner of the building, I picked up the first hints of the elf's magic. Conveniently, this drew me away from the main thoroughfare. Well, it was convenient for me. I knew that even with the two teenagers tagging along, an elf wasn't going to get the upper hand over me easily. But she could quite easily force me to expose the magical universe to the fine residents of Whistler. And even I wasn't going to get away with that level of transgression.

Maia was gazing overhead. I followed her eyeline to a crow perched on an upper balcony, overlooking a narrow lane to my immediate right. The crow dipped its beak and shuffled along the railing, peering down at the lane.

"Can the crow see the elf?" I asked Maia.

The teenage skinwalker sneered. "What? You think I can talk to crows? Because I'm First Nations, I must commune with animals?"

Well ... it wasn't a completely stupid assumption, was it? I laid on an equal amount of snark myself. "I was thinking it might be a secondary ability. What with your changing into a raven and all."

Peggy stifled a giggle.

Maia scowled. Then she begrudgingly said, "Yes. Something shiny wanders this way."

Laughing under my breath, I stepped into the narrow lane that cut between the buildings. The cobblestone alley led to the road that ran out of the village proper and onto the highway. It was just wide enough for a couple of ATVs to get through. Actual vehicles didn't drive through the pedestrian-only retail section of Whistler Village except in emergencies.

Halfway down the lane, magic rippled around me. It tasted of an evergreen forest after a rainstorm...and something else I couldn't immediately identify.

One moment, I was walking on cobblestones, with snow packed against the walls of the buildings to either side. The next, I was standing in an atrium with soaring, vaulted ceilings—and that churned with magic. I'd never seen anything like it, except maybe for renderings of grand cathedrals or glass castles in fantasy movies.

I might have been a little too hasty with that 'not easily gaining the upper hand' boast. I really had to learn to keep my mouth shut, even in my own head.

Peggy gasped, pressing a shaking hand to her temple. She looked pained, as if she'd just been stabbed in the head. "Something is wrong," she murmured, peering around. Her eyes were narrowed in discomfort, as if the muted daylight was suddenly too bright.

"What gave it away?" Maia asked snarkily. "The purple water?" The skinwalker jabbed her finger toward a stream that now appeared to be twisting along the edge of a black stone path. The purple-tinted creek wove through strange plants and trees, leading us forward.

"Water? Where?" Peggy wrapped her hand around my elbow. Her sweet blackberry-imbued magic slipped through my personal shields with the physical contact. "Oh! Pretty!"

I sighed. Apparently, the telepath could use me as some sort of seeing-eye dog. "Did you ask permission to touch me? To use your power on me?" I side-eyed Peggy, who was even cheekier about Adept etiquette than I was. I really had no idea how her adoptive mother, Angelica, kept her brood from getting slaughtered by easily offended Adepts on an ongoing basis.

Oh, right. She'd moved them all to Vancouver. A problem shared was now annoyingly my problem.

Peggy widened her sky-blue eyes, then blinked at me with feigned regret. Apparently, I also shielded her from whatever had caused her instant headache.

I shook my head. "If I have to move quickly, you're going to get hurt."

"I'll let go."

Stifling yet another sigh, I slowly traversed the path that had been apparently laid out just for us. I could still feel the cobblestones under my sneakered feet and the cold morning air on my exposed neck, rather than the warmth that visually radiated from all around us. So apparently I was walking through some sort of illusion. And since Peggy was also a truth seeker, which I loosely understood to be some sort of human lie detector, the fact that she'd felt the change but didn't see the illusion until she touched me made sense.

"No birds," Maia murmured, scanning left to right in a way that seemed to mimic the raven form she could wear. "Or animals."

"I think we're indoors," I said. "Or at least we're meant to believe we are."

I rounded a tree, or maybe it was a really large bush, whose red-veined blue flowers dripped with what looked like malicious magic. "Don't touch anything," I belatedly murmured to my young companions. I still wasn't accustomed to being the babysitter. You know, what with my own childish tendencies. Which included grabbing anything magical within my reach.

The atrium opened up before us to a wide area covered in opalescent black tile, easily large enough for a hundred elves to congregate. The purple stream dropped into a pool near the far side. A dais topped by a single chair rose beyond that short waterfall. Actually, it was a massive throne—and along with the dais itself, it was carved out of some metal that shone with foreign magic.

I slowed, reaching back and physically tucking my two companions tightly behind me. They complied without protest. Seriously, I was just in town to open a damn bakery. So I didn't need an elder of the local First Nation band and the rest of the itchy-trigger-fingered Talbots gunning for me because I'd led their kids into an elf slaughter.

I didn't call forth my knife, which was strapped as always in its invisible sheath on my right hip. All my instincts told me I should. But I actually wasn't certain what sort of tableau we were creating outside the illusion. Would a nonmagical passerby see us standing huddled together in the narrow lane, gazing off into the distance? If so, then waving my blade around like a maniac would really put a dampener on the grand opening to come.

"I know this game," I said, cutting through the bullshit with snark instead of my knife. "I haven't played it. But I get the gist. I'm supposed to ask who sits on the throne."

I glanced around, searching for the elf who'd drawn me out of the cozy interior of the bakery. Waiting for an answer, I scanned the overflowing greenery along the edges of the atrium, seeing nothing other than layers and layers of magic. And Maia was right—I couldn't hear anything natural within the space either. I should at least be able to hear the waterfall. So the illusion somehow blocked out the sound of the busy marketplace behind me, but it didn't come with its own audio. Either that or the elf wielding the illusion magic wasn't strong enough to completely enthrall me. Or she was limiting the display to give me a false impression.

There were too many unknowns. And I wasn't particularly interested in games where someone pretended to be something they weren't just to secure my attention ... or to distract me.

Though I couldn't hear anything within the vision created for me by the elf I'd followed out into the cold, I could feel that I was surrounded by her magic. Her particular power was apparently different than the magic the elf in the park had wielded. Either that or he hadn't bothered showing off—thinking I was easy prey, perhaps.

Feeling the teenagers behind me becoming restless, I wrapped my hand around the hilt of my knife. Someone was going to have to teach Peggy and Maia to be patient hunters. Sadly, I was concerned that that person was supposed to be me, and I was honestly getting bored myself.

I broke the weird silence again. "The thing is, I'm a little busy, and using magic on an Adept without permission is seriously frowned upon in this dimension. So this is strike one for you."

"Ahead to our right ..." Peggy whispered. "You have someone's attention. I can feel the weight of it."

Using the telepath's direction as a focus, I tracked the eddies of magic running up and around the atrium's arcing walls and vaulted ceiling, sensing a possible source about twenty feet ahead and slightly to our right. Still keenly aware of the scene I was possibly putting on for pedestrians who weren't caught up in the illusion magic, I gathered the power simmering underneath my feet, coaxing it upward to curl around my left hand. I kept my right hand still loose around the hilt of my knife, just in case I was about to instigate an attack.

When I'd drawn enough of the elf's power firmly into my grasp, I tore the energy free, ripping through the illusion with strength and will, no blade necessary.

A massive tear appeared, slicing across the black-rock path and the purple river to expose the cobblestones underneath. Through the rupture, I could once again see the cedar-shingled buildings that sided the narrow lane, and the tidy piles of snow edging their concrete foundations.

Maia gasped.

Peggy giggled, quietly delighted.

I allowed the effervescent magic—now tasting of bark and moss—that I'd ripped from the illusionist to collect in my knife. Storing it rather than absorbing it fully. Then I reached for another handful.

The illusion collapsed before I could touch it again.

The elf was standing at the spot where I'd sensed her magic, and the lane around her was otherwise thankfully empty. She was supporting herself with one hand propped against the corner of a building sided in naturally weathered cedar shingles. Though she appeared winded, possibly hurt, she locked her fierce gaze to mine.

"In this dimension, we introduce ourselves before attacking each other," I said. "It's just polite."

She curled her lip in a snarl.

"You were trying to be friendly, yes?" I asked mockingly. "What with the smiling and beckoning?"

The elf pushed herself away from the wall, her gaze flicking to Peggy, then to Maia, both of whom were peering around my shoulders. "Perhaps you should see to your young, witchling." Her accent was an echo of Pulou's British lilt, similar to the elf in the park but less labored. Perhaps she'd spent the last three months in ESL classes. "We shall play another day."

"I'm not interested in—"

The illusionist elf spun away, running with swift, light-footed strides.

Apparently she wasn't a fan of banter.

I followed, jogging as I assessed her path but not breaking into a full run.

She darted across the main road, Whistler Way, zigzagging through the slow-crawling traffic. Leaping onto the sidewalk on the other side, she nearly slipped on a patch of ice. Then, somehow, she stepped into the crowd at the crosswalk and disappeared.

Another illusion.

I paused at the edge of the road, hoping to catch sight of the elf before I crossed it. Just in case she was doubling back and around.

Peggy and Maia slammed against me, realizing too late that I'd stopped. Their slow reaction time reminded me that I wasn't backed by my usual companions—powerful, quick-healing Adepts who'd been severely injured the last time we'd tangled with an elf. I occasionally caught Kandy rubbing her ribs as if they still ached from the warrior elf's blades. And while the fledglings seemed fully prepared to follow me into whatever skirmish awaited us if we caught up to the illusionist elf, their magic practically sparking off them, neither of them wielded any offensive power. At least not any honed magic useful in a toe-to-toe tussle.

And still, I'd been completely ready to abandon my responsibilities and drag Peggy and Maia into danger.

The elf certainly had my number.

Maybe that was what the glittery display of magic was about. Enticement—and of me specifically, because with my companions off skiing, she'd thought I was alone. So exactly how closely had she been watching me? And for how long? I wondered whether she'd followed me to Whistler.

All without me picking up any hint of her magic.

Because that was troubling. And seriously irksome.

"We have a bakery to open," I murmured, calling myself back to the present and to the teenagers shuffling their feet behind me.

But before I turned back to the bakery, I ran my fingers along the hilt of my knife, stirring up the magic I'd stored within the blade. At a minimum, the elf's power was capable of making me think I was seeing things—and at its worst, she was invading my mind without me feeling it. So, tasting the magic I'd torn from her, I allowed the knife to absorb it completely. She wouldn't be able to trick me again so effortlessly.

The fledglings at my back were another story, though.

And, silly me, I'd deemed it overkill to install wards on the new bakery.

"Why show us that?" Peggy asked. "That room?"

I didn't have an answer for her. But I did have an idea that it had something to do with whoever sat on that throne. Someone who liked having the buffer of the purple pool between them and their subjects. Their followers? Citizens? I really wasn't a fan of anyone who thought they deserved to sit on a throne carved out of magical metal. And yeah, I understood how totally judgemental that was.

"It was a test," Maia said.

"Maybe," I murmured, turning back to the bakery and drawing her and Peggy with me. "That's what it felt like."

A test. To see what I would do. How I would react. But had it been a test of my power? Of my willingness to engage? Or—much more potentially foreboding—had it been a warning? Because though I had no concrete evidence either way, I felt pretty certain that the illusionist elf wasn't the person who sat on that throne. Because if that was the case, why wouldn't she have revealed herself perched there?

So was she attempting to intimidate me...or was she trying to help me?

"If the elf comes around when I'm not here, I don't want to be rescuing you after the fact." I looked pointedly at each of the teenagers in turn. "You got it?"

"Sure, Jade," Peggy said.

Maia snorted. "Like I'd be that stupid."

Right. Maybe it was just me who dashed out into the street to follow beguiling magic whichever way it led.

Maia picked up the pace, sprinting as the bakery came into view. Peggy was at her heels. The sight was so carefree that I had to smile. They had just faced off against an elf—a mythical creature from another dimension—and hadn't batted an eyelash.

Me? I churned the scene over and over in my head and fretted. Because they didn't know how quickly pretty magic could lead to bloodletting, neck snapping, and utter despair.

Bryn opened the bakery door, peering around and looking a bit panicked. But she smiled as Maia and Peggy barreled by her, already stripping off their outerwear as they tumbled into the storefront.

"Ready, Jade?"

I returned Bryn's smile. "As ready as I ever am."

At least I had new cupcakes and hot chocolate waiting for me. Elf or no elf, that was something to relish.

Chapter Two

A broad-shouldered dragon with dark-blond hair filled the doorway, blocking out the final rays of the cloud-filtered afternoon sun. The gold of his magic glinted across his blue-green eyes as he caught my gaze while reaching for the door handle. And even though we'd been apart for less than twelve hours, my heart hitched.

Warner.

Mine.

Well, in less than a week he'd officially belong to me. And yeah, I knew that idea was a little inappropriate. But I wanted to claim him. To pronounce that he was mine to have and to hold, to cherish. And not because I thought marriage was the most epic thing I would ever do in my life, but because it was a massive declaration of my choice, my desire. Of how I wanted my life to be. Or at least those parts of my life I could control.

My husband-to-be was accompanied by Kett and Drake. All three were decked out in ski gear—jackets in various shades of blue and gray, ski pants, and boots. They would have left their skis locked up on one of the racks strategically placed all over the village.

I passed a tray of mini-cupcakes to Peggy. Early afternoon sales had slowed as skiers returned to the mountain for the last runs of the day, so I'd had a chance to slip back into the kitchen and bake another round of minis. We would give those away for the rush I anticipated after the hills closed for the day.

Making sure my hair wasn't a complete mess, I stepped around Maia, who was helping a customer navigate the often overwhelming array of cupcakes the bakery sold. I always made sure to group selections by cake bases, and for new customers, I usually just pointed out the swath of chocolate occupying the center of the display case to get them started. Maia had been utilizing this technique all day with great success.

Warner opened the door, allowing a gust of freezing air into the storefront. We had invested in a heat lamp that would counter the chill at the exterior door, but hadn't managed to get an electrician to install it yet. Thankfully, I couldn't sense the cold at all over the tantalizing taste of his delectable black-forest-cake magic.

Drake shouldered past my fiancé before he even had one ski boot on the large rubber mat set into the slate-tiled floor. In the summer, Bryn would replace the mat with something pretty and not so necessarily waterproof.

"I fell off a cliff!" the dark-haired fledgling guardian crowed as he barreled toward me, seemingly anxious to tell the tale of how he'd conquered skiing the face of the mountain. Almost as tall as Warner now, and just a month shy of his eighteenth birthday, Drake was sporting a wickedly puffy black eye. I knew it must have been the remnant of a much more severe wound, simply by how it hadn't fully healed in the time it took for the three of them to ski down the mountain and walk to the bakery. Unless Drake had actually tumbled all the way down.

Warner and Kett stepped into the storefront, casting their respective gazes around the seating area. Warner was likely looking for troublemakers, and Kett might possibly have been looking for Jasmine, who he practically kept locked in her room when he couldn't be around. Okay, that was an exaggeration. The newly turned, golden-haired vampire seemed more than content to be left to her own devices. Literally. Devices, as in laptops, tablets, phones...yeah, I was hilarious with the wordplay.

Drake veered abruptly right, completely distracted by a telepath with a tray of mini-cupcakes. Peggy meeped as the fledgling guardian appeared before her. He was already examining the cupcakes with the attention scholars usually reserved for one-of-a-kind ancient texts.

Drake looked Peggy straight in the eye, hitting her with a massive grin. "Tell me the tale of the delectable treats you carry with such grace, oh telepath."

Peggy opened her mouth as if to answer. But instead, she just sighed and appeared to melt before the onslaught of...well, Drake. And everything that came with him—power, intensity, strength, vigor. To be fair, to anyone with a thing for almost-eighteen-year-olds, Drake was intriguingly, if boyishly, handsome. Tall, dark-haired, and dark-eyed, with gloriously long lashes.

"Chocolate?" Drake prompted, pointing at the array of *Chill in a Cup*. "And?" He pointed at the *Tingle in a Cup*.

Peggy nodded as if she would have loved to answer but had no idea how to speak English. A blush flushed her cheeks.

Drake tilted his head at her questioningly. Then, as if he'd sussed out her game, he grinned conspiratorially. "Would you like to whisper the answer in my mind?"

"No!" Peggy blurted. Then she glanced around as her blush deepened.

I met Warner's disgruntled gaze over Drake's shoulder, shaking my head. Then I stepped back around the display case, grabbing a full-sized cupcake and instantly snagging Drake's attention with it.

He accepted my offering, lifting it before him so he could admire it like a piece of art.

"Remember where you are, Drake," I murmured.

"Of course, dowser," he said agreeably—and completely missing my point about talking magic among the crowd of nonmagicals in the bakery.

"Chocolate-mint cake with mint buttercream," I said, shaking my head a second time but letting it go. "*Tingle in a Cup.*"

"Mmm," Drake said. "Chocolate and mint ..."

Practically pressing against my shoulder as she watched Drake savor the first bite of his cupcake, Peggy groaned quietly. She presumably thought it impossible for anyone to hear her.

I gave her a quelling look.

The telepath snapped up to her full height—she was actually taller than me by an inch—as if I'd caught her stealing cookies. Then, attempting to cover her ogling of Drake, she offered the tray of mini-cupcakes to Kett with a pert smile. "Cupcake?"

The vampire didn't even condescend to look at her.

Warner reached over, plucked a miniature *Chill in a Cup* off the tray, unwrapped it, and tossed it into his mouth without looking away from me. "Try the humans, fledgling."

Peggy nodded, scrambling away from us.

"You're blocking my way to my woman, Drake," Warner said.

He was being deliberately incendiary by calling me his 'woman,' so I gave him the glare he was practically begging for. At the same time, my insides went all mushy in reaction to being so blatantly and brashly claimed.

Drake stepped aside, mowing through his cupcake while following Peggy into the bakery seating area.

Warner moved forward, brushing a chaste kiss across my lips in deference to the bakery being a place of business. Of course, he clandestinely managed to grab a handful of my ass at the same time.

"How was skiing?" I asked, finding that I also needed to remind myself I was at work.

"Invigorating." Warner purred the word. Deliberately.

As he'd undoubtedly intended, my reaction twisted through my belly—along with another tantalizing taste of his magic. Ignoring the desire to wrap myself around him, I laughed quietly, reaching over to touch Kett's shoulder in greeting. "Jasmine's still upstairs."

"I know," the vampire said coolly.

"Well, you don't have to be such an ass about it. I was being polite."

Warner stifled a laugh.

"Thank you for babysitting, dowser," Kett said stiffly. Then he drifted across the bakery toward the fireplace.

I glanced at Warner, casting my voice low. "Did something happen?"

"There was a brief moment where Drake appeared to be badly hurt."

I frowned, not connecting Kett's current mood to Drake deciding to ski off a cliff. Without even knowing the particulars, I was certain it had been a deliberate choice on the fledgling guardian's part. He and Kandy had been watching extreme skiing videos the previous evening on YouTube. "And?"

Warner laughed under his breath. "You have to ask? How would you have reacted? If the vampire had shown up with Drake over his shoulder?"

I would have been seriously pissed. Completely irrationally, of course, because I knew how futile it was to try to keep tabs on the young dragon, and blaming Kett or Warner for Drake's actions would have been ridiculous. And ... if Jasmine had gotten hurt under my watch, I would have felt just as responsible.

I met Warner's gaze, a little sadly. "I don't like it when Kett's unhappy."

Warner kissed me lightly. "You don't like it when anyone is unhappy."

"True."

"But the vampire is fine. Possibly as happy as he can be. Happier here with you, with us. Rather than the alternative."

I nodded doubtfully. After the engagement party, I had thought that Kett and Jasmine might return to New England with Wisteria and Declan, but they'd remained in Vancouver. As far as I was aware, Whistler was the farthest the executioner of the Conclave had traveled from the city since then.

"We're going to shower, and then we will join you for closing," Warner said. "I'm thinking a bittersweet hot chocolate, a *Lust in a Cup*, and a seat by the fire might be a delightful way to end your day."

Yeah, he was deliberately trying to distract me with the mention of chocolate. And it worked. I lifted up on my tiptoes and kissed him properly—allowing myself more than just a taste of his black-forest-cake-infused magic, propriety be damned. But even as I did, the memory of my morning intruded on my thoughts.

"Oh, and an elf paid us a visit."

Warner went absolutely still, waiting for me to elaborate.

"I didn't kill her," I said, a little belligerently. Honestly, you killed one deranged, immortality-seeking dragon, then an elf who'd tried to murder two of your loved ones, and you totally got labeled. "I had two fledglings with me. And a bakery to open. She's skilled in masking her magic. And masterful at illusions."

"She just walked into the bakery and confronted you?"

"No. She drew me away from the bakery, apparently to show me an elaborate illusion of a throne room. But she got a little testy when I ripped through her magic, then she disappeared into the crowd on the far side of Whistler Way."

"Disappeared, as in within another illusion?"

"That's what I was thinking." I glanced around, slightly concerned about being overheard, but the few customers nearby seemed enthralled with the cupcakes. Which was a good thing for multiple reasons, including a successful launch for the bakery. "But I couldn't taste her magic. Not until she actually cast the full illusion."

Warner nodded thoughtfully.

"Do you think that's how they've been hiding in Vancouver for the last three months? I was beginning to think they'd fled immediately, which would have made total sense. Especially after we took out the warrior in the park."

"We?" Warner playfully mocked my implying that he and Kandy had played a part in the elf's demise.

"You both wounded him to begin with."

He grunted, not completely agreeing. But not arguing either.

"Maybe she's returned for some reason. Or she only got as far as Whistler and decided to stay here?"

"Elves don't set up house. No ..." Warner swept his gaze across the front windows, taking in the still-bustling marketplace beyond. "They've been biding their time."

I didn't bother repeating the questions we'd been asking each other for months. Namely, why would the elves have chosen to stick around? What could they possibly have been waiting for? "None of the chronicles I read mentioned anything about elves wielding illusionist magic."

"No, they didn't. And I haven't encountered anything like that either." Warner, along with my father and Haoxin, had been dealing with minor incursions from demons and elves ever since Shailaja attacked Pulou, almost a year ago now. The treasure keeper had been injured so badly that anything personally sealed by him—prisons, dimensional pockets, and doorways alike—had been compromised. But those incursions had lessened recently. Warner hadn't been called away in over three weeks.

"You haven't seen another elf since the one in the park, right?"

Warner shook his head, snagging another mini-cupcake off Peggy's tray as she crossed back around the display case, then started helping the next customer in line.

"So they're in hiding?"

"Or we've established appropriate boundaries."

Appropriate boundaries ... meaning we slaughtered any being that threatened our dimension. Granted, that was the job of the guardians, but ... well, I was glad it wasn't my destiny. No, my destiny was to wield the instruments of assassination. And, honestly, I still had no idea what that really meant in the long term.

Warner gently brushed his fingers through my curls, smiling softly. "I'll be right back."

I laughed. "After you shower? Or after you hunt the elf?"

"What do you think?" He grinned. Kissing me briefly—almost bruisingly—he turned back toward the door without another word.

Kett appeared at his side, his expression suddenly almost joyful. It was more than an easy guess that the executioner had overheard every word of our conversation. And he had been seriously peeved that I had done away with the elf in the park without at least getting the chance to lay eyes on him. The vampire had even gone so far as to suggest that we utilize Peggy and Gabby—a telepath backed by an amplifier—to form a mind link, so that he could see the event directly in my memory. Purely for research purposes, of course. But even before I could protest, Kandy had gotten all prickly about using any of her so-called misfits in such a way.

Warner and Kett, two of the most dangerous Adepts I knew, exchanged a look. Then they stalked side by side from the bakery. Drake appeared behind them, following closely as they exited. Once outside, they split off in different directions, intent on tracking an elf who was probably long gone.

I brushed my fingers along the invisible knife sheathed at my hip. And for a painful but thankfully brief moment, I had to force myself to stay behind. I would remain in the comforting coziness of the bakery instead of charging out into the evening cold. And my regret wasn't for fear of the elf hurting anyone. Rather, it was because I wouldn't be there if they got into a tussle. I wouldn't be testing my strength, wielding the weapons that were both my destiny and my doom—and which were literally hanging around my neck.

As I turned back into the kitchen to collect the final tray of mini-cupcakes, I wondered—and not for the first time—whether holding myself back, holding my instincts at bay, would always be a struggle. Or would I eventually come to some sort of understanding with the instruments—and all the destructive potential that came with them?

Preceded by her bitter-dark-chocolate magic, Kandy shouldered her way through the crowd that had descended on the bakery as the sun fully set and the majority of the ski lifts stopped running for the night. I glanced up from the box I was packing for a happily exhausted, sandy-haired woman with two off-the-wall-excited children. She had asked me if I had anything with an extra kick to it—meaning alcohol, which I didn't use in my baking. But I'd winked at her as I nestled a *Sin in a Cup*—spiced cake with a generous swirl of kick-ass mocha buttercream—among her other more child-appropriate selections.

Audrey and Lara paused to one side of the entrance as Kandy slipped around the display counter and sidled up to me. Audrey was outfitted in sleek cream-colored skiwear, while Lara was swathed head to toe in purple, as usual. Though there weren't any wards on the bakery, there was still a certain protocol when entering the territory of another Adept. So even though we'd greeted each other formally in the apartments above the bakery the previous night, I smiled invitingly at the beta of the West Coast North American Pack. Audrey nodded back but remained by the door.

"Have you kept us some treats, dowser?" Kandy was already scanning the cupcakes in the display case. "Or should I make Lara stand in line?" My werewolf BFF was wearing neon-green ski wear, including a head-band that covered her ears but forced her green-dyed hair to flop over its edges like a mop. I could feel the potent magic of the rune-scribed gold cuffs she always wore, currently tucked away underneath her ski jacket.

I laughed. "I've kept some. Warner, Drake, and Kett are showering. Assuming they're back from tracking the elf."

"Elf, huh?"

I nodded.

"Interesting. But since you don't currently appear to be under attack, let's circle back to that." Kandy was never easily distracted from being controlled by her appetite first and foremost, so she returned to her most pressing concern. "And hot chocolate?"

"You have to ask?"

She laughed huskily. Then, pressing her lips to my ear, she whispered, "I brought champagne for Bryn. Ask her to stay?"

I nodded, smiling at my friend's thoughtfulness.

"So...elf?" Kandy kept her voice low, but her anticipation at possibly being able to settle a three-month-old score was more than obvious. "He have swords and such?"

"She was female, I think." I smiled at my customer, passing her boxed-up cupcakes over to Peggy to ring through the register. "Showed up this morning, flashing pretty magic. Illusions. No sword that I saw. She ran off."

"Illusions, huh?" Kandy scoffed. "All the easier to smell her."

"My, my, what big teeth you have," I murmured playfully.

Kandy chuckled darkly. "You know it, babe."

Clearing her throat pissily, Maia deliberately stretched her arm in front of Kandy, reaching for a *Blitzen in a Cup*. There were only two of the seasonal eggnog-buttercream-topped mocha cupcakes remaining. I'd have to make a note of that for Bryn, and add another half-dozen to her daily baking list.

"Employees only," the skinwalker said snottily to the werewolf.

Kandy snapped her teeth about an inch from Maia's neck. "Move me yourself, little birdie."

Maia jutted out her chin, then looked pointedly at the long line twining through the bakery seating and toward the door.

Kandy laughed, then toyed teasingly with one of Maia's long braids. "Fortunately for you, it sounds like I've got bigger game to play with. Maybe next time."

Kandy was gone before Maia could offer up a rebuke, crossing toward the two werewolves still standing sentry by the door.

Stifling a smile, I grabbed another box, returning my attention to the next customer in line while folding it.

But I didn't miss the anticipatory grin that spread across Audrey's face as Kandy informed her that a possible elf hunt was in progress. A gleam of green rolled across Lara's eyes as she glanced my way and waved.

Though I had no doubt that Gran and Warner would have preferred to keep this new information only within the Godfrey coven and among the dragons, Kandy had previously made a heavily edited report to the pack about our confrontation with the warrior elf. She was, after all, obliged to protect the pack—both as

an enforcer and simply because it was the right thing to do. She hadn't mentioned the prison or the guardian connection, but she had included the possibility that two more elves were at large. Desmond, the pack alpha, had once sneeringly suggested that elves were nothing more than myth—though the werecat had also put the guardian dragons in that same category at the time. Kandy and I both believed that the pack deserved to know that elves were actually real. And potentially deadly.

Letting in another blast of cold air, the werewolves stepped into the cobblestone street to join the hunt. A moment later, they were swept from my sight within the still-teeming crowd.

Chapter Three

Three werewolves, two dragons, two vampires, a telepath, a skinwalker, and Bryn lounged around the sleek gas fireplace at the far end of the bakery. Plus me, of course. Two empty bottles of champagne and a white china platter dusted with cake crumbs had been abandoned on a low table nestled between the couch and a close grouping of chairs.

I was pretty sure that Bryn was asleep. Truthfully, I wouldn't have minded snuggling up to Warner and napping myself. The werewolves were busily plotting something nefarious—judging by their chortling—in the corner by the window. Hopefully not my bachelorette party.

Though before that became an issue, I still had to get through the bridal shower my mother was hosting the following afternoon.

To the disappointment of more than half of the gathered Adepts, the elf hadn't made another appearance. Even the three werewolves hadn't been able to pick up any trace of her magic. All the hunters had showed up just as the bakery closed, Warner settling on the couch, thoughtfully quiet. But Kandy, Lara, and Drake had happily drowned their sorrows in chocolate and cupcakes while exuberantly trading outrageous tales of their skiing exploits.

Jasmine had been coaxed out of the upstairs apartment, but as always, she was more interested in communing with her laptop than in conversing. With her eyes perpetually glued to the low-lit screen, her long, dark-blond curls formed a barrier between her and the rest of the bakery's occupants. But at least she'd decided to join us. I knew what being surrounded by this much magic was like for a person who felt out of place—and I didn't have to worry about accidentally biting anyone if I got overwhelmed. Unless stabbing someone with my jade knife counted as an equally inappropriate reaction. If so—been there, done that.

At a table next to the fledgling vampire, Drake and Kett were engaged in a chess game. Judging by Drake's increasingly determined grunting, I was fairly certain the executioner was beating him handily.

Snow had begun falling in earnest about an hour earlier. It was accumulating so quickly that the windows were already edged with tiny drifts, and the cobblestones had been completely covered despite the foot traffic that had remained steady throughout the evening. If we were going to get back to Vancouver, I was going to have to leave the last of the cleaning to Bryn and Maia. Conveniently, though, the Whistler bakery was going to be closed Sundays and Mondays for the immediate future, so they wouldn't have to polish every surface that night.

Warner shifted off the couch to settle on the coffee table in front of me, grabbing my calf and shucking off my sneaker. He began to massage my foot with the focus he usually reserved for gutting demons ... or for sex.

I stifled a pleased groan, but there were way too many people in the room—including an actual telepath—for me to let my thoughts wander. Though Peggy seemed otherwise occupied, engaged as she was in some interaction with Maia that included a lot of references to their phones and taking pictures of each other. The telepath had spent the entire evening studiously avoiding any and all conversation that included Drake. A smart move on her part for multiple reasons, including the fact that Drake appeared to be more intrigued by magic than people. As such, if Peggy misread his intentions, it might easily lead to her having her heart broken.

With the lone exception of my mother and father—who had created me in the mix—dragons didn't seem to have relationships with anyone but other dragons. Assuming they even had those kinds of relationships at all. I expected that had a lot to do with simply being stronger, faster, and more powerful than every other type of Adept—and the fact that unbalanced relationships didn't have much longevity. Even an eighteen-year-old dragon thought of future plans in terms of decades, not years or months.

"What am I being buttered up for?" I whispered to Warner. I didn't want to disturb Bryn, who was lightly dozing beside me.

He chuckled quietly as he continued to work on my foot. "Kett wishes to continue with his elaborate plans for my bachelor party."

"Okay …"

Warner leaned forward. "And if I'm about to leave the country, I'd like a moment alone with you. Upstairs, perhaps?"

Placing a hand on his chest, I pushed him slightly away. He accepted it with a grin that told me he was content to be compliant. For the moment, at least. "You're leaving the country? With Kett?"

He shrugged. "We're bringing Drake. And your father and Qiuniu are joining us at some point. So what could possibly happen?"

I said nothing, just letting my mind momentarily boggle at all the craziness that might occur under those exact circumstances.

Warner removed my other sneaker, digging into the tender muscles of my left arch. "Don't fret. We'll be back in time."

"I should hope so. The wedding isn't for five days."

He chuckled, then sobered thoughtfully. "But you'll text Kett if the elf surfaces again. I'm not a fan of games. I'm only a portal away if you need me. And your father would be happy for an excuse to visit Vancouver."

I glanced toward the windows, eyeing the snowfall. "We need to take off soon if we're going to make it back to Vancouver ourselves."

A sly grin slipped across Warner's face. "I'll help you pack."

I laughed quietly, downed the final sip of my hot chocolate, then nudged Bryn awake. "Hey, babe. Good opening."

She laughed, blinking her dark-brown eyes sleepily. "Yeah, I think the bakery is going to do okay."

"We're going to have to abandon you, though," I said. "I'm concerned about the roads."

She nodded, stretching. "I'll tally the sales in the morning and send you an email."

"Boo-yah!" Drake crowed, slamming down a chess piece on Kett's side of the board. Possibly his queen? I wasn't exactly an aficionado of the game, so a lot of the pieces looked the same to me.

Peggy and Maia both flinched.

Drake pumped his fists in the air, holding them aloft as he looked at all of us, silently declaring his victory.

Kett eyed the fledgling guardian. Then he slowly and deliberately lifted his hand and slid his castle across the board with a single finger. Or maybe that was a queen as well? "Checkmate."

"What?" Drake cried. "No ..."

Kandy started guffawing. She sprang out of her seat, catching Drake in a headlock. Warner threw his head back and laughed. Then Kett joined in with a warm chuckle—a thing I wasn't sure I'd ever heard from him before.

Jasmine looked up from her computer, shocked. Then, smiling softly, she closed her laptop to watch Drake and Kandy playfully tussle.

And for just that moment, I felt completely, utterly blissful. I breathed the feeling in. Soon, we'd be splitting up and racing the snow back to Vancouver. Then all the annoying bits of the final wedding prep would intrude on my life, including my grandmother's disappointment over every choice I made—from the tiny guest list, to the color of the flowers, to the fold of the napkins.

But for right now, Bryn and I had just opened a second bakery that appeared to have been well received, and the evening was filled with friends and laughter, chocolate and cupcakes. I was surrounded by the family I'd chosen, for love and friendship. Not the one that had been foisted upon me by the circumstances of my birth. Though obviously, I loved Gran, Scarlett, and Yazi as well. But this was a gathering of people I would die for. People I would never, ever willingly hurt.

And it was perfect.

Then someone rapped their knuckles on the glass front door.

Every predator in the room fell into silent alert mode. So, like, all of us, excepting Bryn and Peggy.

A group of people stood huddled in the snow outside the bakery. Surrounded by so much potent magic within the storefront, I hadn't tasted the separate tenor of the newcomers' magic as they'd approached. But I could taste it now. Sorcerers. And—

"Who's that?" Bryn asked.

"Oh," Peggy cried, flinging herself off the couch. "I was supposed to text when I was done work. We're staying the weekend. Skiing!"

Yep. Another Talbot—most likely Angelica—had just knocked imperiously on my bakery window. What other Adept would have had the courage to startle the amount of power lounging around the fireplace?

I sighed, regretfully tugging my foot from Warner's grasp and pushing myself up off the couch. I was going to have to be pleasant to sorcerers. Especially these ones, who were not only under my protection but partly in my employ. And although he wasn't currently with the rest of the family members gathered on the other side of the glass door, Liam Talbot had proven to be a more-than-useful associate over the past three months, using his connections with the city police and the RCMP to try to track the elves by nonmagical means in and around Vancouver.

Liam was currently investigating an odd series of break-ins around the city, during which nothing appeared to have been taken and the property damage was so minimal that it would normally barely rank as a police matter. It seemed likely that the events were nothing more than teens goofing around, but we were all wary enough that we would grasp at any straw.

All the magical means we'd used to try to find the elves—including the witches' grid—had come up with zilch. This was especially and utterly annoying to my grandmother, since identifying and tracking magic was the primary reason the grid had been created. I had overheard Gran and Scarlett frostily trading words on more than one occasion about my mother's insistence that Burgundy take my place at the Kits Beach anchor point three months before. Gran insisted that tying in my dowsing abilities would have increased the sensitivity of the grid. The argument never went anywhere, mostly because my mother refused to engage. But also because no one else agreed with Gran, including me.

I didn't bother with my sneakers as I followed Peggy through the seating area to greet the rest of her family. Her twin sister, Gabby, was among them, so I assumed they'd left Vancouver as soon as the amplifier's shift had ended at Cake in a Cup.

Peggy unlocked the door, letting in a frigid gust of air. "I'm so sorry. I forgot to text!"

"It's all right, Peggy." Stephan Talbot pushed back the hood of his ski jacket. "We knew where to find you." The telepath's adoptive father was dark-haired with medium-brown skin, but he spoke with a brash French Canadian accent. It was an interesting combination.

I hadn't spent much time with the patriarch of the Talbot family, though he'd come to the bakery to introduce himself when he'd arrived in Vancouver about a week after I met the rest of his clan. He ran a business that had something to do with technology, but what exactly he did had immediately gone over my head. Whatever it was meant he needed to travel a fair bit. He was also a former member of an American chapter of the sorcerers' League, which he had declared emphatically alongside introducing himself. And he'd worked with Henry Calhoun multiple times in that capacity.

Why he'd quit the League likely had everything to do with why he'd moved his entire family to a different country. But I didn't pry for details that weren't any of my business.

Vancouver had always traditionally been witch territory, which should have made it an odd place for sorcerers to settle. But it was apparent that the Talbots put their family above all the dreary, obsolete politics of the Adept. Another reason to like them.

Except for Tony, that was. I saw the dark-haired junior sorcerer trying to get a look at everyone hanging out in the bakery—but without actually stepping out from behind his parents. He met my gaze and hitched his backpack up on his shoulder, no doubt unconsciously concerned that my magic would trash the tech within it. Then he looked away, which was fine by me.

"Jade." Stephan cleared his throat, smiling hesitantly. "We are well met … yes?"

Right. I was pretty much blocking the door … and eyeing their son like I was thinking of leaving him outside in the cold and denying him cupcakes.

I smiled, stepping back. "Of course. Peggy mentioned you were planning a ski trip. I forgot in the … bustle of the day."

As they tamped off their boots and brushed off their coats before entering the bakery, I was reminded that the Talbots originated from somewhere where snow was more common than it was in the Pacific Northwest. Then the entire family minus one invaded the storefront.

I smiled and started making introductions, rather than sighing heavily and being pissy about the delay.

See? I could be a grown-up. Well, on occasion.

"Would you like to take a look at the kitchen?" I asked Angelica, with a pointed look Stephan's way. The Talbots had started putting their jackets back on as part of making a move toward the door and an early dinner out.

Angelica nodded, though she didn't look particularly pleased to follow me through the swing doors into the kitchen. Bryn's kitchen, really. My business partner had chosen white granite with thin veins of gray over stainless steel for her workstation. To our immediate right, the industrial dishwasher was piled high with muffin tins and mixing bowls.

"Very nice," Angelica said, quickly scanning and dismissing the entire kitchen—her tone polite, but still frosty around the edges.

I swallowed a nasty retort. The kitchen was freaking gorgeous, and it didn't make anyone the lesser to admit that.

"The double ovens especially," Stephan said, much more earnest in his praise.

Tony slipped through the double doors, settling his back against them so they wouldn't continue to swing. He cleared his throat, darting a look toward his parents, then addressing me. "This is about the elves?"

I eyed him before I nodded. "Yep." I wasn't the youngest Talbot's biggest fan, even though Tony was helping with Liam's investigation into the elves. I had actually carried a slash of red across my chest for a couple of days after he'd hit me with some sort of electricity-based sorcerer spell in the Talbots' basement. And sure, his magic had been seriously amplified at the time. But still.

"What?" Angelica's tone suggested that she clearly thought I'd actually asked if she wanted to admire my kitchen, rather than having some other reason for pulling her and Stephan away from the group.

I leaned back against the main counter, talking to Tony since he was apparently more in tune with the situation. "An elf skilled in illusion made an appearance this morning. Then disappeared."

Tony grunted, pulling out his phone and applying his thumbs to it. Presumably taking notes.

"Disappeared?" Stephan asked. "Or left town?"

"Your guess is as good as mine."

"We obviously don't have the same information you have." Though her outward demeanor remained dismissively judgemental, Angelica's brown-sugared shortbread magic churned around her, as if agitated. Perhaps being offish was a coping mechanism for the sorcerer.

"The elf appeared to be trying to make contact, rather than setting up an attack. As best as I can tell, anyway. Peggy can fill you in with the details when you're away from Bryn."

"Peggy?" Angelica gave me a look suggesting she was considering strangling me.

I knew that feeling. But I simply waited, giving her the time to articulate her displeasure. She chose to keep her complaints to herself instead.

"We were planning to stay through Sunday, re-turning in the evening," Stephan said.

"The bakery will be closed, and I seriously doubt the elf will return. She seemed focused on me. But I wanted to give you a heads-up."

"Thank you."

"I'd appreciate it if you kept in contact with Kandy through the weekend and let her know of any unusual activity."

Stephan gave Tony a look. The younger sorcerer nodded, acknowledging his father's silent directive with-out even looking up from his phone.

"I've been doing some research for Liam," Tony said. "Compiling and comparing elf myths. Searching for fact within the fiction."

That was news to me. "And?"

"Nothing really lines up with what you've told him. There's a lot of elf lore, but nothing that feels legit. I'd guess that no firsthand accountings have made it online yet."

I glanced Stephan's way. "And the talk among sorcerers? Within the League?"

"Nonexistent. As far as I've heard." He glanced at Angelica for confirmation.

She nodded. "Mythical creatures. Just like the guardians themselves."

Tony snorted as if Angelica had made a joke. If she had, she had a wickedly dry sense of humor. To me, she sounded more chastising than jovial.

"I know you came to Vancouver for protection," I said. "And the elves weren't part of the deal."

"No." Stephan waved his hand. "You cannot control who threatens your territory. And we're glad to help if we can. It is a...blessing to live somewhere where we are...valued. And the girls ..." He looked over at Angelica.

His wife nodded, her expression softening slightly.

"The girls have never been happier."

A sweet warmth bloomed in my chest in response to that. "I'm not the best role model. But I...like having them around. Gabby and Peggy fit in well at the bakery."

Stephan laughed, as if I was now the joker in the group. "They have never been so focused, so eager to be social, to be among other Adepts. They feel safe in Vancouver. With you." He reached over, offering me his hand. "You and Kandy."

I was surprised at his offer to touch me. Adepts often didn't like to make contact with other Adepts. But I wrapped my hand around his in response. His buttery, nutty magic—a smoother, creamier version of Liam's peanut butter punch—tickled my senses, making me crave honeyed peanut butter cookies that I hadn't baked in years.

He smiled, patting the back of my hand. "Thank you."

I cleared my throat, suddenly and oddly emotional. "Please be careful this weekend."

"We always are." Angelica was back to being a little stiff around the edges, but she slipped her arm through Stephan's and gazed up at him sweetly. The Talbots had sacrificed a lot for their adoptive children, though I knew they might have disagreed with that observation.

"Enjoy your dinner," I said.

"Enjoy your wedding festivities." Then Stephan turned with his wife, wandering back through the swing doors to the storefront.

Tony turned to follow his parents, but I called him back quietly. "Tony."

His shoulders stiffened, but he paused, looking back at me.

"You might want to discuss your findings and how you're gathering information with Jasmine."

"The vampire?"

"Yeah," I said, heavy on the sarcasm. "The vampire is a tech wiz."

"Okay...cool then."

"Right. Cool then."

He offered me a crooked smile, then stepped through the doors.

Leaning back against the counter, I listened to the excited murmur of voices beyond the swing doors, thinking once more back through the encounter with the illusionist elf. If she'd been laying out clues or taunting me somehow, it had pretty much gone over my head.

The door swung open and Maia poked her head inside the kitchen. "Hey, Jade."

"Maia."

"I'm going for dinner with the Talbots."

"Great."

"And, um, thanks for today."

"Thank you for today. I think it was a great success. I'm glad Bryn has you to help her out."

Maia frowned. "Not that. I mean, yeah, selling cupcakes is cool and all. I meant, thanks for not, you know, being pissy about the elf thing today. Thanks for including me."

"Right ... about that ..."

"Don't mention it to my grandmother?"

I laughed. "Actually, please do mention it. Then maybe pick her brain about elves? Or any creatures from First Nations history that might have actually been elves?"

"Cool, yeah. There's none I can think of, but Grandmama might have ideas."

"Thank you."

She nodded, retreating back through the doors.

"Oh, Maia?"

She poked her head back in.

"But maybe don't mention it to anyone else."

She snorted, as if I were an idiot to even think she'd gossip about facing off with an elf. Apparently, I was the only one with the big mouth in this group.

Warner, true to his word, helped me pack. Problem was, he apparently thought the clothing I was currently wearing belonged in my overnight bag. And no matter how quickly I might move on even my best days, he always moved quicker.

I didn't manage to find my voice…or my breath…until we'd made it into the shower and my dragon proceeded to soap up every inch of me. Then he brought me through and over the peak of pleasure a second time while I was pressed against the tile wall.

"What did I do to deserve such tender treatment?" I murmured, relaxing into the aftershocks of my orgasm.

Warner didn't answer. Instead, he angled the showerhead perfectly so that the hot water cascaded over my shoulder and across my chest, streaming over my belly and between my legs.

I laughed shakily, opening my eyes to find my fiancé gazing at me intently. He traced the path the water formed over my collarbone, around my left breast, between my lower ribs…then dipped lower through the slick curls at the apex of my thighs.

"I might need a minute."

A smile teased his lips, but the shimmer of golden dragon magic across his eyes let me know he was feeling serious. Running my fingers through his hair, I gently massaged his temples, then down the back of his neck.

He groaned, letting his head slip forward to rest on my shoulder and grant me better access.

"What is it?" I whispered.

He shook his head slightly, brushing off my concern. But then he reached up and hooked the tips of his fingers into two of the wedding rings attached to my necklace hanging between my breasts. His parents' rings. Dragon magic stirred at his touch. The instruments of assassination remained dormant where they were also attached to the necklace's thick-linked gold chain, as they always did until I called them forth. Otherwise, it would have been difficult to make love to a dragon without removing the necklace. And I never, ever took the magical artifact off.

Originally crafted to simply be a pretty trinket I could hang around my neck, the chain now contained so much power that some days I worried it wasn't safe even with me. The treasure keeper had wanted the necklace locked up in his chamber for safekeeping, along with my knife and my katana. And maybe he was right. But the instruments apparently had their own ideas.

Now, claimed by me and adhered to my necklace with my own alchemy, they were my responsibility. And though he had never expressed any concern over my becoming the wielder of the instruments, Warner being the sentinel of the instruments meant that I was his responsibility.

"I'd prefer not to leave," he finally said.

I stroked my thumbs lightly down his throat, then firmed my touch across his shoulders, trying to loosen his tense muscles. "Because of the elf?"

I had shared more details about the illusion with everyone earlier, when Bryn slipped away to the washroom. Maia and Peggy had chimed in with their observations as well. Which was good, because we needed to have any and all information on the elves we could accumulate. I was seriously done with blindly barreling into dangerous situations. I had too much to lose.

Warner just made a noncommittal noise, though, lifting my left hand from his shoulder and sliding the smaller of the two rune-carved wedding rings up to the first knuckle of my ring finger. We had discussed using his parents' rings for our own nuptials, but Warner had preferred that they remain around my neck, for the power they brought to the collective whole of the necklace. Instead, we'd ordered stacked rings from a goldsmith on Granville Island. Three bands, each with a slightly different shape and width, of twenty-four carat white, rose, and yellow gold. Gold that would be perfectly receptive to my alchemy for whatever 'extras' I chose to add to the wedding bands.

Warner was to pick the rings up on Wednesday morning, and his custom-tailored suit that afternoon. I had a final fitting for my dress on Monday, and the flowers were being delivered on Wednesday afternoon. The ceremony was scheduled for Thursday at sunset. I'd opted for getting married at Gran's. Yes, under some duress. In all honesty, I'd really wanted to use the bakery, because that was where Warner and I had first met. Well, technically, we'd met in the alley behind the bakery. And sure, he was unconscious at the time. Then we met again inside the bakery when Warner trashed my safe, got pissy about me having the dragonskin map that led to the instruments of assassination, and sneered at my cupcake pajama pants. But still.

In the end, getting married at the bakery had been seriously kiboshed by my grandmother, who'd wanted the complete opposite—a large church wedding and a huge party in a grand hotel ballroom. So we'd compromised.

"I'd prefer to never leave," Warner murmured.

"Tell me," I said. "Just tell me whatever you need to tell me. Did you open Rochelle's sketch?" I was referring to the drawing that was still tucked beside the bed in my apartment, and still in the art tube in which it had been presented to me. An engagement gift from the oracle that I hadn't found the right time to open.

Okay, fine. I hadn't found the courage to open it.

Warner lifted his gaze, still lightly stroking his thumb across the wedding ring at the end of my finger. His expression was still too serious despite the mutual pleasure we'd just shared. "Of course not."

I smiled. "The gift tag has your name on it as well."

He brushed his lips across mine. I lightly nipped at his lower lip, which finally resulted in him smiling. Though it was fleeting.

"I have no doubts about you, Jade Godfrey. You will open the oracle's sketch when you wish. But I will be marrying you in five days, no matter what is pictured within."

I darted my tongue into his mouth, indulging in the taste of his dark-chocolate-cherry-and-whipped-cream magic.

Pulling back from me slightly, he kissed my hand, tugged my finger from the ring, then allowed the necklace to fall back between my breasts. "I simply do not like the game the elf played today. Deliberately drawing you away when the rest of us were otherwise occupied, and you were away from your power base."

"Do you think something else is coming? Like whoever sits on the throne she showed me?"

Warner shrugged, feigning casualness while meeting my gaze earnestly.

Yeah, I knew that look. And every time I saw it, I tried to not react childishly. And failed. Sixteenth century needed to say something to me that he knew was probably going to get his head torn off.

He grimaced ruefully. "Will you renew your request for an audience with the treasure keeper?"

I squelched my instantaneous instinct to lose my mind. Pulou had ignored my last two requests. Other than vaguely acknowledging—to Haoxin, who'd then informed Warner—that he had, in fact, dropped three elves into Vancouver without anyone's knowledge. Confirming that it wasn't some other mixed groups of Adepts.

"You think I should update him about the elves? The illusionist and what she showed me?" See? I could keep my cool.

"He might have some insight."

"But is he willing to share it?" I asked caustically. "With me?" Okay, so…still not completely petulant, but…

I took a deep breath, reaching for the stillness I'd been cultivating. A peacefulness that allowed me to co-exist with the instruments without charging off into battle at the first hint of confrontation. Well, most days. "Fine. I'll ask Blossom to carry another message."

With a satisfied grunt, Warner grasped my hips, lifting me up until my legs were wrapped around him. "Just because I trust you to handle the situation, it doesn't mean I like running off with the vampire. You know he tries to be friendly with me only because he loves you."

I gasped as Warner slipped inside me without renewing the foreplay. All my nerve endings were still sensitive from my earlier orgasm. So much so that all I could do for a moment was cling to his shoulders as he pressed me back against the tile and settled into an achingly slow rhythm.

"Kett does things for many different reasons," I finally managed to say.

"The almost-immortal always do." Warner darted his tongue teasingly into my mouth. "But you aren't some passing fancy. Some pretty little magical thing for him to collect in the moment. He's afraid of losing you."

"To you?" I asked, honestly confused.

Warner laughed huskily. "No. He doesn't appear to be jealous. Of anything."

"And you, sentinel? Are you jealous?"

Warner trailed kisses down my neck instead of immediately answering. Then he lightly sucked and nibbled his way back up along the same path.

I lost track of the conversation.

"I am jealous," Warner whispered against my ear. "Jealous of every moment I'm not with you. Yes. Every moment I don't get to have you in my sight, by my side. Can you blame me?"

I groaned. "Take me to the bed. I want to feel your weight. I want to be underneath you."

He chuckled. "You'll want to dry off first."

"The bathroom floor then."

He turned the water off with a slap, then stepped out of the shower. Somehow, he managed to settle me down on the shower mat with the very cores of our bodies still connected. Looming over me, his hair was darker when wet, dripping across my face, neck, and chest. He tugged a towel down from the counter, setting it under my head to cushion it from the hard floor, and all the while continuing his slow pace.

But I wanted to be crushed, to be consumed by his touch and his magic. Pressing my feet to the tile, I sought out the leverage to match his, then increased his rhythm with my own upward thrusts.

I cinched my arms around his shoulders and neck, pulling him tightly against me so I could bury my moans in his warm, wet skin. "I love you, Warner."

He groaned, then allowed himself to finally give in to the pleasure building swiftly between us.

And there weren't any more words spoken after that.

I jotted a note to the treasure keeper on the back of the take-out menu that had come with the dinner we'd ordered the previous night, after everyone had gathered in Whistler. Yes, there was a helpfully lined section on the final page, where the restaurant encouraged potential customers to make note of their favorite dishes. It was also just enough space to inform Pulou about the illusionist and the throne in concise, just-on-the-edge-of-pissy prose.

Sealing the missive with one of the Cake in a Cup stickers Bryn had printed for the opening, I tucked it into my overnight bag. Seemingly an odd choice for a letter I intended to have delivered. Except that Blossom's newest favorite activity was cleaning and obsessively ironing my clothing. Yes, including my jeans and T-shirts. Not that I'd ever caught her with an actual iron.

But I had no doubt that sometime later that night while I was sleeping, the brownie would unpack my bag, find the letter, and deliver it to the treasure keeper. Just as I had no doubt I wouldn't hear anything in return.

Still, just because Pulou was a huge jerk, it didn't mean that Warner wasn't right about keeping him informed. The elves were his freaking escapees, after all. And in truth, before the elf sighting that morning, part of me had begun to think the guardian had simply scooped the last two elves up and locked them away somewhere—snickering to himself all the while at my ineptitude, then conveniently forgetting to mention it to anyone.

But apparently that wasn't the case.

The elves were still at large, and that both thrilled and worried me. I mean, who wouldn't crave a fight where you didn't have to hold back? But there were a lot of people I cared about who might get caught up in the tussle and be seriously hurt. Again.

So I wrote the note, wishing I had time to order spring rolls, and grinning while I imagined the treasure keeper's confusion over my choice of paper.

I could be a jerk too. I was just more playful about it.

Chapter Four

Jasmine was completely peeved to be traveling in a vehicle with three werewolves and me, rather than riding in Kett's SUV and getting set to jet off to some international location that the vampire was keeping a secret. But unfortunately for the golden-haired vampire, the only way Kett could participate in Warner's apparently three-day-long bachelor party—which for some reason he'd taken upon himself to plan—was if she stayed with Kandy and me. Or if she went to London.

Even though the tech-savvy vampire wasn't a fan of being babysat, it was heartwarming that Kandy and I ranked higher than the big bad of London—in her mind at least. That big bad was Kett's granddaddy, who'd banned me from the city. Actually, he'd banned me from all of the United Kingdom. I had no idea how enforceable that was, but had no desire to test it either.

Rumor had it—via Kandy via Benjamin Garrick via the ancient vampire chronicles that Ben was gobbling up as part of his recent remaking—that Big Bad was far more powerful than even the executioner. The unique powers he wielded were said to have allowed him to hold London for himself and his children for centuries. True to form, Kett had never gone into any of those particulars in all the years I'd known him. And remaking Jasmine and mentoring Benjamin hadn't made the close-mouthed executioner any chattier.

Still, those unsubstantiated rumors were apparently enough to result in Jasmine being pressed up against the back passenger door, hunched over her iPad, and making certain that no part of her body came into contact with mine. I'd been relegated to the middle seat between Lara and her, while Kandy drove the hulking black SUV and Audrey rode in the front passenger seat.

By the time we'd exited the apartment, and after Kandy had taken in my wet curls with a saucy grin, it was snowing so heavily that Kett's white SUV was practically invisible. As we headed out of the village, I was glad I wasn't the one driving. The highway that cut through the mountains from Whistler to West Vancouver, then to Vancouver beyond, had been improved many times over the years. But parts of the winding, steep grade still dropped off to nothing at multiple points before the road flattened out near Squamish. And most drivers took the curves way too quickly, Kett included. The white SUV holding the vampire, Warner, and Drake had disappeared ahead of us moments after he'd turned onto the highway.

Of course, no one but me apparently had any concern over being caught in the middle of a blizzard. The werewolf trio had spent the better part of ten minutes teasing me about it when we'd climbed in the SUV. For everyone else, the snowfall was 'light' and 'pretty.'

What could I say? I knew a dangerous situation when I saw one.

In Vancouver, even a light skiff of snow spelled trouble for driving. But unbeknownst to me until fifteen minutes before we set out, Kandy had apparently driven in snow on a regular basis her whole life. My werewolf BFF wasn't big on sharing childhood details, though.

Actually, anything to do with her past was pretty much off the table.

"Where are you going on your honeymoon?" Lara asked.

It took me a moment to realize she was addressing me. The werewolves had been chatting quietly among themselves—gossiping really, and always about people I didn't know—and I had dropped into a light doze.

"Oh…um, Warner is taking me to Stockholm. He has a house there. It's slightly bad timing with the delay in opening the Whistler bakery, so I'm actually going to have to close Cake in a Cup for the days that—"

"What is that?" Audrey growled from the front seat. She jabbed a finger toward the front window, indicating something on the side of the road up ahead of us.

All I could see was blowing snow swirling in the headlights.

Kandy tapped on the brakes lightly. "Where?"

"There!" Audrey pointed more emphatically. "Is that an animal?"

Kandy tapped the brakes again. She and Audrey leaned forward, peering through the blizzard that encased the vehicle. Well, from my vantage point in the back seat, anyway.

"Is that a wolf?" Audrey's tone was low, stressed. "There?"

"Maybe," Kandy murmured. She slapped on the hazard lights and slowed the SUV to a crawl.

"Pull over there," Audrey commanded.

Even though Audrey was the beta of her pack, Kandy normally wouldn't have responded well to that particular tone. But the green-haired werewolf carefully pulled over onto the wide shoulder of the road.

Lara unbuckled, climbing over my lap to perch between the seats. All three werewolves were watching something outside, completely alert. I could feel their magic shifting, rolling between them.

"What's going on?" Jasmine whispered, belatedly looking up from her iPad.

No one answered her.

"There," Kandy murmured. "Twenty feet to the right?"

"It's hurt," Lara moaned. Then she scrambled backward, elbowing me in the left breast as she threw open the back door before anyone else could respond.

"Ow!" I cried.

"Lara!" Audrey snarled, looking back. The green of her shapeshifter magic had overwhelmed the natural color of her eyes.

"Um, I hate to be the voice of reason," I said, rubbing my wounded chest and peering out the front window. "But I don't see anything, and maybe it's a bad idea to go tramping off through the woods without—"

Kandy glanced at me in the rearview mirror. Then she exited the SUV without a word, Audrey close behind her.

All righty, then. Apparently we were going out into the blizzard to track down a wounded wolf. Delightful. What the hell we were supposed to do with it once we caught it, I had no idea.

"Jackets might have been a good idea," Jasmine muttered, slipping her iPad into the satchel tucked between her feet.

"By the magic I'm feeling, I'm fairly certain that fur coats are on their way." I begrudgingly pulled my green ski jacket out of the back hatch as I prepared to follow the wolves out into the night.

Jasmine eyed me, twisting her lips wryly. "I guess blindly following you out into a snowstorm goes with the whole hero-warrior thing?"

"You're more than welcome to stay," I said pertly. "No one expects you to be a warrior, fledgling. Plus, according to you, this is just a dusting of snow."

The red of Jasmine's magic rolled over her eyes as she curled her lip into a snarl. She grabbed for her coat without looking away from me.

I laughed.

The vampire looked a little chagrined, figuring out that I'd been playing with her. No one could accuse Jasmine of being slow though—that was still my territory. She was just easily distracted. And who wasn't? Though technology certainly didn't hold the same fascination for me as it did for her.

Together, we climbed out of the toasty-warm vehicle to follow three werewolves into a blizzard. Because nothing could possibly go wrong with that scenario, right?

A car whipped past me as I stepped out. I pressed back against the side of the SUV, cursing under my breath. Then, feeling like an idiot, I shimmied around the front of the vehicle, finding Jasmine crouched on the sheltered side. She was peering down at three sets of tracks in the snow, leading off into the forest.

I zipped my coat up as high as it would go, leaving it uncomfortably snug under my chin. I brushed partially frozen hair from my face, seriously wishing I'd done more than towel-dry it. Vanity had stopped me from using the regular hair dryer I'd found in the en suite. I hadn't wanted Warner's last look of me—for three days if Kett's epic bachelor party went according to plan—to involve a frizzy head.

"At least it isn't just sheer cliff face through this section of road," I said.

Jasmine straightened, tucking her wild hair into a cable-knit hat, then pointing straight ahead of us. "It actually drops off in about seventy-five feet." She was wearing a dark-brown ski jacket with fake-fur trim around the hood. I was pretty sure I was going to completely lose sight of her among the trees.

"You can see that far?"

She shook her head. "Barely. But the trees just disappear there. So I assume there's an edge. How far is the drop?"

"Far. Like, 'straight mountainside all the way to ocean level' far. Though I'm actually not certain where we are right now. Somewhere between Whistler and Squamish."

A howl cut through the night, quickly answered by two others. Based on the direction of the calls, the werewolves had separated to track the wounded wolf they'd spotted.

"Do we follow?" Jasmine asked.

I sighed. "Yeah. We follow. You behind me."

"I can see better."

"Well, I can slaughter elves better. And I don't know about you, but a wounded wolf hanging out at the edge of a highway? Seems a little far-fetched."

Jasmine narrowed her bright-blue eyes at me. "I'm reserving judgement." Then she quirked her lip. "And ... I have been practicing."

"How's that going?" I knew that Kett would be a hard trainer. Unforgiving, and not terribly encouraging.

"Just fine," Jasmine said primly, never one to speak against her master. Though I wasn't sure if her reticence had more to do with the magic that tied her to Kett, or the fact that she was speaking to me.

I snorted in disbelief. Then I stopped my dithering and clambered up across the deep snow piled at the edge of the road by daily plowing. Breaking through the icy top layer, I immediately sank to my knees into the hard-packed snow beneath. I bit back a snarl of curses.

Jasmine snickered behind me. Then she promptly twisted her ankle a couple of steps later on some hidden rocks.

Lovely. We were going to make a great pair, stumbling after each other in the freaking dark while the werewolves ran amok.

After about ten minutes of slogging and blundering through the snow, Jasmine and I caught up with Kandy. The green-haired werewolf was still in human form, standing in a clearing among fir trees. I'd chosen to follow the taste of her berry-imbued-bittersweet-chocolate magic because I far preferred to meet my BFF in a dark forest, rather than Audrey.

The moon, if there even was one that night, still hadn't made an appearance. The cloud cover was low and thick, blocking out the stars, though the snowfall had actually eased. My night vision wasn't great to begin with—the vampire and the werewolves were far better predators after sunset than I was. And to make it worse, the snow blowing in my face and collecting underfoot had surpassed annoying five minutes previously and was steadily on its way to becoming hazardous. Ah, to be able to snap my fingers and conjure light. But no. I wasn't that sort of witch.

Kandy turned as Jasmine and I approached, her eyes blazing green and her head tilted to one side as she listened.

"Something's wrong," she whispered. She sniffed the air intently.

"With Lara or Audrey?" I asked.

Kandy shook her head but didn't elaborate.

Jasmine was scanning the clearing, turning in a slow circle. Her diligence reminded me that she had formerly worked as an investigator for the witches Convocation. Before getting to know her better, I'd assumed that whatever she'd done in her past life had all been tech based. But you know what they say about assuming...

"What do you sense, vampire?" Kandy asked.

"It's what I don't sense that matters," Jasmine said mildly.

"Out with it, then," Kandy snapped.

"Did you follow the hurt animal you saw here? By sight?"

"The wolf. Yes."

"Where are its tracks?" Jasmine gestured around us.

The only tracks I could see were made by human feet, some clumsier than others. No other signs of movement marred the thick blanket of snow in the clearing.

"What?" Kandy snarled. Her face rippled for a brief moment, as if her wolf form was close to the surface, threatening to overtake her human visage.

"The wolf's tracks?" Jasmine repeated.

Kandy glanced around. Excepting Jasmine's and my messy trail, and the green-haired werewolf's more precise steps in the snow, there weren't any other tracks leading to or from the small clearing. At least from what I could see of it, surrounded by snow and tall trees.

"You must have walked over them, morons," Kandy snarled. Then she checked herself, frowning. "I'm...that ..." She looked down at her bare hands. The taste of her magic intensified, and claws appeared at the ends of her fingers.

Jasmine went very still beside me.

Kandy clasped her hands together, taking a moment to breathe. Her claws retracted and her shoulders relaxed. She shoved her hands in the pockets of her ski jacket as she pinned her still-glowing eyes on me. "You think I'm seeing things?"

"Did you see the hurt wolf? A werewolf? And you saw its tracks?"

She nodded, stepping back to join us.

"Can you smell the wolf?" I asked, remembering that the illusionist elf had blocked out the sounds of the bustling Whistler village, but that the illusion itself hadn't come with any other sensory information. "Or just see it? And its tracks?"

Kandy paused, thinking, while I scanned her for any unusual magic. She appeared to have herself under control. Perhaps it was just stress, rather than foreign magic that was calling her inner wolf out.

"No," my BFF admitted sheepishly. "I...I can't smell wolf. Didn't smell it...and if it's hurt ..."

I nodded. A wounded animal should actually have been easier for Kandy to track, even in the dark and through the snow. "Okay. So...maybe the animal you thought you followed here was actually an illusion?"

"And the prints?" Jasmine asked. "They what? Faded?"

"Perhaps the illusionist has a range." I paused to actively scan the immediate area with my dowser senses. I sought any hint of the mossy magic I'd absorbed into my knife, but found nothing. "If the wounded animal was manifested by the elf, then she's not nearby. Or at least she's not actively wielding her magic. I can taste you and Jasmine. Then farther away, I can pick up hints of Lara and Audrey."

"So...then there is a wounded animal out here." Kandy pivoted slowly, surveying the clearing. "Maybe I just lost track of it?"

"Maybe. But whether or not I can taste the illusionist's magic, it seems odd. A hurt wolf at the edge of the road just as we're driving past? And...you three. Your...reactions. Do you normally split up when hunting?"

"Tracking," Kandy snapped. Then, recognizing her tone as being a little on edge again, she shook her head and scrubbed her hand across her face. "No...that's not normal for wolves."

"Pack hunters," Jasmine murmured.

"We just covered that, baby girl." Kandy shoved her hands in her pockets. Again. "Sorry. I let Audrey's stress and Lara's instincts influence me. Let's head back."

I nodded, turning to follow the trail we'd carved through the snow back toward the SUV.

Jasmine's phone buzzed. She freed it from her pocket, reading the message on the brightly lit screen and completely destroying her night vision. Well, destroying my night vision. I had no idea if a vampire's eyes worked the same way.

"Kett," she murmured. "Wondering why we stopped."

I laughed. "You think he's tracking the SUV?"

"They weren't that far ahead of us," Kandy said. "Tell old toothy we're fine—"

A terrible, pained howl came from somewhere to our far left, back toward the parked SUV, but possibly farther out. The cry cut off sharply.

Kandy took off through the deep snow. I lost sight of her as soon as she darted through the fir trees.

Running basically blind, I grabbed Jasmine by the back of her coat and started hauling ass toward where

I could taste werewolf magic converging. All of the werewolves. Though whether that was three or four, I couldn't tell.

"My phone!" Jasmine cried, tearing herself from my grasp and ripping her coat in the process. Apparently, she'd dropped her cell.

I let her go, still chasing after Kandy and hoping I didn't catch my foot on any fallen branches or rocks hidden underneath the snow.

A terrible, lingering whine of pain cut through the chilled air. Sensing Kandy adjust her course somewhere ahead of me, I did the same.

Low branches scored my face and tangled in my icy hair. I twisted my ankle, stumbling and slamming my shoulder into a massive tree. My unintentional assault of the evergreen released an avalanche of snow onto my head and neck, which immediately began to melt as it dripped down my back.

Delightful.

But despite the combined forces of nature and winter attempting to keep me at bay, I continued to chase after Kandy until the thick tree line opened up before me.

And then, suddenly, there was nothing underneath my feet.

Just a vast, dark space.

I would have sworn to God that I hung suspended in the air for a moment. A final breath.

Then I fell.

Straight down into a swirling vortex of darkness and snow.

Something caught me, yanking me backward. I slammed against what felt like a sheer rock wall with a pained snarl, smacking the back of my head against craggy granite. Pinpoints of light exploded in front of my eyes. Apparently, I had inadvertently found the cliff face.

"Some help, dowser." Jasmine spoke from somewhere above me, sounding strained.

I reached up over my head, blindly seeking, then finally finding the golden-haired vampire's arm. She was holding me with one hand.

Jesus.

I scuffed my heels against the rock behind me, looking for and finding footholds. Taking some of my weight, I managed to twist around and find a handhold, still gripping Jasmine's arm with my other hand.

Then the fledgling vampire hauled me back over the edge of the cliff, dropping me face-first into the snow and collapsing on her ass beside me.

"You're heavier than you look," she said.

I heaved myself up to kneeling. "I'm going to take that as a compliment."

She plucked at the sleeve of her jacket. It was shredded. "You ruined my jacket."

"You should see the shoulder." I pushed my frozen curls out of my face.

Jasmine stretched her arm out to the side, as if testing it for injury.

"Thanks for the rescue," I said, gaining my feet and holding my hand out to her.

She hesitated, then grasped my hand and allowed me to haul her to her feet. As she disengaged, she glanced down at her also-ruined pants. The knees were shredded. "I thought I might go off the cliff with you."

"Yet you didn't hesitate."

She met my gaze. "No. Kett would have been displeased."

I grinned at her. If she wanted to justify her actions—aka rescuing me from grievous injury and possibly death—by using Kett as an excuse, I wasn't going to argue.

She laughed quietly. "You probably would have survived the fall."

"Probably. But it would have seriously hurt."

A pained whine filtered through the trees. It was coming from the same direction, somewhere to our left, but the sound was weaker. Fading away even as I strained to pinpoint its location.

Snow continued to fall from the dark sky, but nothing else moved. Jasmine stopped breathing—which, of course, she didn't actually need to do except to speak.

Then a single shout cut through the frozen night.

Kandy.

Jasmine met my gaze questioningly. With a nod, I allowed her—and her ability to actually see in the dark—to take the lead. Together, we carefully stepped along the edge of the cliff.

Twenty steps brought us to Kandy. Thankfully, she had seen the edge of the rock outcropping. She was pacing, her magic once again blazing in her eyes.

"Dowser," she shouted when she spotted me. Then she pointed over the edge of the cliff.

I crouched where she'd indicated, peering over the edge. "I don't see anything."

"Right there," Kandy snarled. "The wolf went over."

I glanced up at my best friend, concerned. "A wolf...just ran over the edge of a cliff?"

"What would a hurt wolf be doing running around at night anyway?" Jasmine peered over my shoulder. "Shouldn't it be holed up in a den somewhere? You know, healing?"

Kandy got up in the golden-haired vampire's face. "What do you know about it!?"

"Whoa, whoa, ladies." I stood up slowly. "Let's take a step back. I already fell off this cliff once tonight. We'll sort this out—"

A dark-gray wolf appeared out of the stand of trees behind Jasmine and Kandy. Then another lighter-gray wolf appeared in the opposite direction.

Audrey. And Lara.

The beta prowled forward. Her green eyes were pinned to me, and her lip lifted in a silent snarl. I became uncomfortably aware of the sheer drop at my back. But taking another step forward seemed like a really bad idea. Lara pressed against Audrey's shoulder, then stalked forward alongside her beta, keeping her blazing green gaze on Kandy.

Jasmine stilled. Smart vampire.

"Did you find a way down?" Kandy asked, stepping forward and drawing the dark-gray wolf's attention.

The beta werewolf regarded her briefly before pinning me with her gaze again and answering with a low, vicious snarl. Delightful. Apparently, Audrey had decided I was the bad guy. Why, I didn't know. I mean, other than the fact that the magic of the instruments of assassination probably smelled like … well, murder. And would have seemed so even more acutely to her wolf form.

Ignoring her beta's pissy behavior, Kandy hunkered down beside me, turning to face forward as if she were preparing to scale the cliff. In the dark. After a snowstorm.

"Kandy!"

"You don't understand, Jade," she snarled.

"Listen, I do. But neither Jasmine or I can see what you see—"

Kandy slipped.

I crouched, grabbing her arm in the same motion.

Then I felt the curl of magic. Elf magic.

As I tasted it again, I understood how I might have missed it previously. It was practically indistinguishable from the scents of the forest surrounding us, even in the snow.

"Let me go, dowser," Kandy snarled.

Audrey was suddenly breathing down the back of my neck. She emanated a low, snuffling snarl that promised much flashing of fangs and rending of flesh.

Lara whined, sharp and conflicted.

"Jade?" Jasmine whispered questioningly.

"Stay calm," I said, addressing all four of them at once. "Smell the magic."

Audrey huffed, her breath hot against my exposed skin. Even in her wolf form, she clearly thought I was an idiot.

"Smell. The. Magic," I repeated. Then, shoving Audrey away with my shoulder, I hauled Kandy back up and over the cliff.

The beta stumbled, then immediately lunged for me. Kandy crouched between us, her head lowered and neck exposed.

Audrey hesitated.

Going against my instincts—I would have seriously loved to kick Audrey's ass—I kept my gaze on Kandy, rather than meeting the beta's eyes.

The dark-gray wolf huffed again, shaking her head but taking a step back. Lara pressed against her shoulder.

Then the five of us clustered together, breathing in the silence deeply. Waiting. Ready. I reached out with my dowser senses, through all the magic I knew well, seeking power that tasted of evergreen forest after it had rained...

The hurt wolf whined again. Closer this time.

Kandy stiffened, preparing to spring into action.

"Wait," I whispered. I caught the tenor of the magic I'd felt earlier, though I still couldn't taste anything. "Over there. In the trees."

"The wolf?" Jasmine whispered.

"No." I sprang up, inadvertently knocking Audrey and Lara away from each other as I twisted, calling forth and throwing my knife. The jade blade spun through the air, slicing across the magic I'd felt.

Elf magic.

Power shimmered in the air, then dissipated as if I'd cut through another of the elf's illusions. The immediate area didn't change in any other way, though. My blade embedded itself in a fir tree.

I stalked forward in the snow with Audrey at my heels, looking for other tracks or any other lingering magic. We found nothing.

Kandy peered over the edge of the cliff. "The wolf is gone."

I retrieved my knife.

Audrey began sniffing all around the base of the tree, then outwardly in larger and larger circles. But I couldn't see or taste anything unusual. No evidence that anyone but us was hanging out on the edge of a cliff in the aftermath of a snowstorm.

I looked back at Kandy, shaking my head.

She nodded grimly. "Someone is playing with us."

"Yep. And either she planted the magic on you three sometime today, or she somehow timed the illusion to trigger at exactly the right point as we drove by. And in either case, her illusions are obviously mobile, at least to some degree. Set and go. Because I can't sense her anywhere nearby."

"Neat trick," Jasmine said.

Kandy curled her lip. "And smart. Not sticking around and getting between three werewolves and a potentially hurt packmate. Two enforcers and a beta. We'd have made mincemeat out of her without thinking twice about it."

"Question is…how did she know a hurt werewolf would get your attention?" I gestured around the immediate area. "How did she know she'd elicit this reaction? You know, what with her being from another dimension and all."

Kandy looked uneasy, briefly meeting Audrey's intense gaze then quickly looking away. "She's been watching us."

I nodded grimly. "Without us noticing."

Audrey snarled, a rippling, vicious sound. Then she took off with Lara at her heels. Back toward the SUV, I guessed. Though presumably they'd stop off wherever they'd stashed their clothing. Because it was going to be much, much easier to tell us all off in human form.

I sighed, tromping after the wolves.

Why did I suddenly feel as if I were back in school, staring at a surprise math test and not even knowing where to start? And, to top it off, the outsiders in this so-called test—the elves, who were out of their element and should have been struggling to catch up—had apparently gathered more information about the Adepts of Vancouver than I had about them in the same period of time.

In the aftermath of a tense drive back to the city, I rolled into my very empty bed, pleased to be back in Vancouver and behind the wards of my apartment—but still out of sorts over the games the elf was playing.

Audrey and Lara were staying with Kandy in her apartment across from mine. After a flurry of text messages with Kett, updating him and Warner about the elf activity, Jasmine had barricaded herself in my second bedroom with a half-dozen electronic devices, including an old, broken laptop of mine that she'd somehow found in the hall closet. I'd meant to recycle it, then had forgotten to actually take it to the depot.

The fledgling vampire had tried to convince Kandy she was capable of spending the night in Kett's and her apartment in False Creek. But with that apartment lacking the wards that protected the bakery and both of our apartments—powered by heavy-duty blood magic, courtesy of yours truly—Kandy had flatly denied the request. Jasmine wasn't under house arrest or anything. But if the elf had actively targeted the werewolves after attempting to beguile me, then the vampire was safer staying in a secured building.

The werewolves' gossipy chatter hadn't resumed after the incident with the elf. Kandy had wanted to continue hunting, but Audrey had decreed that we would return to the city. By the baleful looks the beta kept casting my way, I figured she was trying to sort out some way to blame the elf fiasco on me. Presumably, dashing out into a snowstorm after nothing but an illusion really wasn't Audrey's idea of a good hunt. What was that saying about getting egg on your face? Whatever it was, the beta of the West Coast North American Pack didn't like the feeling.

As I reached over to turn off the bedside lamp, I spotted the art tube from Rochelle tucked up against my bureau.

Slowly, I climbed out from underneath the covers and crawled to the corner of the bed. I brushed my fingers against the plastic cap that sealed the tube, feeling a tingle of oracle magic.

Then I hesitated.

For the umpteenth freaking time.

I was getting married in five days. Whatever Rochelle had deemed an appropriate engagement gift had to just be a confirmation of the future I'd chosen for myself. Therefore, I was acting ridiculous, giving the sketch contained in the art tube far too much power over me.

Unless... unless the oracle had a warning that she'd wanted to wrap in ribbon. You know, to soften the blow.

I withdrew my hand.

Yep, I was being utterly absurd. Reading into whatever Warner hadn't fully articulated in the shower. Fretting about the elf. And now not opening the oracle's sketch, when I knew everything was going to be okay. Because no matter what happened, it was always eventually okay.

Eventually.

But not always without casualties.

I crawled back under the covers, tucking in with my phone and texting Kett.

Kiss my dragon goodnight for me.

I had barely closed my eyes before the vampire replied with his typical brevity.

>Done.

I threw my head back and laughed. I felt the magic of the instruments on my necklace, then felt the energy of the wards that coated the walls ripple and roll in response.

Then, under the comforting weight of both, I slept. I knew that I needed to be rested, what with the fact that my mother was hosting a bridal shower that my grandmother had insisted was her inherent right to host, as the head of our family and the head of the coven. But because I'd already begrudgingly allowed Gran to throw us an engagement party, I'd overruled her.

So the following afternoon would be filled with tea, petit fours, and polite conversation, all underlaid with the disquiet that constantly simmered between Pearl and Scarlett, mother and daughter.

Certain types of Adepts, if not most, became more powerful with age. And my mother was no longer hiding her power, or her influence, underneath a thick layer of charm and charisma. I'd actually heard her refer to herself as 'Scarlett Godfrey, member of the Convocation, mother of Jade, dowser,' twice in the past three months, when normally she'd introduce herself as the daughter of Pearl Godfrey.

So, yeah. Even beyond elves running amok, the tenor of Vancouver was changing. And it always got worse before it got better, didn't it? The trick was getting through the worst of it without losing anyone in the process.

Or without murdering anyone.

And I had yet to pull off that feat.

Chapter Five

Strawberry-blond tresses tumbled over my mother's shoulders as she leaned forward, reaching for me with both hands before I'd even made it to the bottom of the front stairs of her newly renovated triplex. She was swathed in a royal-blue wool dress that fell demurely to just below her knees, and which displayed a generous hint of cleavage. By the wattage of her smile, paired with a lingering discordant spike of her underlying grassy witch magic, I got the distinct sense that Scarlett had thought I might not have shown up for my own bridal shower.

But my werewolf pack had hauled me out of bed only a few hours after I'd fallen asleep, and together we'd gotten pedicures and gone for brunch. Audrey was reserved as usual, but Lara and Kandy had bantered away, seemingly unaffected by our run-in with the elf. Jasmine opted to stay at the apartment, tinkering away with her tech projects. Apparently, neither brunch nor being touched by estheticians was high on the vampire's list of likes.

After getting back from the pedicure, I'd flicked through the unusually tidy hangers filled with jeans and T-shirts in my closet, finding a green-and-brown plaid kilt I'd completely forgotten I owned. Blossom's obsessive need to organize every inch of the space she deemed her territory came with bonuses beyond that of a pristinely clean kitchen. I paired the skirt with a slim-fitted, hand-knit dark-green sweater and tights, setting off my green knee-high boots perfectly. The Mezzo Dallas Fluevogs came with my favorite two-and-a-half-inch wrapped leather heel and had two rows of antique silver studs running up the fronts. The skirt was a trifle short for afternoon tea, but I looked damn cute.

I grasped my mother's hands, stepping up to brush a kiss across her cheek. Energy shifted between us, and the taste of her strawberry magic filled my senses. "What's wrong?" I whispered.

"Absolutely nothing, my darling. I love the boots."

I glanced down to admire them with a grin. "I got them on sale!"

My mother laughed quietly, then reached around me to shake Audrey's hand as the beta werewolf joined us on the front patio. "The pack honors us with their presence."

Audrey nodded imperiously. "The pack is always pleased to express their friendship with the Godfrey coven."

My mother's smile stiffened, but she deliberately turned her attention to Kandy and Lara, greeting everyone formally in the order their rank required.

So it was going to be one of those sorts of afternoons. Painfully polite politics paired with thinly veiled threats and subtle games of dominance. And I'd thought I was just showing up for the treats.

Jasmine had once again chosen to stay behind, having declared she was busy fixing and improving the laptop I didn't actually need. And after she'd repeatedly and grumpily sworn that she'd text one of us before she left the apartment—and the protection of its wards—Kandy and I had agreed. Though a heated argument had erupted among the wolves when Kandy suggested that Lara could stay with her. Apparently, the suggestion that one of the pack enforcers would babysit a vampire was an utter affront. According to Audrey, at least.

And in truth, I was worried that on top of the in-bred animosity that continually percolated between vampires and werewolves, a gathering of witches might have been too much for Jasmine. The strength that being remade with Kett's blood had given her—strength of both mind and body—was considerable. But she was still a fledgling, learning how to handle that strength. When she'd caught me, then hauled me back from a blind drop over a cliff the previous night, it had seemed to surprise her as much as me.

Thinking about that moment again, I realized I shouldn't have been all that surprised that my mother had thought it was possible I wouldn't show up for my own bridal shower.

Kandy and Lara followed Audrey into the main level of the house. My mother linked her arm through mine, holding me back for a moment as the werewolves removed their coats and knitwear in the small entrance-way. The triplex was split from front to back, with the two upper units sharing the main and top floors. Bedrooms were above the living area, and the lower garden-level unit occupied the entire basement foot-print. Scarlett had opted to follow Vancouver's Heritage C guidelines, picking her paint colors and other finishings based on specified options. As such, the exterior was a deep purple offset by white pillars and window trim.

As the werewolves wandered in, following the murmur of voices toward the living room, my mother and I stepped inside, arm in arm. It was almost shockingly warm. Scarlett had to release me to close the door, and I shucked off my jacket and scarf, hanging them up in the coat closet. A colorful oil painting by a renowned local artist, David Wilson, depicting Vancouver in the rain, held a place of prominence on the wall opposite the closet.

My mother had been nomadic throughout my entire life, but she seemed to be enjoying finally settling down and slowly filling her abode with collectables from local artists—paintings, pottery, and handmade furniture. Her taste skewed to understated and modern, despite the heritage status of the house, but she didn't shy away from color.

A glimmer of magic drew my attention to an ornate wrought-iron umbrella stand tucked beside the door. Reaching through what appeared to be an invisibility spell—one that tasted distinctly of my mother's strawberry-infused witch magic—I brushed my fingers across what felt like the pommel of a sword.

At my touch, an almost delicate-looking rapier sheathed in worn, rune-etched leather appeared before me. The cross guard was an elaborate twist of gold-plated metal, designed to deflect blows and protect the wielder's hand. It was set with sapphires almost the same color as my mother's eyes.

As my eyes.

The weapon tasted of smoky dragon magic. I gave my mother a pointed look.

She shrugged delicately, smiling.

I released the pommel, and the weapon disappeared behind the invisibility spell again. "I suppose he offered to train you as well?"

"It would have been irresponsible not to," Scarlett said smoothly.

My mother and I had never discussed—and hopefully never would discuss—what relationship she and my father had rekindled after I'd met him for the first time almost four and a half years before. Or if there even was a relationship. Though I had long suspected that Yazi at least visited my mother, and I'd seen my father wearing a scarf that looked like one my grandmother had knit.

Warner had implied as much during our conversation in the shower the previous night, when he'd suggested that my father wouldn't mind an excuse to visit Vancouver. To see me, yes, but I was fairly certain Yazi also wanted to see my mother. He didn't appear to use the portal in the bakery, so I honestly wasn't sure how he was coming and going. But either way, without really intending to do so, I'd made sure that my relationship with my father and my mother wasn't tied to whatever form their … connection took. At least not beyond the one thing they had in common—me.

I couldn't imagine anyone trying to maintain a romance of any kind with a guardian dragon—especially not my father, the warrior, who helped guard all the territories at the other eight guardians' behest. Though now that I was thinking about it, I imagined that dating Chi Wen, the far seer, would probably be more difficult.

Then there was the fact that my mother, even though a powerful witch, definitely wasn't a demigod. Her mortality added a difficult dynamic to the equation. Which was maybe part of the reason behind the gift of the sword.

"Well," I said, breaking the silence that had stretched between my mother and me as I sorted out the ramifications of the rapier's appearance in the umbrella stand. "Bring it to me when you have a moment and I'll tie it to you. So no one else can wield it without your permission."

Scarlett smiled, brushing her fingers against the back of my hand. Her magic curled up across my wrist—but for the first time in a long while, I didn't allow it past my personal shielding. Normally, I would have greedily collected the lick of strawberry-imbued power and hoarded it in my knife.

My mother's smile faltered. "Am I so weak that you think me unworthy of him?"

Startled, I met her strangely sad gaze. "Why would you think that it's you I'd deem unworthy? Or that I'd think that of either of you?"

"I know he…your father is …" She seemed unable to complete her sentence.

And I knew how she felt. Having a demigod for a parent was a little overwhelming, and a whole lot of pressure. "Mom. I was…he's just not the most reliable. That's all."

"He would do anything for you."

"But this isn't about me, is it?"

"Isn't it? Warner isn't exactly known for his availability. You take him as he comes, and for whatever time he's able to spend with you. Isn't that the hallmark of a solid relationship? That you both do your best? That you love each other for what time you have?"

I shifted uncomfortably under my mother's soft gaze. The conversation had rather abruptly taken a turn into territory that I wasn't particularly prepared to discuss. Not Warner's and my relationship, or my mother and father's.

"The difference is…I am…the wielder of the instruments of assassination." The pronouncement of my title, of my magical prowess, felt lame the moment I uttered it, but I didn't know any other way to express my reservations.

My mother smiled proudly, then she reached up and lightly rested her hands on my shoulders. And this time, I allowed her magic to settle on me, easing the tension that had become stifling in the small entranceway.

"That you are, oh daughter of mine," she murmured. "You are a kind, lovely soul. Fair-minded but fierce when you need to be. I'm blessed to call you my own."

Tears of joy suddenly threatened the edges of my eyes. I laughed quietly. "And I bake the tastiest cupcakes."

My mother chuckled. "Don't worry about your father. He does his duty, and I happily do mine. Here with you. If we meet in the in-between, we are both pleased to do so. Our relationship is separate from our individual connections with you. I wouldn't have it any other way."

I nodded, still a little too overwhelmed by her declarations to articulate any actual thought.

"Come now, my Jade. I've collected all your favorite treats."

"But you'll bring the rapier to me? That is a lot of power to leave propped by your front door."

"Tomorrow, darling. Tomorrow. Your father bade me to leave it there, and you forget how few could see through that spell."

A cold shiver ran down my spine. "He bade you? As in...he knows...or rather, the far seer knows...that you'll need a weapon easily at hand in the near future?" I didn't articulate the thought further, but my mind was suddenly churning with possible scenarios that would require a dragon-wrought sword to be accessible at any moment beside my mother's front door. Each wild scene I conjured was more terrifying than the last.

Scarlett paused. Her indigo gaze was thoughtful but not concerned. "I didn't question him. I assumed that it was … playfully intended."

I nodded, opting to let the subject drop—even though I was fairly certain the warrior of the guardians didn't lightly gift deadly magical artifacts, not even in order to woo the mother of his long-lost child. And if my father was following a directive, or even just a suggestion, from the far seer?

Well … I inhaled deeply, settling my thoughts. The future unfolded whether I understood what was coming or not. And if a rapier tipped the balance in my mother's favor? Good. I'd make sure no one could take the blade from her, and I would try to find peace with the idea.

Because what I really wanted to do was to charge back to the bakery and through the portal, demanding answers. But I was trying to avoid angry hysterics as much as possible. It was difficult to embrace being a brat at heart when you were also the caretaker of the only three ways to kill a guardian dragon.

So that was another thing to be bitchy at Chi Wen about. I wouldn't have minded having a few more years of unfettered brattiness before taking up that mantle.

Ignoring my introspection, my mother tugged me through the short front hall into the living room. I allowed her to pull me out of the disconcerting moment, though she couldn't have physically moved me without my willingness. I certainly wasn't going to play games with my mother, not when she never played them with me.

That said, my grandmother was another ball of wax/kettle of fish/brouhaha altogether. The implied power of the dragon-forged rapier in the umbrella stand, whether it was simply a gift or a precursor to a future unfolding, would not sit well with Pearl Godfrey, chair of the Convocation. Not one bit. And it saddened me that my mother could offer me unconditional love when her mother had never felt the same for her.

Not that I'd known either of those things while I was growing up. The eternal underlying tension between my mother and grandmother was yet another reason that I could have happily stayed a blissfully ignorant, self-centered brat for a few more years.

Yeah, I had lots of things to thank Chi Wen for. So blaming the far seer for my needing to grow up seemed to fit onto that list just fine.

The only time I ever drank tea was when it was served in fine china and paired with crisp layers of pastry and buttercream—specifically, the impossibly delicious offerings of Notte's Bon Ton. And that was exactly what my mother had arrayed across the sleek cherry-wood table that bisected the dining room portion of her open living room. Tiers upon tiers of pastries, plus the most heavenly scented teas.

Based on the sheer volume of pastry, I wasn't certain how many guests my mother had anticipated hosting. Though it was a safe guess that the three werewolves alone could have cleared the table given a solid hour or so.

After greeting Gran, who was already deep in conversation with Audrey, I chatted briefly with the group of witches who'd commandeered the green velvet love seat and twin recliners. Those included Burgundy, Mory's friend; Olive, whose hair was twisted up in a gaudy orange scarf; and Kelly, who was knitting something large—possibly a lace blanket—with a thick, natural red-brown yarn that I assumed was from her alpacas.

I winked at Rochelle, who had wedged herself in the front window seat with Mory as a buffer between her and everyone else. Then I made a beeline for the treats.

The junior necromancer was also knitting, but her thin yarn matched her purple-and-red-streaked hair. She was working on another tube—meaning probably more arm warmers, or maybe socks. She never seemed to have enough of either. According to Gran, knitting was a way for some witches—and apparently at least one necromancer—to visualize how their magic worked when they didn't see magic, as I did.

The oracle had opted for a baggy, loose-knit black sweater that hung off her petite frame and likely fell to her knees when she was standing. It also covered her increasingly rounded belly. Yep, Rochelle was six months pregnant. That was the news she'd wanted to share at my engagement party. Kandy had been teasing her endlessly about having tiger twins, suggesting with much mirth that not even her oracle powers would be able to help her raise two shifters.

The oracle's white-framed tinted glasses might have hidden the magic simmering in her eyes from sight, but I could still taste her tart apple power as it intermingled with the grassy base of the witches. I hoped it was just the situation—being surrounded by Adepts—rather than an oncoming vision that had Rochelle's oracle magic percolating. I was already unnerved by the appearance of a rapier in my mother's umbrella stand, meaning I'd likely overreact to anything else. And I didn't want to ruin the afternoon for everyone.

Okay, to be fully honest, I didn't want anything to occur that might cause the treats to go to waste.

I set up camp by the dining table, waffling over pouring a cup of *Chocolate Rocket* from DavidsTea—which

I honestly would have carried with me everywhere for its scent of chocolate, almonds, and raspberries—or the *Forever Nuts,* which paired perfectly with any and all desserts, especially with its undertone of sweet apple.

My mother had commissioned the cherry-wood table, matching chairs, and sideboard from a local woodworker who displayed his work on Granville Island. She'd taken delivery of the set just in time for the bridal shower. The linen napkins and the handblown glass vase, currently holding a white orchid and sitting in the center of the table, were also from local artisans, but the sterling silverware and the china were antique.

Kandy sidled up to me, pilfering one of the three *Florentines* I had already perfectly balanced on my plate, so as to keep enough space for at least two more selections. The decadent petit four boasted two layers of dark-chocolate buttercream sandwiched between three caramelized almond-and-candied-fruit cookies, with the bottom layer dipped in chocolate. The green-haired werewolf could have easily grabbed a *Florentine* from the dozen plus still adorning the china platter. But for her, stealing my food was much, much more satisfying.

I flashed her a grin, content to play werewolf dominance games if she so desired. Despite her easy manner during brunch and pedicures, I was still a little concerned with how my BFF had been affected by the elf's illusion of the injured wolf. Plus, I knew that having Audrey around was always tension inducing. Kandy could have been the beta of any shapeshifter pack she'd desired. But she had chosen Vancouver instead, and a pack of magical misfits that happily included me. So despite all of that, I was pleased she was still feeling playful.

Also, there were more than enough treats to go around, or I might have had to fight her for it. Best friend or not.

"Politics," Kandy muttered, her narrow-eyed gaze fixed over my shoulder.

I glanced back to see that she was eyeing Gran and Audrey, standing close together, framed in the pocket door that stood open to the kitchen. They were having some sort of intense discussion. Lara stood politely just off to the side of her beta's shoulder, but she looked bored. I picked up enough of their softly exchanged words—*Whistler…snow…wolf…elf*—to get the gist.

"I'm sure the pack is simply filling the coven in on last night's encounter," I said, not particularly interested in eavesdropping further. "As per protocol."

"Sure, sure," Kandy said, deceptively agreeable. "Except, of course, you were the senior Adept on site, so doing any sort of so-called report to the head of the Convocation is technically your call. Especially since you exposed the plot and all by unearthing the elves in the first place."

I laughed under my breath, taking a deeply satisfying sniff of my tea. I had opted for *Chocolate Rocket*. "I'm sure Audrey is offering a detailed accounting. And that Gran is pleased to be kept informed."

"Right …" Kandy shrugged her shoulder, snarling sarcastically. "Including how she knew that something was off from the moment she saw the hurt wolf. And that the entire incident didn't smell right."

I gave her a look, nibbling around the edges of a two-tiered, powdered-sugared almond cookie with a chocolate buttercream center—aka a *Japanese* pastry. "Why did you invite Audrey in the first place? Lara would have come alone." I had put the purple-loving enforcer werewolf on my personal guest list—as one of the twelve people I'd wanted to invite to my wedding, including my parents and my grandmother. Warner's list had consisted of five names. Two of those had doubled mine—Drake and Kett. Two, he considered friends of some sort—Haoxin and Qiuniu. The last was pure obligation—Jiaotu.

The guardian of Northern Europe held the power that the sentinel's mother had once wielded, and controlled the territory in which Warner maintained his ancestral home. Thankfully, all three guardians had declined attending the actual ceremony. Their schedules were difficult to predict. But Haoxin and the healer had both expressed a desire to drop by the dinner afterward, if possible.

"Lara would have gladly come by herself." Kandy curled her lip. "But Pearl requested the beta's presence."

"Oh, yeah?" I'd assumed that the addition of Audrey's name—along with Desmond's, who'd also declined—had come from Kandy. I mulled this new information over, eyeing my grandmother. She was looking rather stately in dark-charcoal wool crepe pants and a wide-collared, off-white silk blouse. Her gray hair was tightly braided and coiled around her head. "And why is that?"

"You tell me." Kandy turned her attention away from Audrey and Gran, casting her gaze across the table.

I paused my pastry indulgence to contemplate why Gran would feel it necessary to shore up the coven's relationship with the West Coast North American Pack.

"Because... you're my wolf?" I asked quietly.

Kandy's lip curled. She had taken to declaring herself the 'wielder's wolf' in recent months. "You know it, babe."

"That doesn't change your position within the pack structure, does it? Like, badly?"

"Nope. But it also doesn't give Pearl any in to the pack through me."

A realization hit me hard. "You're mad at Gran. Over tying me to the grid."

"Yeah, I'm mad as hell."

I watched my grandmother again as I finished up my almond cookie pastry. Then I dug into a slice of *Dobos*, which consisted of three thin layers of dense cake and chocolate buttercream, all enrobed in a hard chocolate shell. And yes, I had filled my plate—first pass, at least—with all the chocolate-buttercream-filled petit fours. "You hide your anger well."

Kandy snorted. "Not well enough, obviously."

"Gran's never been particularly concerned about building relationships with other Adepts before. Not that I know of, at least. Witches usually keep to themselves, shoring up power in their covens."

"Most Adept sects do, except the smaller, rarer subsets. Like your necromancer and your oracle, who need to make strategic alliances." Kandy nodded toward Mory and Rochelle, still seated separately from the witches, but who now appeared to be nibbling on tea sandwiches.

Ignoring Kandy's use of 'your' when referring to the two of them, I turned my attention back to the table—where I spotted sandwiches and other delicacies I hadn't noticed before, nestled among all the pastries. I was hoping for peanut butter and banana.

"Rumor has it that the Gulf Coast Pack has a telepath and an amplifier among their membership."

"Well, so do we," I murmured, distracted by a fillet of smoked salmon and a mound of cream cheese—both just out of my reach.

"Yep. Which should make the Godfrey coven one of the most powerful Adept sects in the world, with no need for other alliances."

That got my attention off the food. "Except ..."

"Except there's you. Pearl never had one of the most powerful Adepts in existence living in her territory before. An Adept who's about to marry another powerful person with unshakable loyalties. And ties outside of the coven. Vancouver...hell, the entire West Coast is no longer witch territory with your grandmother as its undisputed leader."

I set down my teacup and plate on the edge of the table, freeing my hands so I could pull the crispy caramelized cookie sections of a *Florentine* apart and lick the chocolate buttercream unabashedly.

Kandy watched me, letting the conversation lapse. "Sorry I'm upsetting you." She hooked her fingers through my bent elbow. "I know you just want to bake and laugh and be...you. And we all want that too. There's just going to be an adjustment period. Right?"

I shook my head, but more in denial of my need to shove my head in the sand regarding the power I carried than about Kandy's assessment. "You hate this political stuff. You don't want to be involved."

Kandy shrugged, popping an entire *Canadian Cheese* in her mouth—a maple-buttercream-filled meringue pastry with a hazelnut crust. "I'm not involved. I'm the wielder's wolf. I'm above it all."

I shrugged off my uneasiness over her tying herself to me with an official title once again. "So you think that Gran is...what? Fortifying her territory from the outside? Why would the pack be interested?"

Kandy snorted. Still chewing, she downed her entire cup of tea. "Witches are useful. And when all else fails, who doesn't want to be able to call up the wielder of the instruments of assassination? You're big league, babe."

"The pack has my friendship, my loyalty, without the games."

"Sure. But Pearl can't bank on things like friendship."

I sighed. "Can we worry about my gran's potentially nefarious intentions later? Or, like … never?"

"There ain't nothing nefarious about it, Jade. She simply wants to protect you from all the things she can't imagine that might be gunning for you. Problem is, what's more powerful than you? And how could she possibly be a help in that fight? Or even shield the coven from it? Hence, the relationship building and the tinkering with the grid. She's shoring up allies, drawing battle lines, in case she has to back you."

I groaned quietly. The last thing I wanted was for Vancouver to become some sort of war zone, with me in the middle of the chaos and my family protecting my back … just like they'd done on the beach in Tofino …

Kandy dropped another *Florentine* into my hand. "Nothing to fret about now, my pretty. Now you get the delightful experience of playing stupid games and wearing a paper hat."

"What?"

"Or maybe it's supposed to be a paper bouquet? I really wasn't listening when Scarlett was planning it all. Though I did find those wooden clothespins she asked for …"

"Clothespins?" Dread crept into my tone. Yeah, I was all Zen when the possibilities included battle lines being drawn, but party games freaked me out. "For what?"

"Don't worry, dowser. You'll get through it. And the bachelorette party is going to be off the hook."

"No weird hats … or games?"

"Nope. Well, T-shirts. You know."

I laughed. Of course there were going to be T-shirts.

Chapter Six

*I*n the end, my mother limited the so-called bridal shower 'games' to three. Though I felt certain that at least one of them had been rigged, because I lost my clothespin almost immediately as punishment for saying the word 'chocolate.' Apparently, I couldn't go five minutes without doing so. But after that, relieved of the pressure of having to watch what I was saying, I enjoyed being surrounded by feminine chatter that had nothing to do with cupcakes, sales figures, or elves.

At one point, the witches got a little rambunctious over the idea of conducting tests with the magical grid, since half the coven—the main part of Gran's whittled-down guest list—was going to be in town for my upcoming nuptials. Then two latecomers showed up—Teresa Garrick, Benjamin's mother, and Danica Novak, Mory's mother. To Mory's utter chagrin, the two necromancers immediately settled down in a corner of the dining room with their tea and pastries, then started cackling about a rare skeleton one of them was adding to her bone collection.

I ignored both conversations, choosing to hang out with Rochelle and Kandy until Beau showed up promptly at 4:00 P.M. That seemed a perfectly acceptable time for a planned retreat, since it had been noted as the end of the gathering on the invitations. The were-cat's appearance—literally, how delectably gorgeous he was—shocked the assembled females into appreciative but polite murmurs. Beau, being rather smart about these sorts of things—and head over heels for his pregnant wife—stuck around only long enough to rescue Rochelle from our clutches. Along with a Tupperware container filled with leftover petit fours, of course.

Leaving the witches to chat and sip freshly brewed tea, the necromancers, the werewolves, and I all made hasty retreats as well. And Kandy was happily laden with two more pastry-filled containers, thanks to my mother's excellent forethought and planning. Mory, looking really put out, climbed into the back seat of an older silver Mercedes driven by her mother. Teresa Garrick took the passenger seat. Other than her daughter, Danica had been the only necromancer in Vancouver before the Garricks arrived. But apparently the two elder necromancers had a lot to bond over and had become fast friends.

Adepts usually stuck to cultivating relationships among their own kind. It must have been nice to be able to share your magic with someone, chat about tips and tricks, and cast spells together. I wouldn't know. But I didn't feel particularly put out for being the only dowser and alchemist around.

Kandy, Audrey, Lara, and I wandered back along West Fifth Avenue toward the bakery as the sun began to set. It was only slightly chilly, the weather in Vancouver being a sharp contrast to what we'd left behind in the mountains. Musing about the weather made me think of the Talbots and their skiing weekend, so I checked my phone for text messages while the wolves dug into the leftover pastries and chattered among themselves.

I had no new messages, from the Talbots or anyone else. And that made me realize that I was hoping Warner and Kett were on their way home. Not because I was worried about the elves, but because I missed them. Yes, even though we hadn't even been separated for twenty-four hours. I might occasionally chafe when my very set routine didn't contain enough knife fighting, but I was a homebody at heart. Whether it was feasible or not, I wanted all my loved ones in the same place at the same time. Didn't everyone?

"Did you check in with the Talbots?" I asked Kandy during a break in the conversation.

"You know I did."

I opened my mouth to continue grilling her, but she raised her hand.

"And Kett. And everyone else who was supposed to check in. Everyone who should be accounted for is accounted for."

"Fine. You don't have to be so bossy about it."

"Apparently I do."

Momentarily satisfied, I stuffed my phone into my sweater pocket, hampered by the handmade bouquet I was still carrying. As one of the so-called games, the guests had constructed the bouquet for me out of the paper and ribbons the shower gifts had been wrapped in. Kandy had gathered the gifts themselves into a large tote bag that was now slung over her shoulder. Though the invitations had indicated that gifts weren't requested, most of the guests had brought a little something, including handmade chocolate-scented soap, lip balm, and body cream from the witches.

Opening the lip balm from Olive—and then gushing over it—was why I'd lost my clothespin so early on. I had a feeling that giving me that particular gift first had been a strategic move on the part of the witches, who liked to win any and all games. Burgundy had come away with the bulk of the clothespins in the end, gleefully winning a gift certificate for a manicure.

I raised the bouquet before me. "And what exactly am I supposed to do with this?"

"Oh!" Lara gushed. "You use it during the wedding rehearsal."

I glanced at Kandy disconcertedly. "We're supposed to have a rehearsal?"

"Don't look at me. I ain't never planned a wedding either."

"Just bring it with you tonight," Lara said, shaking her head at our collective ineptitude.

"You want me to carry it around with me?" I frowned down at the trail of curled gift-wrap ribbons that fell to my knees. "What if I have to pull my knife?"

Lara laughed. "At dinner? Or while we're dancing?"

Kandy growled. "Shut it, big mouth."

Preceded by her sweet peppermint magic, Jasmine stepped onto the sidewalk at the corner of West Fifth and Larch, gazing intently at me. Lara flinched as if the golden-haired vampire had just appeared out of nowhere, but she'd apparently been tucked behind a tall laurel hedge for some odd reason.

"I'm here," Jasmine murmured, darting a look at the three werewolves.

"So I see," I said, confused by the intimate wariness of her tone.

"You were supposed to text if you left the apartment," Kandy snipped.

Jasmine frowned. "Jade texted me."

"I didn't."

She fell into step with me, pulling her phone out of the pocket of her figure-hugging brown suede jacket.

The two pack werewolves dropped back a few steps, as if deliberately separating themselves from association with the vampire. Audrey whispered something that sounded derogatory, but I didn't bother to work out the actual words. Lara snickered.

Jasmine flicked a backward glance at them, but she ignored the cold shoulder. Kandy tucked up slightly behind my left shoulder. The three of us wouldn't have been able to walk abreast otherwise.

Jasmine unlocked her phone and stared down at her screen. "I...that's odd."

"No text message?"

But instead of answering me, the golden-haired vampire looked up abruptly, glaring past Kandy and at the other werewolves for no reason I could discern.

"What are you looking at, vampire?" Audrey asked with a sneer.

"I'm not certain," Jasmine said condescendingly. "But it appears to be roadkill walking."

Lara snarled. The green of her shapeshifter magic rolled across Audrey's eyes.

"Whoa, whoa!" I kept my pace steady in the hopes of continuing to draw Jasmine with me without having to grab her. Something was definitely up with the vampire, but I didn't want to exacerbate it unnecessarily. "It's a party, ladies. Not a catfight."

Lara opened her mouth to snarl something back at me—presumably regarding the cat comment, which I belatedly realized might have been construed as disparaging by a werewolf. An unfortunate choice of phrase on my part.

"Enough," Kandy snarled. She spun around to walk backward, her bittersweet-chocolate magic shifting around her with the command.

Lara snapped her mouth shut.

Audrey pinned Kandy with her green-hued gaze—and her gait slowed. For a brief, panicked moment, I thought the green-haired werewolf was going to throw down with her beta. Which would have been a seriously bad idea for Audrey, because Kandy would most likely win—magic cuffs or no magic cuffs. And Kandy didn't want the rank that would have come with that victory. Or the relocation to Portland.

"The weather is nice, isn't it?" I tried to sound deliberately perky though something was clearly going on, continuing to stroll down the sidewalk. "Snow on the mountains but practically sweater weather in town."

Kandy rolled her shoulders, then turned her back on Audrey, stepping up just behind me again.

Jasmine had reverted her attention to her phone.

The three of us crossed Balsam Street without further incident. Only a block and a half to the bakery. And maybe, once we were behind the security of wards, I could figure out what was up with Jasmine. And the testy wolves, though Audrey was always on the edge of—

"I can hear you, assholes," Jasmine snarled, spinning so suddenly to face the werewolves that I got a mouthful of golden curls. "If you have something to say, try saying it to my face. See how that goes."

Audrey practically threw herself forward, snapping her teeth only an inch away from Jasmine's nose. "You're hearing things, bloodsucker. If I bothered to address your kind, I'd do it with tooth and fang. You're not worthy of my words."

"Technically," I said, "you're talking to her right now, beta."

"Stay out of it, dowser," Lara snarled.

Kandy laughed sharply, drawing Jasmine's attention. The red of her magic was ringing the vampire's bright-blue irises. Something was seriously up with her.

Audrey turned her shoulders away, as if stepping back from the situation. Jasmine shook her head oddly, perhaps trying to clear it. Then Audrey shifted her weight, spinning back with her hand raised to slap Jasmine.

I stepped forward, blocking the vampire from the blow she was too inexperienced to expect. So Audrey backhanded me instead. Aiming for Jasmine's cheek, she got my jaw and upper neck because I was about two inches taller. A bunch of the small bones in her hand snapped, the sound sharp to all our ears.

I turned my head with the blow, hoping to mitigate its effects. For Audrey, that was. I barely felt it myself.

Audrey froze, more wary than frightened. Her hand hung suspended in the air between us.

Lara moaned quietly.

I met the beta's brown-eyed gaze, unable to keep the challenge out of my look. "Care to try again, wolf?"

Audrey lowered her hand, flexing her fingers as her shifter magic rolled over it, likely healing the multiple breaks. "You move quickly, dowser," she said, deceptively mildly.

"You ain't seen nothing yet, werewolf." I smiled. Possibly nastily.

"Jade." Kandy's whisper was muted but tense.

I nodded, trying to temper my tone. I didn't particularly like being hit, not even if I was the one who'd stepped into it. "In Vancouver, we try to figure out what's going on with our friends when they act out of character. You know, before ambushing them."

"Like a coward," Jasmine added.

Kandy closed her eyes, pained.

Audrey's chocolate-infused magic rose again—bitter and punctuated by the earthy taste of mushrooms and some sort of nut…brazil nut, maybe. The bones in her face shifted. Dark, wiry hair appeared and disappeared on her neck. She gritted her teeth, fighting the transformation.

Lara pressed her shoulder against her beta's, but she kept her gaze downcast—likely so I didn't think she was challenging me.

"I told you." Jasmine peered over my shoulder. "They're conspiring against me. Against you, dowser."

"The vampire is obviously out of her mind," Audrey said. "Not unexpected, for her kind."

A wide grin spread across my face. Again. I wasn't particularly friendly with Audrey, but Jasmine automatically earned my loyalty because she belonged to Kett, and because he'd asked me to watch over her.

Audrey actually stepped back. Most likely because I'd wrapped my hand around the hilt of my knife, though I left it sheathed. For now. Even the beta werewolf wasn't stupid enough to tangle with my blade.

"We're supposed to go for dinner," Kandy said, stepping between me and the other two werewolves. She pinned me with a mournful gaze. "Then dancing."

"How can you blame this on me?" I cried.

"The vampire needs to be shown her place," Audrey snarled. "You allow her to be too familiar."

"You once thought that about me, beta." I laughed darkly. The magic of the instruments of assassination sleepily curled around my necklace, egging me on. "Maybe you still do?"

"A leader should understand, Jade." Audrey squared her shoulders, lifting her chin imperiously. "Your example governs the fledglings in your territory."

I narrowed my eyes at her. It felt as if the conversation was veering seriously close to some sort of lesson—but the beta was in no position to school me.

"Time and place, beta," Kandy said, keeping her tone neutral. "I'm certain your insights would be welcome when requested."

"You're crossing a line, Kandy," Audrey snapped.

Jasmine thrust her arm in front of me, showing me her phone. "See?" she cried. "It's right there. I've uncovered evidence."

The screen of her phone was blank.

I glanced at Kandy.

She leaned over to look at the phone, then peered at Jasmine. "There's nothing on the phone, baby girl."

Frowning, Jasmine withdrew the phone, muttering to herself and fiddling with the screen.

Turning my back on the stupid pissing contest with the werewolves, I grasped the golden-haired vampire by the elbow, steering her swiftly toward the bakery. Well, as quickly as I could without drawing attention from the homes lining either side of the street. It wasn't dark yet, and people would be coming home from work soon.

The werewolves followed, Kandy at my heels with Audrey and Lara only a step behind.

Energy tickled the back of my hand. Just a hint of something foreign, almost hidden underneath the vampire's riled, sweet-peppermint magic.

Possibly elven magic by its tenor. But, as far as I could tell, not the illusionist's power.

"Elf ..." I whispered it without otherwise reacting, knowing that Kandy would hear and understand me. "Something's going on. Like with the injured wolf last night."

Jasmine's head shot up. "Elf? Where?" She hissed it through inch-long fangs, which had abruptly made an appearance.

"Keep moving, Jasmine," I said, smiling as if we were just chatting amicably. "Like we're in a hurry, but not like we're panicked. Yes?"

"Yes." The vampire sounded agreeable enough, but I didn't like that she was showing fang.

"Circle back a block at the corner," Kandy whispered to Audrey and Lara behind us.

"Why should we?" Audrey sniffed condescendingly.

"Use your nose, beta," Kandy murmured.

As we approached the corner of Vine and West Fifth Avenue, Kandy said brightly, "We'll meet you two back at the bakery. We just have a few things to pick up first."

Then the three werewolves peeled off in different directions without another word.

As much as I desperately wanted to be leading the elf hunt, I steered Jasmine to the left, heading north to West Fourth Avenue instead.

The disoriented vampire was fiddling with her phone again. "It was right here. Here? No. Right here."

I didn't pick up any more of the magic I'd tasted when I first touched Jasmine. And I couldn't taste any of the illusionist's magic either. Which seriously bothered me. I had learned to rely on my dowser senses in such situations. You know, when my friends were being hunted—though the elves were taking it a step further if they were managing to influence Jasmine somehow.

And with the vampire compromised, I couldn't even pause to dowse for the elves' magic. Not out in the open. Not without first getting Jasmine away from the werewolves, who she seemed to be fixating on. I was hoping that getting the vampire behind the wards of the bakery would mitigate whatever was going on with her.

Thankfully, though, we still had a couple of hours before dinner. So hunting elves wasn't completely off the menu yet.

I paused at the crosswalk at West Fourth Avenue. The traffic was thick, both vehicle and pedestrian. Jasmine pressed up against me, looking around furtively. Involuntarily, I thought.

I gripped her arm slightly more firmly, trying to impress her with the fact that she'd have a difficult time getting away from me. You know, just in case she was contemplating grabbing an unwilling snack. Then the light changed and I wove through the throng of people crossing the road, dragging Jasmine alongside me.

Up ahead, Kandy jogged across Vine Street, darting into the alley behind the Whole Foods at the corner to scout ahead of us. I followed the green-haired werewolf, meeting up with her by the back door of the bakery just seconds after Lara, who had approached from the opposite direction.

"Nothing," the purple-clad werewolf said. "Only humans for a block in all directions. Audrey's doing another—"

Without warning, Jasmine wrenched free from my grasp—leaving the arm of her suede jacket in my hand. The vampire attacked Lara, latching onto the werewolf's neck and slamming her against the green recycling bin.

I lunged forward to slip a finger into the side of Jasmine's mouth. Then, hooking her like a fish, I wrenched her away from Lara's neck.

Kandy grabbed Lara, holding her upright while pressing a hand to her badly bleeding neck. Lara's shifter magic exploded around us as she instinctively started to transform into a shape better suited for taking on a vampire. A form that wouldn't remain hidden behind the recycling bin for very long.

"No!" Kandy pressed a hand to Lara's face, gazing deeply into her eyes. "You're okay, my friend. You're safe."

Leaving the hurt werewolf for Kandy to manage, I dragged a snarling Jasmine toward the exterior door of the bakery. She twisted and fought against my grip the whole way. Thankfully, the door opened to the touch of my magic, rather than needing to fumble with an actual key. That allowed me to get it open one-handed, then to thrust the vampire through the wards.

I glanced back at Lara and Kandy. The purple-clad werewolf's neck was no longer gushing with blood. She looked completely pissed, of course. But at least she was still human.

Looking through into the kitchen, I realized I was still holding the sleeve of Jasmine's jacket, though I'd lost the paper-and-ribbon bouquet somewhere. The golden-haired vampire was standing a few steps away from my stainless steel workstation, wearing her ruined jacket and a dazed expression. Thankfully the bakery was closed for the day.

A hulking, hairy monster abruptly appeared behind me, scoring my back with its wicked claws before I could step aside.

"Audrey!" Kandy cried.

Pulling a page from the beta's own playbook, I took a step over the bakery threshold, then pivoted to backhand Audrey.

Carefully.

She was in her half-wolf, half-human form, first stumbling, then snarling, then coming at me with teeth and claws bared. Yes, right out in the freaking open space of the alley.

I slammed both hands over Audrey's massive maw, squeezing her jaw shut. Then I tucked my knees and rolled backward into the bakery, pulling the huge werewolf with me. Audrey flipped ass over head, slamming down onto the edge of the workstation. Its stainless steel crumpled underneath her massive, clawed feet.

I stood motionless for a painful moment, cringing at the damage I had just inflicted on my haven.

Unfortunately, I'd also forgotten about Jasmine.

As Audrey staggered to her feet among the wreckage of my steel counter, the golden-haired vampire flung herself around the werewolf's neck, dangling there like a pretty ornament. Her fangs had retracted. Her blue eyes were wide but determined. Whatever magic had influenced her previously appeared to have been negated by the bakery wards.

Unfortunately, a newly made vampire—even with Kett's powerful blood running in her veins—was no match for a beta werewolf. At least not a match for Audrey in her half-beast form.

Snarling, the massive monster trashing the tile floor of my kitchen with her clawed feet reached up to engulf Jasmine's face in her hand. Holding her by the head alone, she pulled the vampire off her shoulder. Then she body slammed Jasmine onto the floor—doing even more damage to my tile, along with what remained of my workstation.

Kandy appeared at my back, but she was trying to hold on to Lara rather than joining the one-sided battle taking place in my kitchen. The wounded werewolf's eyes blazed green as she desperately struggled to thrust herself into the fight.

Jasmine, still on her back, slammed a kick to Audrey's leg. I heard bone snap, but the beta barely paused. Snarling viciously, Audrey bit downward, making an earnest attempt to decapitate the vampire with a single chomp.

Jasmine rolled out of the way at the last moment, leaving a tangle of curls between Audrey's teeth.

"Jade!" Kandy cried.

Spotting an opening, I lunged forward, getting between Audrey and Jasmine before either had a chance to see me move. I grabbed Audrey in a chokehold. My arm didn't even come close to circling her neck, but my strength made up for my lack of grip. The beta grabbed my shoulders, but she couldn't shake me off.

"Get back!" I said to Jasmine, who was looking like she was thinking of wading into the tussle again. The vampire crab-walked backward, clearing the immediate area.

"Dowser!" Audrey snarled, the word mangled by her not-quite-perfectly aligned jaw. "Step aside."

"The pack has a perfect right to extract revenge, dowser," Lara said from behind me. "The vampire has broken covenant with us!"

Kandy shook Lara harshly, so much so that the wounded werewolf appeared dazed—though that might have been due to the amount of blood she'd lost.

I shoved Audrey a few steps back as I let go of her. "Jasmine, child of Kettil, the executioner and elder of the Conclave, is under my protection."

Audrey's magic welled up and around her. Suddenly, I was looking at the gorgeous, sleek-haired beta in shredded and stretched clothing, instead of the toothy monster. She raised her chin regally. "No matter her lineage, she's transgressed against the pack."

"Under the influence of elf magic."

Audrey curled her lip dismissively. "Elves. Hogwash. Show me some evidence."

Kandy stepped up beside me. She was still holding Lara, though the wounded werewolf appeared to have calmed down. "You don't want this fight, beta. You want a cooler head. And to remember the report I sent three months ago."

"Also," I said snottily, "the illusion that had you hanging your ass off a cliff last night." Yep. Unable to keep my mouth shut, as always.

Audrey eyed me. "I believe that was you, Jade."

"The title is dowser, or even alchemist, if you believe me to be lying, werewolf. Wielder of the instruments of assassination if you'd like to challenge me. Again. Only friends call me by my first name these days."

Audrey's face blanked of emotion. She wasn't necessarily afraid of me, but she was definitely thinking through the consequences of continuing to push me. The beta of the West Coast North American Pack was usually much more diplomatic, which made me even more certain that the foreign magic I'd picked up earlier was at the root of this unfortunate skirmish.

I glanced over at Kandy. "How badly did your beta ruin my sweater?" I asked, allowing the tension to ease out of my voice and body language.

Kandy laughed. "The back is completely shredded."

I gave Audrey a peeved look, but kept my tone playful. "Merino, cashmere, and silk. Hand knit by my grandmother, beta."

The dark-haired werewolf offered me the hint of a smile, taking my lead and softening her demeanor. "I'd be happy to offer compensation."

I nodded seriously. "See's Candies will do. When you're next in town."

"Your wish is my command ... Jade." Her using my first name again was a deliberate claim. Of my friendship. And possibly my loyalty.

I nodded, then turned back to the more pressing issue. Namely, the vampire who'd suddenly decided to attack a werewolf.

Jasmine was still on the ground, her back pressed against the wall beside the open door to my office. She regarded me with a steady blue gaze through her mass of riotous curls. "My head feels like it's been split open."

"You're lucky, vampire," Lara snarled from her corner of the kitchen. "The beta should have torn it off."

Kandy cringed, and for a moment, I thought Lara was going to renew her attempts to attack Jasmine.

Then Audrey stepped into my eyeline, her gaze on Lara. "Surely I misheard, my enforcer," she purred. "You couldn't have just thoughtlessly used the term 'should have' in reference to a choice your beta made."

Lara dropped her gaze. Then, obviously deeming that to not be a strong enough reaction, she dropped to one knee and tilted her head to expose her neck.

A bruise was forming around the bite Jasmine had inflicted. The wound was still seeping blood.

Jasmine moaned quietly. "I'm so sorry. I don't know why I did that. I wasn't even hungry. I've never bitten anyone before."

A look of distaste overtook Audrey's stern features.

"It's okay, Jasmine," I said. "Figuring out the why is next on our list of things to do."

"I can…I can fix it. Heal it." Jasmine bit her lip, making the offer to me rather than Lara. "At least, I think I can. I've never…tried. Never needed to …" She stopped talking, glancing around at all of us in uncomfortable dismay.

"What the hell do you eat, then?" Kandy asked.

I elbowed my BFF in the ribs, reminding her—with no particular subtlety—that Jasmine wasn't going to be comfortable talking about her still fairly new feeding habits. Especially not in front of Audrey and Lara. Plus, I already had an inkling of the answer, based on Kett's need to continually shore up power.

Jasmine reached up and touched the gold chain at her neck. It had come loose from her blouse in the tussle. The tiny reconstructions hanging from it flared at her touch, and a hint of nutmeg teased my senses. I wondered whether she could still feel the magic of the cubes in her new form. Or whether touching the necklace was simply habitual. Comforting.

"My saliva should heal the wound," she whispered, not answering Kandy's question.

"Absolutely not!" Lara snarled as she looked up at her beta. "I'll shift, and it will be nothing but a nasty memory by tomorrow morning."

"It's your choice, wolf," Audrey said. "I, for one, wouldn't choose to remain weakened when in the territory of another. Not with elves running the place."

That last bit was a dig at me. I let it go without comment—though not without silently deciding that Audrey would be paying for cupcakes henceforth.

Lara looked aghast. "You'd let a vampire... lick you?"

"I wouldn't have allowed one to bite me in the first place."

Lara's face crumpled, then almost immediately hardened.

Jesus. Being a werewolf was a perpetually demoralizing lifestyle unless you were at the top of the pecking order. I glanced over at Kandy. She shrugged.

"If there's a magical trail to follow, we need to get on it," I said. "Plus, the display in the alley might be an issue."

"I didn't see any windows open," Kandy said. "Most likely due to the weather. You were partially hidden by the garbage bins. And I didn't see anyone walk by or drive into the alley. I triple-checked."

I nodded. "Moving forward, then."

Jasmine held out her hand to Lara. She was still sitting on the cracked tile floor—yeah, I was actively ignoring the state of my kitchen so I didn't melt down. But she kept her gaze somewhere around the werewolf's knees.

"The elf screwed with us last night," Lara said. "And I couldn't smell any magic." She glanced at Audrey and me for confirmation.

Kandy nodded. "Even the dowser missed it."

I huffed out an indignant breath. "I never pretend to be infallible."

"You skewered that elf in the middle of the forehead in the park." Kandy's tone was edging on accusing. "After he took down Warner and me. I'd think you'd know the taste of his magic."

Lara, Audrey, and Jasmine all looked at me.

"Hey! Apparently they have different magic, like Adepts do. And the ability to mask it. Or maybe it's because it's not of this dimension. So my senses aren't, like ... tuned up or calibrated to it."

Audrey laughed. As in, throwing back her head and howling.

Apparently, comparing my magic to getting a car serviced really got her going. Honestly, if I were the one standing around half-naked, I'd be just a little more circumspect.

Ignoring her beta's outburst, Lara stood and stepped toward Jasmine.

The vampire rose in a perfectly fluid movement—the same movement that accompanied everything Kett did.

"No biting." The purple-clad werewolf wagged her finger sternly, as if talking to a puppy.

Jasmine nodded, glancing questioningly at me, then at Kandy.

Nodding, the green-haired werewolf stepped around Lara, laying her hand along the back of Jasmine's neck. It was a gentle touch that could turn rough in an instant—backed, if necessary, by the magic of the cuffs she always wore.

Lara smoothed her hair away from her face, gathering it together at the back of her head. Then she stepped closer, offering her bruised neck to Jasmine. The two deep gouges there were still weeping blood.

The vampire reached for Lara's shoulders. Then she curled her fingers in, as if she were afraid of hurting the slightly shorter werewolf.

"Let's not take all day," Audrey said. "Elves to hunt and all."

Instead of closing the space between them, Jasmine leaned forward, running her tongue up Lara's neck without otherwise touching her. Then she paused as if observing the wound. I couldn't see fully through her cascade of curls.

The vampire gently licked Lara's neck again. And this time, the wolf sighed softly. Intimately.

Jasmine stilled for a moment. Then she carefully began lapping at Lara's neck.

Lara twined her hands through the vampire's hair, curving forward into her embrace. Jasmine placed a hand on the werewolf's lower back.

And suddenly I felt like a voyeur.

Kandy glanced over at me with wide, questioning eyes.

Lara sighed again.

"You taste good, wolf," Jasmine murmured against Lara's neck. Heady magic was laced through her words, likely some form of compulsion. "Strong. Vital. Sweet."

"Is that enough, vampire?" Audrey's question snapped through the kitchen like a whip. Or maybe that was her own magic, claiming her dominion over her enforcer.

Jasmine quickly pulled away from Lara. Then she tried to step back.

Only Lara wouldn't let her go.

Kandy reached up, untangling Lara's fingers from Jasmine's mane of golden curls. Lara moaned disappointedly. But she stepped back readily enough, pressing her hand to her neck though it appeared to be completely healed.

She grinned at Jasmine. "Nice, vampire."

Jasmine laughed, but quickly glanced away. "It's a trick, really. My saliva, combined with the residual venom in the bite, makes you feel good."

"Mmm." Lara swayed in place. "Being bitten by Kett was much the same."

Jasmine's head snapped up. "Kett bit you?"

"With permission," I interjected.

"Werewolves aren't food, vampire," Audrey snapped. "As I understand the situation, the executioner was badly wounded. Enough to hurt many innocents. Two of our wolves sacrificed some of their strength in order to quell and heal him. Nothing else."

Jasmine glanced at me.

I nodded, confirming Audrey's version of the incident in which Kett had tangled with a zombie and nearly lost. Then he'd attempted to drain me dry, forcing Desmond to come to my rescue. Though that extra detail was best left between those who already knew it.

"I think I might need a nap now," Lara murmured, swaying on her feet again.

"Sorry," Jasmine muttered.

"You can access Kandy's apartment through mine," I said, gesturing toward the open stairwell. "Just up the stairs and through the front door."

"Yes," Audrey said with a sniff. "We did sleep there last night, dowser."

"Right." I forced myself to continue being polite, though apparently doing so made me an idiot in the beta's mind. "No one should see you, but if you'd like to grab a bathrobe …"

Giving me a look, Audrey rearranged her shredded clothing so that it better covered her important bits. Then she slung Lara's arm across her shoulders. Without another word, the beta half-guided, half-carried her enforcer up the stairs to my apartment.

Jasmine watched them leave, utterly chagrined. "Kett's going to be so pissed."

Kandy howled with laughter. "Oh, yes!" She clutched her belly, trying to talk at the same time. "Oh, please, God. Let me be there when you tell him."

Jasmine twisted her lips, looking slightly nauseated. She hadn't mastered Kett's detached aspect yet, though perhaps that took decades, if not centuries. Either that or Jasmine was a particularly unique vampire emotionally.

"I need to go look for the damn elf," I said.

Kandy sobered, shaking her head. "Lara, Audrey, and I circled twice, doubling back over each other. No elves. At least none we could smell."

"Yeah, I was worried about that." I stepped closer to Jasmine, thinking about how I'd felt the elf magic when I'd grabbed her elbow.

She smoothed her hand down her ruined suede jacket—the second one I'd helped her destroy in as many days. Though if she found a good tailor, she might be able to get the arm reattached.

"May I touch you?" I asked. "I don't know how you were spelled ... if you were spelled."

"It didn't feel like magic, but ... I wasn't naturally talented like that ... even as a witch."

Kandy stepped up beside me, leaning in to sniff Jasmine. After an initially disconcerted moment, the vampire remained still. "Smells like vamp," the green-haired werewolf muttered. "And the necklace. Witch magic."

"Wisteria," Jasmine murmured. Then she smiled softly.

I brushed my fingers across her shoulder, then down her arm. Trying to taste beyond her sweet peppermint and that unknown spice that clearly marked her as a vampire, I breathed through the scent of Wisteria's nutmeg magic in the reconstructions on the necklace. "I tasted elf magic briefly outside when I touched you."

"Maybe we need to step outside," Jasmine said. "Through the wards again."

"No," Kandy said. "Not without finding the source of whatever was influencing you. We don't need Kett pissed at us as well."

I nodded, only vaguely listening to them as I brushed my fingers down Jasmine's other arm. Then I found what appeared to be a small plastic dot stuck to the cuff of her silk blouse. Almost on the very edge. A section that would have been exposed even before she'd torn off the sleeve of her jacket.

I had to actually touch it to get even a glimmer of magic from it. Which made sense, since its hold on Jasmine had been severed once I'd gotten her behind the bakery wards. Still, the idea that something so small could be powerful enough to make a vampire see things—even a fledgling—was disturbing. And even as a guess, this tiny touch of elf magic might have also exacerbated the antagonism between Jasmine and the werewolves. And the power that backed that sort of reach was chilling.

Brushing the supposition off as unhelpful until it was verified, I carefully peeled the dot off Jasmine's cuff. It was the size of the tip of my middle finger.

"What the hell?" Kandy leaned in to sniff the dot. "What's that? Plastic? Like one of those bumpers you put on a cupboard door? Or underneath something so it doesn't scratch your coffee table?"

"It isn't plastic," I said grimly. "It's a drop of elf blood. At least that's what I think it is."

"Blood?" Jasmine whispered. "As in... blood magic?" Witches had an ingrained thing against blood magic—apparently to such an extent that Jasmine was forgetting she wasn't a witch anymore.

"Yeah. I mean, I'm guessing. But elf blood is thick and clear like this. I've seen it turn to a fine powder, like pulverized crystal, when removed from their bodies."

Kandy snorted. "Well, that one time at least."

I nodded thoughtfully. "And the illusionist's magic does seem to work completely differently. So... I really am just guessing."

"But ..." Jasmine hesitated. "If you want my opinion ..."

"We don't stand on ceremony here, vampire." Kandy wagged her fingers toward Jasmine, encouraging her to speak.

I laughed. "We're usually in the dark for way too long as it is, even when everyone is contributing."

"Okay. I don't think I was seeing things. Like, not illusions, at least."

"What about the text messages?"

"Yeah, sure. But then they weren't there, right? And can the illusionist even confine her magic to only one viewer like that? We all heard the wolf on the cliff, right? The werewolves' reaction was just stronger."

"Just because you two don't care about a wounded animal," Kandy grumbled snarkily.

Ignoring her, I spoke to Jasmine. "What did it feel like? I know you don't feel magic like I do. But?"

"Like I was going crazy," Jasmine whispered. Her attention was trained on the solid dot of elf blood at the tip of my finger.

I glanced at Kandy. She shook her head once, grimacing ruefully.

"Telepath?" I offered up the suggestion hoping I was wrong.

Jasmine nodded. "Maybe. Could be. But not just any mind reader. Someone capable of creating a psionic dissonance and planting complex scenarios based on my own ... concerns, obsessions ..."

"Jesus," I muttered. "An uber-telepath who works with some form of blood magic. As what? Something that broadcasts magic, like Wi-Fi? Except personalized?" I refocused my questions to Jasmine. "Why did you go out tonight? Because of the text message you thought you got from me?"

"No. And if being behind the bakery wards severed the connection ..."

"Then the elf wouldn't have been able to trigger the spell and manipulate you until you'd left the building. He or she must have been waiting, and then ... simply brushed up against you without you noticing."

Jasmine nodded. "I'm sorry."

"Sorry is what sorry does," Kandy drawled sardonically.

"Helpful, my wolf."

Kandy grinned toothily, like a wolf smiles at a bunny.

"So … you left the bakery, then what?" I asked.

"Then I remembered I was supposed to text you, so I stopped on the corner … and saw I already had a text."

"From me."

"Yes." Jasmine hesitated. "I thought I might try to come in … for the bridal shower. Scarlett, your mother, did invite me, and I was okay hanging out with you all in the bakery in Whistler last night. But …"

"But?" Kandy prompted.

"But, um, you're all … I thought it might be harder around witches and the necromancers …"

"Weaker prey," Kandy said matter-of-factly.

Jasmine nodded.

"You might be surprised," I said. "Especially by the necromancers." I thought about the bone bracelet with which Teresa Garrick was practically torturing her son, Benjamin. Then I sighed as I laid the puzzle pieces out before us. "What are the chances that an elf skilled as an illusionist would also be a masterful telepath?"

"In the Adept world?" Jasmine asked. "No chance at all. Both are mind magic, obviously, but they're completely different skill sets. Hell, they're different genealogies."

"Yeah," I said grimly. "I thought you were going to say that."

"The third elf." Kandy tugged her phone out of her back pocket.

Yep. The freaking third elf.

"And …" Kandy added, drawing out the word in a way that let me know I really wasn't going to like what came after it. "The telepath's magic doesn't register on the witches' grid."

Ah, the freaking grid.

"They are other-dimensional beings," Jasmine said helpfully, attempting to get a look at Kandy's phone. The werewolf belligerently angled her screen away from the vampire. "Do you have the grid up and running on your phone?"

Kandy eyed her for a moment. "Like how? With a live feed?"

Jasmine grinned, then shrugged. "I guess you're going to have to let me look at it. See what I can do."

Kandy offered Jasmine one of her patented nonsmiles.

Jasmine's grin widened. "And I might be able to figure out how to tweak it so it can register the elves' magic."

"How?" I asked.

Jasmine nodded toward the solid dot of blood on my finger. "Exactly like that, but in reverse. But I'm … ah … it's not blood magic if it's elf blood, right?"

"I don't think the Convocation would come after you for it," I said wryly.

"Well, I wouldn't be able to cast anyway. I'd need a witch. Maybe Wisteria?"

Kandy eyed her. "Would Kett want us asking the reconstructionist to fly into Vancouver? With him away?"

Jasmine set her jaw, then spoke begrudgingly. "Scarlett will do."

"Not Gran?" I asked.

Jasmine looked aghast. "I'm not asking the head of the Convocation to mess around with this sort of stuff. What if it doesn't work? Plus, um, I haven't actually been face to face with her, since … you know."

Right. Jasmine meant since she—a former tech witch—had been remade as a vampire. I hadn't realized she'd managed to avoid Gran all this time. But then, Kett managed to do so well enough.

I indicated the spot of what I hoped was dried elf blood on my fingertip. "I assume this isn't enough of a sample?"

Jasmine shook her head.

"Okay, then. We'll have to deal with that later. But first, I need a change of clothing ..."

I crossed to and flicked on the light in my office. An older green hoodie was hanging on one of the hooks behind the door, kept around for the exceedingly rare occasions when I got chilly while baking or had to step out into the alley during a snowstorm.

Jasmine appeared beside the desk, opening a few drawers until she found and liberated a half-dozen safety pins I hadn't even known were there. The golden-haired vampire then tugged off her suede jacket and began meticulously reattaching the arm with the pins.

"Planning on starting a new fashion trend?" I asked, swapping my sweater for the hoodie—and attempting to not lose the dot of elf blood in the process.

Jasmine grinned without responding. She followed me out of the office with her head still bowed over her task, managing to not trip over her own feet.

Seriously, that was skill. I could barely eat and walk at the same time.

I stepped back into the kitchen. Kandy was perched on the counter beside the oven—the only counter that appeared to have survived the tussle with Audrey unscathed. My BFF jumped down, stuffing the last pastry from a container into her mouth. She placed the empty Tupperware in the industrial dishwasher, then brushed her hands together with great satisfaction.

Damn it. I wouldn't have minded another *Florentine* myself.

Steadfastly ignoring the trashed state of the kitchen, I crossed to the exterior door, opening it and stepping through the wards. "Let's see if we can turn the tables on the elf. Assuming she's stupid enough to leave us a drop of her blood."

Kandy laughed snarkily.

"How?" Jasmine asked, following us out into the alley while tugging on her hastily repaired jacket. Somehow, she'd completely hidden the safety pins from sight. Skilled in tech and tailoring. Nice.

"Dowsing, baby girl," Kandy said. "That's what Jade does, after all. Want to go hunting with us?"

Red rolled across Jasmine's eyes, and she grinned wickedly. "I sure do."

Lovely. "Though let's keep the biting to a minimum, eh?"

Kandy laughed quietly, then whispered to Jasmine behind my back, "She always says that."

Well, this was sure to go delightfully.

Chapter Seven

Evening had taken hold of the city, even though it was just after 5:00 P.M. as I stepped out into the alley. I crossed through the wards that I was assuming had cut the hypothetical telepathic elf off from tapping into the magic embedded in the drop of solidified blood. Or, more accurately, the magic I hoped was embedded in the blood. Otherwise, I had no leads—and no easy explanation for Jasmine's behavior.

I had a sinking feeling that Audrey wasn't going to let the golden-haired vampire's unprovoked attack go. Meaning that without evidence pointing directly at the elves, the relationship between the pack and the Conclave was going to get even tenser. How this political crap had even become my concern, I didn't know. But now it was all on me to keep everyone friendly, by trying to track a being that was supposedly mythical.

Holding the elven blood magic aloft on the tip of my finger, I paused a couple of steps from the exterior bakery door, gazing up at the dark, cloudy sky. It wasn't raining, but if not for the apartment blocking my view, it was a sure bet that the craggy tips of the North Shore Mountains would have been completely obscured. I focused my dowser senses on the elf blood magic that I hoped I was holding. I'd feel pretty damn stupid if it did turn out to be a plastic bumper.

I could taste Kandy's bittersweet chocolate and Jasmine's sugary-sweet peppermint magic behind me, but nothing from the elf blood. And as the moment stretched, I found myself inwardly and sarcastically applauding my supreme arrogance. Why had I even suggested that I could track the elves through a single drop of their blood? Assuming that was actually what I was holding in the first place.

"What if the elf activates whatever magic she used on me?" Jasmine whispered. "Won't it affect the dowser?"

Kandy snorted condescendingly. "Watch and wait, baby girl."

Sounding a little put out, Jasmine said, "I imagine it was tailored to me specifically, anyway."

"Which, again, makes me wonder how they got near enough," I said. "Not only to drop the spell on you earlier today, but to take the time to watch you. To figure out your obsession with your phone and the natural enmity that vampires and werewolves have. That would have taken … weeks, maybe."

"Thinning the herd," Kandy murmured. She was scanning the alley and the rooftops across from us.

"I am not a cow, werewolf," Jasmine snarled, falling into the antagonistic-species byplay without thought.

Which maybe answered at least one of my questions—though, again, only if the elves were able to get close to us without any of us noticing, and for long periods of time.

I sighed. "Kandy means that it's possible that the elf, or elves, watched the rest of us go to the shower, then homed in on you as the easiest to access. Similar to how the illusionist attempted to draw me away from the bakery yesterday when everyone else was skiing." And if the elves deemed studying our behavior worth their time ... well, that said something interesting about the interlopers. That they were patient and manipulative.

And completely different than I'd assumed when I crossed blades with the forthright warrior elf in the park.

So how much of my exchange with him had been contrived to distract me? Taking him down had been easy. But had it been too easy? Had he actually sacrificed himself?

No.

The elf had wounded Kandy and Warner seriously enough that he'd put some effort behind it. There would have been no reason to randomly decide to pull his punches with me, who he'd deemed the weakest member of the group.

But he had placed himself deliberately in our paths. Even his attack on Burgundy had felt contrived—something that would force us to react, though perhaps elves just weren't particularly chatty to begin with. So were the remaining elves—with the illusions and the telepathic manipulation—currently testing us ... or distracting us? And if so, to what end?

Magic shifted across the tip of my finger. Just a spark—as if the elf who'd cast that magic had just pinged the connection. Similar to how I could reach out for my alchemy, whether in my wards, in Kandy's cuffs, or any of my own creations.

"Got you," I murmured. Then I took off at a light jog, cutting onto Vine Street, then down the hill toward Kits Beach.

Kandy whooped quietly, falling into place behind me without another word. Jasmine was at her side.

The slightly chilly breeze reminded me that it wasn't really the right weather to be jogging down to the beach. Also, speaking of being stupid, I was still wearing my pretty boots. I should have changed them before we left the bakery. If it came to an all-out brawl, I was going to have to remember to take them off, because I certainly wasn't ruining them over elves playing games.

Though clearly, what I'd taken to be games so far—in Whistler and in the snowstorm—could have had malicious objectives that we'd all just been too savvy to fall for. This wasn't the first time I'd been hunted—and the previous times hadn't turned out well for the hunters.

But I knew the odds dictated that someone was eventually going to be faster, stronger, and smarter than me. And it went without saying that I had more to lose now. Or was that more to protect?

I lost touch with the elf magic, pausing at the corner of West Second Avenue. Kandy continued across the residential street, then turned right, intent on looping the block. Jasmine stayed at my side. We were mostly surrounded by older three- and four-storey apartment buildings. A single red house with cream dentil moldings sat on the corner, with its tiny cream picket fence guarding dormant rose bushes. It was one of the rare remaining houses in Kitsilano, though of course, it had been converted into suites years before.

"Can you tell how close they…the elf…is?" Jasmine spoke quietly, as if worried she'd distract me.

I shook my head, waiting…waiting for someone to try to use the magic stored in the blood drop. The elves were playing games with powerful Adepts—first me, then the wolves, and now Jasmine. As if they'd spent the last three months watching us, and were now testing us, one by one. With the illusionist, I'd inadvertently proved that I could tear through elf magic. And now with Jasmine, even with the change in the elves' tactics, I had thwarted their attempt. Though, to be fair, I hadn't figured out what was up with the golden-haired vampire terribly quickly.

But what was it they were attempting? Internal discord?

"Why do I suddenly feel like a hamster?" I murmured.

"How so?" Jasmine asked. "You aren't in a cage. You aren't even prey. Far from it."

I nodded, though I'd been referring specifically to the idea of endlessly running on an exercise wheel that went nowhere.

Kandy appeared on the sidewalk to our right, padding silently through the pools of light that formed underneath the regularly spaced street lamps. She slunk in and out of deep shadow, as predatory as if she were wearing her wolf form. Her eyes were blazing green, but she shook her head at my questioning look. So she'd scented nothing.

"Maybe it's time to update Kett and Warner?" I asked. I wanted to keep my attention on the hunt—but I also remembered my promise.

"Already ahead of you," Kandy said.

"Where the hell are they, anyway?"

"Do you really want to know?" Kandy wagged her eyebrows.

I laughed quietly. "Are they heading back?"

"You think we need their help badly enough to interrupt their fun?"

I grimaced ruefully, but I shook my head. The telepathic elf was a concern, for sure, but not enough of one to call in reinforcements. Not yet, anyway. I just wanted Warner back in town for purely selfish reasons.

The magic in the elf blood shifted, tugging me north again. From what I could tell, that was the same orientation as before—implying that the elf was stationary. So far.

"So …" I said. "They've laid a trap?"

Kandy flashed me a toothy grin. "Let's hope."

Jasmine glanced between us. "You two are a little crazy, you know."

Kandy shrugged. "You'll get it, baby girl. When you're all grown up and never meet your match."

Jasmine twisted her lips wryly, tugging her phone out of her jacket pocket. "I've already met him."

Kandy laughed huskily, shaking her head. "The nearly immortal are more vulnerable than us three, darling. They've forgotten they can die. And it's the possibility of death that keeps us sharp." Kandy tapped her temple.

Emulating her master, Jasmine raised one eyebrow at the green-haired werewolf, texting without looking at her screen. "Thanks for the life lesson, wolf."

Kandy snapped her teeth. "You can owe it to me, vampire."

I laughed. "Shall we continue?"

Kandy swept her hand forward, indicating that I should lead the way. I jogged across the street, covering two more blocks and reaching Cornwall before the magic tugged me north again. But also a little to the left. Toward Kits Pool.

And also toward Gran's house.

That couldn't be good.

Kandy, Jasmine, and I had just passed the administration buildings that backed Kits Pool when the magic in the dot of blood ebbed again.

I slowed, then paused, taking in the well-lit and busy neighborhood against the darkness of the night.

Vehicles streamed steadily by us on Cornwall—we'd opted for the roadside path, not the seawall—likely filled with commuters heading home from work. The closer we came to Gran's house, the more expensive the vehicles and homes became. Single strings of Christmas lights along the occasional apartment balcony or roof-line became showy displays, replete with white wire deer and light-twined trees so tall that they would have taken a cherry picker to decorate.

"Signal died again?" Kandy asked.

Nodding, I stepped off the paved path, giving way to the joggers and bikers trying to get some exercise on a nonrainy day.

A misplaced shadow shifted along the eaves of the recreation building that blocked our view of the pool and the seawall beyond—Freddie, the shadow leech, showing itself but not approaching. Though I hadn't seen the leech since before I'd gone to Whistler, I'd left a set of magically charged coins for Freddie's consumption on my bedroom's Juliet balcony that morning, swapping them for the three pieces of sea glass currently in the pocket of my hoodie. I had salvaged the sea glass from my ruined sweater, carrying them with me everywhere infused them with my magic.

Since the leech had taken part in the incident with the elf in the park—and, specifically, the way Freddie showed that it understood the elf was an enemy by trying to protect Burgundy—I'd gotten less worried about the risk of it breaking my 'no siphoning magic from Adepts' rule. I also suspected that it had been getting fed by another hand over the previous few months—Mory's hand, to be specific. I couldn't prove it, though, and as long as the shadow leech remained friendly, it seemed overly controlling to intervene. Mory felt like I hovered too much already.

"Hey, Freddie," I whispered to the creeping shadow.

Kandy flinched, instinctively shoving herself between the leech—which she couldn't actually see—and Jasmine.

"What?" Jasmine hissed, looking around frantically for an attack she couldn't see coming.

Ignoring them both, I stepped closer to the building. I pulled out my phone, trying to look as though I wasn't talking to thin air by staring down at the screen. "Have you seen any elves around?"

"Who the hell is she talking to?" Jasmine asked.

"The bloody leech," Kandy said. "Little creep." Then she softened her tone. "Except for that one time."

Freddie poured down the side of the building, clinging to the red-brown brick just above my shoulder. I raised my hand, palm up, and the leech reached out a tentative curl of shadow to touch me. The taste of burnt cinnamon toast tickled my senses, but it was muted.

"The elves?" I murmured, not expecting an answer but trying to create a sense of connection nonetheless. Shailaja had been able to communicate with the shadow leeches, but they were her creations, not mine.

Freddie chittered so quietly that I barely heard it, then it withdrew from touching me. The leech sounded mournful, and I didn't like the muted nature of its magic.

"I left you coins," I said. "On the balcony." It was early in the evening and Freddie avoided daylight, so maybe the leech hadn't fed yet. Or it wasn't feeding enough. And that didn't seem like a good idea.

Slitted red eyes appeared in the center of Freddie's amorphous body. The leech blinked, slowly. Maybe showing that it was listening.

"Okay. Go eat, then." I said it a little gruffly, feeling like an idiot for trying to have a conversation with the leech. "Then...check in with me." I glanced over at Kandy. "We might have a job for you."

Freddie chittered again, flashing needle-like teeth at me before it disappeared.

"A job for it?" Kandy echoed.

I shrugged, tucking my phone back in my satchel. "The leech is another set of eyes, isn't it?"

"You don't even know that it understands you."

"It understands me. I just...don't understand it."

Kandy sighed heavily, muttering something about "shadow creeps" and "magical suck-faces" under her breath.

Jasmine was looking back and forth between us, far more incredulously than anyone who'd grown up around magic should have been. "You know it looked like you were talking to yourself?"

"I covered," I said lamely. "With my phone."

"You totally didn't."

Kandy snickered.

"What is a leech exactly?" Jasmine asked.

"You don't want to meet Freddie if Jade's not around." Kandy shuddered, likely in remembrance of her last encounter with the leeches—when they were under Shailaja's control. "Ask Kett."

Jasmine twisted her lips. "Honestly, my unanswered list of questions for him is already longer than my to-be-asked list."

Kandy barked out a laugh.

"Benjamin is writing a chapter on Freddie," I said, completely empathizing with Jasmine. I knew what it was like to feel as though you were constantly asking questions and only getting half answers. And from Kett, specifically. "Or at least an entry. For his chronicle."

"Benjamin?" Jasmine echoed, clearly having no idea who I was talking about.

Kandy and I glanced at each other.

"Garrick," I said, opting for a casual tone—even though I was pretty certain I was filling the golden-haired vampire in on information she should have already known. "The vampire that Kett is mentoring. Teresa Garrick's son."

The red of Jasmine's magic rolled across her eyes. "Benjamin Garrick is in Vancouver." Her tone was low and dark, but then she shook her head. "No, I…actually, I should have known that…Wisteria arranged it. I'm not sure…why …" She trailed off, looking down at her phone but not texting anything.

But what she'd been about to ask was an easy guess. Why wouldn't Kett have introduced her to Benjamin? I'd have been wondering that as well if I were her. Except, of course, Kett liked to keep all aspects of his life more than simply boxed up. The executioner erected steel walls that only he could shift when necessary, as when he'd finally introduced Jasmine to Kandy and me.

"Maybe he didn't think it was a good idea …" Jasmine muttered to herself, trying to justify Kett's actions. "With both of us being young and all …"

"Don't make excuses for him, baby girl," Kandy said. "Kett does what Kett does. He has reasons, of course, but they're only relevant to him. The only thing you control in any situation is what you do."

Jasmine's face blanked, as if realizing that she'd said too much. She didn't like to talk about Kett. At least, she didn't like to talk about Kett with me. But that was fair enough, because I didn't bring the executioner up in conversation either.

"Benjamin Garrick is writing a chronicle about ... you?" Jasmine asked.

"Crazy, huh?" Kandy gave me a side-eyed look.

"It's actually about the modern world of the Adept," I said. "Benjamin says all the books Kett has been lending him are antiquated."

"You can say that again," Jasmine muttered. "But still ... that's potentially dangerous information."

"Ah, yeah?" Kandy mocked. "What did I just say?"

Jasmine's phone buzzed in her hand. She tapped the screen, opening the message.

"What's old toothy up to?" Kandy asked knowingly.

Jasmine snorted, shoving the phone in her pocket without replying to the text.

Kandy laughed under her breath.

"Did you tattle on the fledgling, my wolf?" I asked teasingly.

"Might have."

I glanced at Jasmine questioningly.

She lifted one shoulder in a casual shrug. "He said, 'Stop biting everyone.' And that 'Werewolves are apex prey, tasty but tough.' "

Kandy choked on her own laughter. "Who else have you bitten?"

"No one," Jasmine said sourly. "He's exaggerating."

"The executioner isn't prone to exaggeration," I said.

Tired of waiting for the elf to trigger the magic in the dot of dried blood once again, I reached out with my dowser senses, scanning the well-lit area with more than just my eyes. I could feel the edge of Gran's house wards, though we were still a couple of blocks away.

"I think I'd know if I were going around biting people, Jade," Jasmine said crossly. "Especially because you'd be first in line." The golden-haired vampire widened her eyes, looking aghast.

"Well, now…that would be a sight to behold." Kandy wagged her eyebrows at me.

"Um, oh …" Jasmine said. "I just mean…you …" She looked a little ill. "Smell…tasty."

Kandy nodded encouragingly. "Like Chinese food."

"What?" Jasmine all but cried out. "She does not! No…no, you just know she'd be sweet but…spicy …" Then she clamped her mouth closed, carefully not looking at me.

Kandy started chortling, having deliberately baited the young vampire into confessing her bloodlust.

"You are very controlled," I said kindly.

The green-haired werewolf started weeping with laughter, bent over her knees. Jasmine eyed her as if she were thinking of going in for a bite. And not just a love nip.

"Very…controlled," I repeated.

Jasmine nodded, looking deliberately away. "Kett's blood is potent. I'm his first child. And he was…concerned about my transition. So he …" She waved her hand.

The gesture could have meant anything, but I took it as a reference to her feeding habits. Specifically, based on the information I'd wrangled out of the executioner when he'd tasked me with watching over Jasmine while he was off cavorting with my fiancé, I understood that she fed only from Kett himself.

This arrangement was so Kett could continually transfer more and more of his magic to her. According to him, human blood wasn't anywhere near potent enough. Or at least it would have taken Jasmine longer to gain control of the bloodlust, as well as hone her own abilities, while on a nonmagical diet. And the executioner wasn't a fan of weakness in any form—especially not in his own child.

This was why Jasmine could tolerate the sun, though she didn't exactly like it. This was why she wasn't a slaughter-focused fiend chained in a basement for the first decade or more of her undead existence. And this was why—or at least I was reading between the lines with this particular supposition—Kett had kept Jasmine in Vancouver and away from London. To give them both time to adjust to their new roles, and to build up their power.

"Kett's careful," I said. "Usually." Then I corrected myself. "With others. Not necessarily himself."

Jasmine nodded, still keeping her gaze away from Kandy as the werewolf's chortling faded.

Then something exploded to my far right. Blocks away.

Something powerful.

Something that tasted of my grandmother's lilac witch magic.

I spun, turning toward the forceful pulse I could feel flooding our way. A wave of residual energy crashed over me, reverberating with decades of carefully layered magic. Gran's wards. Reacting to an assault of some sort.

"What the—" Jasmine cried out, actually stumbling with the flash flood of energy.

Kandy took off down the paved pathway in the direction of Gran's. I followed, tight on the werewolf's heels but letting her lead. Leaving Jasmine's question unasked and unanswered, we ran, completely heedless of moving too swiftly along the edge of a busy road filled with evening commuters.

Another wash of energy came from the direction of Gran's house. Perhaps the result of a secondary attempt to breach the wards. And with it came the taste of rain and the depths of an evergreen forest.

"Elf," I said, taking the lead from Kandy without effort. "Maybe more than one." And if I couldn't wipe the grin of anticipation from my face? Well, who could blame me?

I rounded the laurel hedges at the top of Gran's drive, skidding to a stop at the edge of the driveway. The wrought-iron gate was open, but the wards were undisturbed.

My grandmother was standing before her front door with her arms extended to the cloudy night sky. Her long gray hair, loosed from its braids, churned with power in a wild halo around her. Blue lightning streamed from her fingers. This breathtaking display of power fed upward into the dome of her property wards, then etched itself across the entire protective boundary. It radiated out through the witches' grid in what I knew was thirteen different directions, though I didn't step back to count. But I could imagine the energy streaking over the city in a vivid display that any Adept who could see or feel magic would stop to marvel at … or to dread.

"Wow," Kandy murmured.

Jasmine slammed into my back. Apparently, she hadn't seen me stop.

Gran locked her blazing blue eyes on me, then she cackled.

Yes, cackled.

"That stung them," she cried gleefully, slowly reining in her magic.

Them.

"Two?" I yelled down the drive and across the front yard, not wanting to risk passing through the active wards.

"At least." Gran smiled at me, full of confidence and pride. "Happy hunting, my granddaughter. Don't be late for your dinner."

"She won't!" Kandy shouted. The werewolf was already pacing along the street-side edge of the wards, leaning down to sniff the sidewalk despite the fact that the neighborhood was bustling with nonmagicals, all of whom were completely ignorant of the skirmish that had just taken place between Gran and the elves. Thankfully, for the most part, they were literally blind to magic.

"Jasmine," I said, already dowsing for the elves' magic myself. "Stay with Gran."

"Stay? Here?" Jasmine echoed incredulously. She was holding her nose as if she'd hurt herself running into me.

"She might need backup."

"Backup? Did you see her? Even I could feel the power pouring from her."

"Jasmine ..." I cranked my head over my shoulder to eye the vampire. She scuttled slightly to my left as I turned, as if she were attempting to hide behind me. "Are you scared of Gran?"

"Who isn't? Even Kett keeps his distance."

I glanced across the yard at my grandmother. She was straightening the strings of Christmas lights twisted around two potted cedars on her front step. She all but radiated a calm composure, except for the cascade of gray hair spilling over her shoulders and down her back. Tinted with the blue of her witch magic, that hair was still writhing slightly, stirred by a nonexistent breeze.

"Hey, Gran?" I called. "Jasmine is going to stay with you. Kandy and I will be right back."

Gran nodded absentmindedly, then waved her hand toward us. The magic of the wards shifted, allowing Jasmine entry.

The golden-haired vampire looked at me as if I were condemning her to a brutal death.

"You wanted a look at the grid command center, didn't you?" I asked coaxingly. Out of the corner of my eye, I saw Kandy pick up a trail at the edge of the street, then dart across Point Grey Road between two slow-moving vehicles.

Jasmine crossed her arms. But the gesture wasn't defiant, more as if she was trying to downplay her reaction to the chance of laying eyes on the epicenter of the witches' grid. "Kett said I was to stick with you."

"And I'm asking you to guard my grandmother," I said sternly, emotionally blackmailing the fledgling vampire thoroughly and completely. Though I honestly did think she could back Gran up if needed.

Jasmine nodded begrudgingly, turning to pass through the wards and jog down the driveway.

"Don't bite any elves," I called after the golden-haired vampire. "Their blood turns weird when separated from their bodies. Might not be very tasty."

Jasmine grumbled something under her breath that sounded like, "One bloody time …"

I laughed. Kandy darted across the street again, walking swiftly back the way we'd come. I jogged to catch up to her.

"At least one of them is hurt." The werewolf paused to peer at the grass along the sidewalk.

I couldn't see what had drawn her attention, nor could I taste any unusual magic in the immediate vicinity. But the green-haired werewolf was a different sort of tracker than I was. Less dependent on her magic, and she could pick up other physical cues as well. It was a skill set I knew I should definitely think about honing at some point—even more so given the recent evidence of how my reliance on my dowser senses was hindering me from hunting down the elves.

Truth be told, I was starting to feel somewhat vulnerable. Even with the firepower I had slung around my neck, I was slightly out of my depth. I had no idea why the elves would escalate from playing games with Jasmine, the werewolves, and me to outright attacking Gran. Or at least trying to take down her wards. Were they trying to distract me with Jasmine so they could attempt to gain access to the witches' grid? Or even disable it? And if so, why? What threat did the grid pose? It couldn't even be used to track them. Not yet, at least.

Though how the elves would have known any of that, I had no idea.

Kandy straightened, continuing along the sidewalk back toward Kits Pool.

"Blood trail?"

"Burned, I think. Judging by the smell, and not really a surprise. I certainly wouldn't want to face your grandmother alone when she goes dark."

When she goes dark. Not *if*. Ignoring the implication of that, I asked, "Did they double back around us?"

Kandy grunted in the affirmative.

Ahead of us, close to Kits Pool, a large chow chow out for a walk began to bark. It was straining against its leash, nearly toppling its owner.

Kandy laughed quietly—a pleased, proactively victorious sound. "It's difficult to hide quite so effectively when you're wounded."

Without needing to discuss our next moves, we each picked up our pace, parting ways where the path split off in three directions. Kandy doubled back along the roadside path at the back of the recreational facility while I cut down to the seawall, passing the gated entrance to the outdoor pool and turning left.

Ahead of me, the seawall ran in a fairly straight stretch. The paved path was roughly four feet wide and only sporadically lit by overhead lamps. It cut between the high chain-link fence that marked the edge of the pool's concrete deck and the two-foot-high rounded cement barrier that dropped down to the rocky beach on my right. The tide was high enough that the churning surf had splashed onto and darkened the top of the concrete.

About a half-dozen feet ahead of me, another dog out for a walk abruptly lost its mind. It was a pretty little mop of a thing—maybe a shih tzu—and was lunging toward the cement base of the chain-link fence as if sighting prey. Though what had attracted its attention, I couldn't see.

The dog's owner, unable to soothe it verbally, swept her agitated pet up in her arms and continued on. As they passed me, the dog was panting, nostrils flaring as it looked back over its owner's shoulder with dark, beady eyes.

I paused near the section of fence that the shih tzu had fixated on, stepping to the side so I wouldn't block the path while I peered through the chain-link wire.

Kits Pool was closed for the season. Its salt-water pool was chemically treated to withstand the winter weather, though it occasionally froze if it got cold enough. At that time of year, it often boasted a large population of seagulls and ducks, but there were no wild fowl in sight.

I glanced both ways. The path to either side was momentarily clear. I leaped forward, springing halfway up the high chain-link fence, then flipping over it. Landing softly, I immediately darted left, hiding in the deep shadows of a massive winter-bare chestnut tree. In the summer, sunbathers often arrived early in the day to secure spots for their towels on the grassy section underneath the boughs of the tree, rather than the wide concrete surround of the pool itself. Behind me and slightly to my left was a small water park for kids.

I waited in the shadows, peering across the serenely still pool and listening. To my far left, the traffic on Cornwall remained a steady drone. To my right, a murmur of conversation ebbed and flowed as pedestrians traversed the path in both directions. Over it all, the surf slapped steadily against the rocky shore and the concrete edge of the seawall.

Another dog—unseen from my vantage point—exploded in a frenzy of barks at the far end of the long pool. Disconcerted shouts from an obviously confused owner followed.

Kandy suddenly appeared, scaling a far section of the fence, then dropping silently onto the smooth concrete that edged the pool. Her eyes were glowing green with her shifter magic. She had turned her neon-green jacket inside out, presumably having decided that the darker fabric of its interior lining would disappear more easily in the dark.

I stepped out of the deep shadow of the tree, revealing myself to her. After catching her gaze, I stepped back, holding my magic in a tight coil around me.

Kandy crouched. Then, picking up whatever trail she was following, she slunk along the opposite edge of the pool, slowly crossing toward the low brick building that housed the change rooms, showers, and administrative offices.

At the far corner of the pool, she disappeared.

Just vanished.

From my sight. And from my dowser senses.

Fear washed down my spine, threatening to freeze me in place. But I stifled it, calling my knife into my hand. Dowsing, no matter how much I relied on it, wasn't my only ability.

Leaving my hiding spot, I cautiously followed the same course Kandy had been walking, but on the opposite side of the pool. The entire area appeared to be empty. But two steps from the corner of the pool closest to the building, I felt elf magic.

The illusionist.

I continued to step sideways, keeping my knife mostly hidden within the folds of my skirt. I was exceedingly aware that I was in full view of any pedestrian who might care to glance over from the seawall. I might have been able to talk myself out of a trespassing charge easily enough. But getting caught waving a jade blade around would be a different matter.

Suddenly and abruptly, I wasn't standing at the edge of Kits Pool in the middle of December anymore.

I was on the rocky shore of a wide purple ocean. Waves sedately rolled across what appeared to be a black-sand beach. Two moons shone brightly overhead, one smaller than the other. A breeze that somehow felt thick, perhaps with salt, rustled my curls.

Damn it. I was so going to ruin my boots.

Assuming that I was now hidden from the sight of anyone nearby—as Kandy had disappeared from my view—I raised my knife before me, setting one foot behind the other, ready to lunge and stab. "More games, elf?" I asked the deserted beach before me. "I believe I've already proven that I can tear through your illusions. And you didn't appear to take that well last time."

The elf I'd seen in Whistler appeared some twenty feet before me. A vicious, blackened burn across her face and neck continued across one shoulder, destroying her pretty blue, puffy jacket.

"Dowser," she said. "We haven't been properly introduced." Her British lilt was most definitely less pronounced, smoother, than the accent of the elf I'd murdered three months previously.

"That's your failing, not mine," I said.

She lifted her undamaged shoulder in an exaggerated shrug. Another learned human gesture, perhaps. "These things aren't my decisions. I'm not the power here."

She wasn't referring to me. Or to Kandy. I was pretty certain she was talking about whoever sat on the throne she'd shown me.

"The telepath?" I asked.

The elf laughed. A low, hearty chuckle. "Is that what you would call her?"

"Why attack Gran's house?"

That question made her pause.

I clarified. "The powerful witch responsible for your wounds."

"Why do you attack anything in a foreign territory?"

I frowned. "I don't."

She tilted her head, but didn't elaborate.

"Are you the distraction?" I said. "Another sacrifice?"

"A sacrifice?" she asked in a whisper.

"Like the warrior in the park."

"Is he dead?"

Now it was my turn to pause. "What did you think happened to him?"

"I was ... I thought you might have captured him."

"He tried to kill people under my protection."

She shook her head. A gesture of sadness, if I was reading her correctly. "Did the guardian come? With the golden sword?"

She meant my father, Yazi. I wondered when and where she'd seen him—or, given the timeline of her incarceration, his predecessor. "No."

She regarded me steadily. "You three were not possibly powerful enough. Four, if I bother counting the lame witch who had already fainted."

I stepped forward, slowly closing the space between us. "It didn't take three."

The elf raked her gaze over me, her expression souring. "You? Impossible."

"Yeah, I get that a lot."

Anger flashed across her face. The center of her burn was already healed to a dark pink, but blackened tissue still radiated out across her pale, finely scaled skin.

"So …" I said, almost within striking range. "Are you another sacrifice, then? A distraction so the telepath can flee?"

"A strategic retreat."

"Sure. Or she's just a coward."

The elf's expression turned stony. "What you should be asking, witchling, is where the wolf is wandering?"

Something large splashed to my right. But other than the soft, rolling purple surf of the illusion, I couldn't see anything move.

Water.

Deep water.

Kits Pool.

And Kandy couldn't swim. By some weird quirk of their magic, shapeshifters' body mass and strength worked against them in deep water.

"What would you be willing to sacrifice, dowser?" the elf asked tauntingly.

I turned, already diving toward the pool that should have been on my right. Though all I could see was a black-sand beach.

The elf ran past me.

I sliced through the illusion hands first, sliding through it into the deep, bone-chilling water of Kits Pool. I couldn't see anything. I couldn't taste anything.

I touched down. I'd hit bottom. Spinning around in the dark water, I caught a glimpse of a wash of gold.

The magic of the cuffs.

I reached for their power, calling it to me. The artifacts responded to my call, dragging Kandy with them. She was thrashing madly, struggling to breathe.

I grabbed the drowning werewolf by the shoulders, slamming my feet down onto the concrete and forcefully propelling us upward.

I broke the surface, gasping for air. Then I dragged Kandy to the edge of the pool.

She grasped the concrete, coughing up a lungful of water. "What the hell sort of chemicals are in this? It's going to completely ruin my hair!"

I tried to laugh, but a shudder overtook it. "Your hair? What about my boots?"

Kandy slung her arm around my shoulders, allowing me to drag her to the concrete stairs at the corner of the pool. Clinging to each other, we climbed out of the freezing water.

Shivering violently, my BFF murmured, "I'm sorry. I could smell the magic, but all I could see was purple water and black sand. Then I was in the pool."

I shook my head. "More games."

"I'm good to pick up the trail."

"It's six degrees Celsius. And we're soaking wet. What's that in American? Minus fifteen?"

"Fahrenheit." Kandy curled her lip, completely affronted. "And more like forty-three degrees."

I laughed.

Kandy shook her head, spraying me with icy droplets of chemical-laced pool water. But at least she was smiling instead of blaming herself for getting caught in the elf's trap.

Shivering myself, I took my hoodie off and tried to wring some of the water out of it. I didn't even glance down at my soaked boots. It wasn't the time for tears. "We'll head back to Gran's. See if the grid lit up at all. If it did, maybe we can track the elves that way. At least it will give us a baseline. Right?"

Kandy looked grim. "Let's hope. I hate to think they can sling that much magic around and have us still be blind to it. It's annoying enough that they can hide from sight and sound. How'd you track the elf here?"

"The dogs on the seawall. The illusionist was badly burned, like you thought. I figured the dogs were picking up her scent."

"Yeah, just that weird smell…no footprints, no magic residual. Not even broken blades of grass. If I could have transformed, I might have scented more." She shivered again, then pushed her damp hair back from her face. "I'm glad I bought those waterproof cases for our phones."

I laughed. "Priorities."

"Exactly."

Kandy slung her arm through mine and we crossed out of the pool enclosure. Skirting the cashier booth, we jumped over the gate at the entrance—and completely startled a couple jogging side by side along the adjacent path.

"Bachelorette party," Kandy crowed merrily.

The couple laughed, easily shaking off their momentary alarm as they kept up the pace of their jog. "Have fun!"

"We plan to!"

Sure. Great.

Right after we dried off, then figured out what the hell the elves were doing.

It wasn't as though we hadn't expected an assault. But it wasn't Warner, Kandy, or me that the elves had attacked. It was Gran. Gran's house.

The anchor point of the witches' grid.

I had thought previously about how the grid might have been their target. Its magic had seemed to piss off the warrior elf in the park—and even though Warner, Kandy, and I were all far more of a threat than Burgundy, he'd attacked her first. Though it still wasn't clear that doing so hadn't just been some sort of feint.

So if the grid was the elves' focus, then why? So far, it hadn't even helped us track their movements. And seeing as how they could almost completely cloak themselves from my dowser senses, what could they be worried about the witches picking up on?

If they were playing us, if they were testing us, then what was the endgame?

Chapter Eight

Sodden and shivering, Kandy and I were intercepted by Gran two feet inside her granite-tiled entranceway.

"Basement bathroom." Gran pointed sternly back through the still-open door behind us.

"Gran," I whined.

"I'll bring you extra towels. Did you find the elves?"

"One. And she pretty much found us. Then got away."

"That last part was my fault," Kandy said.

Gran harrumphed, then actually tapped her foot while eyeing the puddles forming beneath us. "Go. I'll bring you something to wear. You can put everything through the wash."

Grumbling, I hightailed it back out of the house. Crossing along the path toward the garage entrance, I jogged past Gran's car, then through the basement door. Kandy chortled quietly behind me the entire way.

"Yeah, hilarious, wolf," I said peevishly. "This skirt is dry-clean only."

Kandy snorted. "You haven't used a dry cleaner in years."

Gran flicked on the lights in the hallway that bisected the lowest level of the house. She was waiting for us at the bottom of the stairs, her arms full of the most beautiful, puffy, and hopefully absorbent towels in the world.

Kandy picked up her pace, grabbing the top two towels from the stack in Gran's arms. "Dibs on the shower!" She pressed a kiss to my grandmother's cheek, then took off down the hall toward the bathroom just off the laundry room.

I sighed, taking a towel from Gran and halfheartedly drying my hair.

Gran smiled at me, briefly touching my cheek. "We'll figure out how to deal with the elves. Jasmine and I have already discussed a few options with the grid."

My stomach sank slightly. I seriously hoped that those 'options' didn't include trying to tie me to the witches' grid again. That wasn't an argument I wanted to rekindle. "Oh?"

Gran laughed quietly. "Come. I'll get you those clothes."

I expected her to head back up the stairs. But instead, she headed down the hall. Halfway along, I paused at the door to the map room, glancing in to see Jasmine sitting in the center of the floor, meditating. I could understand her urge to do so. The power literally etched into the walls in black paint was awe-inspiring.

"Jade?"

I glanced down the hall. Gran was standing in the door to her storage room, holding a large box.

"You should be able to find something in here."

I closed the space between us, and Gran pressed the box into my arms. Then she immediately began hustling back down the hall toward the stairs. "I'll put on the kettle."

I glanced down at the box. It was unlabeled. I set it down at my feet, then tore off the strip of tape that held the flaps closed.

Various items of clothing—jeans, T-shirts, socks, underwear—were neatly folded within. I picked up a hand-knit sweater, catching the scent of the lavender laundry soap that Gran favored. She had knitted the black cardigan years before, adding a touch of red in a geometric motif reminiscent of runes around each wrist, just above the ribbed cuff.

It had been a Christmas gift.

For Sienna.

Hot tears spiked at the edges of my eyes.

Gran had kept Sienna's clothes. Or at least some of them. It was an uncharacteristic display of sentimentality, especially given that she never discussed her former foster daughter. Not a word about the twelve years she'd spent raising her. Or her descent into darkness.

I had long wondered whether Sienna might have been another item on the list of things that Scarlett held against Gran. Because if Pearl hadn't always insisted on underestimating people, my foster sister might have practiced and grown into her magic safely. In fact, Gran having decided to mentor Burgundy seemed to indicate that that difficult lesson might have actually had an impact on my grandmother. Burgundy was only a quarter-witch by blood, with a talent for healing spells and charms. The sort of Adept that Pearl would once have disdainfully all but ignored.

Kandy padded around the corner, wearing only a towel. Of course, a bath towel pretty much covered the slim werewolf from armpits to knees, and even wrapped around her twice. "Your turn, dowser. Clothing?"

I cleared my throat, straightening. "Yeah."

"Everything okay?"

"Yeah. Gran's making tea."

Kandy hunkered down and started digging through the box. "I'll debrief Pearl and baby girl while you shower. I tossed my wet clothes in the washer already."

I nodded as I turned away. Then I stepped back and gently tugged the black cardigan out of Kandy's hands.

The werewolf frowned playfully. "Not your color, dowser."

"I know … it was Sienna's …"

Kandy went stock-still. Then she stood up swiftly, pulling me in for a fierce hug. Only for a moment. And just as quickly, she let me go, digging through the box of clothing again.

And I went and took a hot shower, knowing that everything happened for a reason, no matter how much those reasons hurt my heart. Without Sienna going dark, I wouldn't have Kandy or Kett. I likely wouldn't have had Warner in my life.

I had swapped a sister for a family of magical misfits. And while most of us didn't completely fit in with the specific Adept sects we were born into, together we had made Vancouver our home.

But it just … just …

It still hurt losing someone who'd held so much of my heart for such a long time.

Since Sienna's clothes were often originally my clothes, I found a pair of light-blue jeans in the box that I could actually do up. Though I did have to lay back on Gran's basement guest bed to get them zipped. But muscle weighed more than fat, right? And yeah, I'd just go on blithely ignoring what that logic had to do with getting jeans on.

The sweater didn't fit, though. I couldn't get the buttons done up over my chest, though I stupidly tried for way too long. So I tucked it back into the box when I put it away again on Gran's tidily organized storage shelves.

Kandy opted for a blue hoodie and dark-gray leggings that were easily three times too large for her trim figure. Naturally, she totally pulled off the oversized look. She even managed to salvage her sneakers with a hairdryer.

I grabbed an old pair of well-worn, lace-up ankle boots that were a trifle tight even with thin socks. Leaving my pretty boots in the laundry sink, I offered up a whispered appeal. I didn't like to make requests of Blossom, but maybe the brownie would take pity on me and condescend to work some magic on my boots. Otherwise, I was pretty certain they'd been completely ruined by my impromptu swim.

Kandy was waiting for me, hovering in the doorway to the map room. The former recreation room occupied over half of the house's basement footprint. All four walls and the edges of the ceiling had been painted with a detailed map of Vancouver—drawn by Rochelle, then carefully painted over in black strokes.

Jasmine had pushed the only piece of furniture, a black swivel chair, over against one wall, choosing instead to sit on the light-gray-carpeted floor in a lotus position. Her computer was in her lap, and she'd set her iPad and iPhone by either knee. With her golden hair cascading from her reverently bowed head, she looked like she was actually communing with her technology, rather than meditating.

"Did the illusion at Kits Pool spike on the map?" I put the question to Kandy, knowing she would have already had this discussion with Jasmine and Gran.

"Yep," she said. "But nothing since."

"So when they actively use magic, it does show?"

Kandy shook her head. "Not necessarily. Volume appears to matter. Pearl wasn't alerted to anything by whatever spell the telepathic elf laid on Jasmine."

"And the tussle with Audrey?"

Kandy pointed toward the southeast wall. "Yep. But the bakery always glows."

I scanned the map, pointing to a couple of other spots that were lit up. "That's Scarlett's house on West Fifth?"

Jasmine spoke without lifting her head from her computer. "The witches all raised their wards after the attack on Pearl. We didn't know if there would be more attempts."

I nodded. "And Rochelle and Beau in Southlands? Geez, those are some heavy-duty wards."

"They're permanent, like at the bakery and Pearl's." Kandy folded her arms, leaning back into the door frame. "Part of how the witches thought they could effectively tie Rochelle into the grid. And it obviously worked. Except not for picking up elf magic."

"The spell on Jasmine might just have been subtle. Even intermittent. And hidden under her own magic."

Kandy grunted an acknowledgement. Jasmine's fingers continued to fly across her keyboard.

I really, really didn't want to ask my next question. But I was wearing my dead sister's jeans, and it was time to be a big girl. "Speaking of the oracle, any new sketches I should know about?"

Kandy shook her head. "Not yet. Not for us, at least."

"But we know that she at least sees the elves," I said.

Rochelle had presented me with a sketch three months before, hand delivered by Blossom. It depicted me holding what appeared to be a large gemstone in the palm of my hand. And though the illusionist elf had a similarly cut stone embedded in her forehead, the gem I had torn from the elf in the park after I killed him had been cracked and its magic destroyed by the death blow dealt by my knife. Conversely, the gemstone in the oracle sketch appeared to be pristine, with what I still assumed were tendrils of active magic attached to it, all rendered in charcoal.

I was fairly certain those differences indicated that I hadn't fulfilled that particular prediction. Not yet. And I was under no illusion that I was actually capable of thwarting any future Rochelle saw for me. Down that road of thought lay madness. For me, at least.

Kandy was watching me. Assessing me. "Well … we know the oracle sees you."

"You spike on the map," Jasmine said.

"When? Just now at the pool?"

"Yep."

"I didn't do anything."

"You didn't pull your knife?" Kandy asked.

Yeah. I had pulled my knife.

Jasmine looked up from her computer, all her attention on the map. "The witch magic is blue tinted. See all of the witches' wards? Different degrees of blue, maybe indicating individual power level? Darkest at Rochelle and Beau's place. But yours is more golden. See the bakery? I've heard that some Adepts see colors that correspond to magic, though I've never been able to. But I guess that's how the map interprets different magic … or … this was drawn by the oracle, yes? Maybe she sees magic in color, and that translated to the map when she drew it?"

I didn't answer—because I actually didn't know. The oracle sketched in black charcoal on white paper, so I had no idea if Rochelle did see magic in color, as I did. Instead, I eyed the bakery depicted on the wall before me. If it was glowing more golden than the other witch magic, it was a subtle difference—to me, at least. But then, I had never been able to see or taste my own magic terribly well, if at all.

Scanning the rest of the map, I pointed to a spot of magic a few blocks northeast of the bakery. "And that? The Talbots?"

Kandy uncrossed her arms, fishing her phone out of her pocket. "Those are the protections the witches put on the entrance to the treasure keeper's prison. The Talbots are still in Whistler, and their house wards aren't active. We've got two hours until dinner. We both need to change."

"Let's borrow Gran's car. Assuming she doesn't need it. I'd like to check on the prison."

"The elves aren't going back to anywhere that nullifies their magic."

I shrugged. "I'd still like a look around."

"Fine. It's after full dark. Baby fang should be on duty."

For the past three months, Kandy had been employing some of the fledgling Adepts who now called Vancouver home in regular patrol tasks. She had Burgundy checking the other twelve grid points, working around her school schedule. Bitsy the werewolf was learning the finer details of patrolling during evening training runs. And Benjamin Garrick was keeping an eye on Pulou's prison and the Talbots' house nearby—with strict orders to stay far away from any elves who might appear. Since Benjamin was rather protective of his newfound immortality, Kandy trusted him to follow those instructions to the letter.

"I'm going to stay here," Jasmine said. "Dinner isn't really my thing these days. And I'm trying to wrap my head around setting up a possible online interface with the map."

Kandy glanced at me. "That youngest Talbot is into this tech stuff."

I grimaced. "Tony."

Jasmine perked up again. "A tech sorcerer? In town?"

"Not this weekend," I said.

"Huh. Might be worth a chat," Jasmine said thoughtfully. "He won't be as good as me…I mean, as good as I was before…you know. But he might be helpful in setting up a command center, at least. Gathering and hardwiring tech and the like."

"Whatever," Kandy said, bored. "But you're joining us for dancing, baby girl. Dancing with Jade is not to be missed, and the more magic on the dance floor, the better."

Jasmine twisted her lips, but she didn't answer.

"Maybe too much magic?" I whispered.

Kandy shrugged. "She'll be the least powerful person there. Audrey and Lara have begged off. So we won't have any repeats."

"I can hear you," Jasmine said crossly. Her fingers were glued to her keyboard again.

Kandy snorted a laugh.

"Begged off? Just from tonight, or from the wedding too?"

"We'll talk about it later," Kandy said, unusually circumspect.

That didn't bode well. I glanced over at Jasmine, but she appeared to be ignoring us again, actually muttering to herself under her breath now.

I stepped back into the hall, leaving the door open while I contemplated making an effort to repair the relationship with the pack, or at least texting Kett to give him a heads-up that the beta and her enforcer might have decided to take exception to his child. Of course, the executioner might not care. I could never really tell with him.

Kandy waved her hand in front of my face. Then once she got my attention, she gestured toward the stairs at the end of the hall. "After you, dowser."

"Ah, are you being sweet?"

"Nah. But if those jeans split, I totally want to be standing behind you. In fact, maybe you should wear them dancing."

Shaking my head, I couldn't help but laugh. Despite her almost drowning, dealing with pissy werewolves, or worrying about elven power plays, I could always count on Kandy to lighten the mood.

Benjamin Garrick, along with the taste of his sour-grape-jelly-bean magic, wasn't the only Adept within viewing distance of the hidden entrance to the treasure keeper's prison. Apparently, Mory was hanging out there as well. After dark. With a fledgling vampire.

Lovely.

I caught the taste of the junior necromancer's toasted-marshmallow magic from the top of the concrete stairs that led to the beach. I then spotted Mory perched on a large driftwood log, only a dozen feet away from the craggy shoreline and the witches' wards. She was knitting, of course and always.

I glanced back at Kandy questioningly.

The green-haired werewolf shrugged, completely nonplussed about a vampire hanging out with a necromancer.

Even more lovely.

Apparently, Benjamin had worked up the nerve to say hello to Mory sometime over the last three months.

I jogged down the stairs with Kandy right behind me.

Mory was wearing the Cowichan-inspired knitted sweater that Kandy and I had bought her for her nineteenth birthday. It was intentionally two sizes too large for her petite frame. The bulky hat tugged down over her currently purple-streaked, bright-red hair matched the cowl tucked into the shawl collar of the sweater, as well as the wrist warmers under her cuffs.

Mory raised her head, eyeing me without pausing her knitting. At best guess, she was working on another hat, though with a slightly less bulky yarn. Plus, it was stranded, which meant she was knitting with multiple colors, each strand leading back to the satchel sitting beside her on the log.

Yeah, I had somehow picked up way too much information about knitting for a nonknitter. But Mory and I didn't have a lot in common, so I tried to talk to her about things she was actually interested in. And, unfortunately, my witty repartee about chocolate, cupcakes, and getting into knife fights bored the hell out of the necromancer.

Benjamin appeared out of the shadows of the cliff side to my left as I stepped down into the sand from the stairs. Hands stuffed in his jean pockets and a scarf knotted around his neck were his only concessions to the chilly temperature—though I wasn't sure he could feel the cold at all. The dark-haired vampire settled his satchel over his shoulder, offering Kandy and me a polite smile.

"The elves have been active tonight," I said, deciding I would treat the vampire and the necromancer as equals, rather than freaking out that they were hanging out together. That seemed like the more mature way to go.

"Nearby?" Mory asked.

"At Gran's. Then Kits Pool."

"The pool?" Benjamin asked. "Do elves have a thing for water?"

"Not unless it's purple," I said.

Benjamin tugged a notebook and pen from his satchel, flipping the book open to a page that was already half covered in neat but cramped handwriting. With his movement, I picked up the taste of the torture device on his wrist—the necromancer working that kept his vampire nature in check, and which drove Kandy's and my protective instincts into overdrive.

"So…nothing happening here." For my benefit, Kandy pointedly turned the question into a statement, since she thought I was wasting our time.

"Ed is just heading back," Mory said.

Ed was the necromancer's red-eared slider. Her dead pet turtle.

"Sorry?" I asked. "Heading back from where?"

Mory nodded behind me. I whirled around to face the hidden entrance to the prison, seeing nothing but the rocky shore.

"We're supposed to keep our distance, right?" Mory said blithely. "And the witches can't take down the wards every night. So Ed scouts."

I didn't want to know…I didn't want to know…

"And then Ed...tells you what's going on inside?"

Mory sneered. "Of course not, Jade. He's a turtle. He can't talk. I see what he sees."

And there was the creepy I'd been expecting.

"He can't go into the cells, of course." Mory continued her explanation, thankfully not noticing me thinking how glad I was that I hadn't eaten since the bridal shower.

I mean, everyone thought seeing through the eyes of a dead pet turtle was super creepy, right? Seriously useful, sure. But creepy as all hell.

Benjamin was furiously taking notes.

Kandy grinned to herself, watching me out of the corner of her narrowed eyes as if gleefully anticipating my eventual freak-out.

Well, I was going to have to disappoint her. "Great, great," I said with completely false perkiness. "Well, keep us informed—"

"He's back."

Ah, damn it.

I turned, my skin already crawling even before I caught sight of the six-inch turtle as he crossed through the witches' wards cloaking the entrance to the cave. Then he continued to shuffle his way through the sand to Mory. The necromancer scooped Ed up, brushing him off and cooing. The reanimated turtle was wearing a tiny amulet around his neck. The charm was constructed out of a dime that tasted distinctly of my mother's strawberry magic. It was presumably what allowed him to pass through the wards.

Delightful. And again, seriously efficient. But creepy.

"So...nothing then." Kandy spread her arms, elbows bent, to the sides, giving me an *All right then?* look.

"No activity here," Benjamin said. "The Talbots left around 3:00 P.M. yesterday for Whistler. And nothing magical has been in the area since. As far as I can tell, of course. Not after sunset at least."

Mory slid off the log, somehow looping her satchel strap over her head without getting tangled in her yarn. She tucked her turtle in her bag. "I'll grab a ride with you guys." She looked at me defiantly. "I'm coming to dinner. And dancing."

I raised my hands in mock surrender. "Why would I try to stop you?"

Mory simply narrowed her eyes at me, nodded a brisk goodbye to Benjamin, and wandered off toward the stairs. And yes, she was still knitting.

I looked over at Kandy. "Really? You thought I'd get pissy about you inviting Mory?"

"Nope," Kandy said. "Kid has her own issues, doesn't she?"

"Um," Benjamin said hopefully. "We were going to schedule that third interview …"

"Nope again." Kandy bared her teeth at the fledgling vampire, challenging him.

He looked nonplussed. "I was asking Jade, actually."

"Be more specific then, Benny boy." The green-haired werewolf turned on her heel to deliberately give the vampire her back, following Mory over to and up the stairs.

"Right," I said, answering Benjamin's question. For the modern-day chronicle he was piecing together, the young vampire had made two earlier attempts to chat with me one-on-one. Problem was, those previous sessions kept getting interrupted. "How about tomorrow?"

"At the bakery again?"

"Yeah. What time?"

"Sun sets at 4:20...so, 5:00 P.M.?"

"Sounds good. Come to the alley door. The bakery's closed tomorrow."

Benjamin smiled, hitting me with a charismatic blast of his vampire magic—his version of the ensnarement ability that most vampires were rumored to wield. Though I hadn't yet felt Jasmine attempt to beguile anyone, and Kett was either careful about it, or he chose to not continually attempt to enthrall his friends.

I grinned back at Benjamin, then jogged through the dry sand to catch up to Kandy on the stairs.

The dark-haired vampire settled down on a log, already bent over the notebook open on his knee. He was likely contentedly transcribing the conversation we'd all just had. Or formulating more questions.

"I'm texting Liam Talbot," I called up to Kandy. "We have time to fit in a chat."

Kandy stopped at the top of the stairs with a put-out groan. "Dowser ..."

"Hey, I'm trying to be responsible. You know?" I opened my text messages and found the thread of my conversations with Liam. "The elves haven't just decided to play games randomly."

Kandy grumbled something under her breath that sounded like, "You hope ..."

"He's on a date," Mory said. She was leaning on the guardrail at the edge of the paved seawall. And yes, still knitting.

"Liam?" I asked.

Kandy nodded, abruptly enthusiastic. "You should definitely text him then, dowser. What's it been? Three days since your last check-in? Anything could have happened."

I gave her a narrow-eyed look. "I probably shouldn't interrupt his date."

"Better than bothering him on shift," Kandy said perkily. "Plus, I wouldn't mind seeing who the detective constable deems worthy of dating."

"He got the promotion then?"

"Just had to pass an exam," Mory said. "After his probationary period. Homicide unit. Though there might have been a bit of magic involved. I heard there isn't normally supposed to be any special treatment for international police officers. But he's back at the same rank he had before, in Boston."

"Boston, eh?" Kandy drawled. "And just how do you know so much about Mr. Stick-Up-His-Ass Sorcerer?"

Mory jutted her chin out belligerently, but she didn't otherwise answer.

I shook my head, choosing to text Liam while the werewolf and the necromancer had a staring contest.

There's been some activity tonight. Would like to chat.

"I thought you were banging baby fang," Kandy said.

"What?" Mory cried, blushing fiercely.

"Aha!" Kandy looked at me triumphantly.

"I am not ..." Mory's voice cracked. "I'm not having sex with Benjamin."

"Aha! Ha! Ha!" Kandy crowed. "I thought Tony Talbot was more your speed."

"What?!" Mory looked over at me for reinforcement, torn between being utterly frustrated and getting seriously angry.

"Liam is a little old for you, isn't he?" I said instead, so very helpfully. "He's what, twenty-three?"

My werewolf BFF chuckled, grinning gleefully at the necromancer.

Mory snapped her mouth shut. Kandy had actually managed to distract her from her knitting, but apparently the necromancer wasn't going to continue the argument.

A text message from Liam pinged through on my phone.

>*I'm available at 9 am tomorrow.*

I'm available now.

Kandy leaned over to look at my phone, then snorted.

Three dots appeared at the bottom of the screen, indicating that Liam was typing something. The dots continued flashing... and continued...

Kandy chortled. "He's telling you off. The sorcerer has balls, all right. But he's a moron."

My phone pinged.

>*I'm at Browns on West Fourth.*

Kandy started guffawing.

"What?" Mory eyed the werewolf with obvious distrust.

"He deleted whatever he was going to text," I said. "Possibly."

"Scared of the dowser!" Kandy whooped, hustling across the swath of grass between us and Gran's navy-blue Lexus where we'd parked on Ogden Avenue.

Mory eyed me. "That's what you want, isn't it? Respect?"

I almost demurred. I almost said no, almost tried to fall back into my old *everyone is a friend* routine. Then I simply nodded. "It's clearer that way."

"And easier to protect everyone, if they know to defer to you." There wasn't any judgement in Mory's tone, but I felt it nonetheless.

I shoved my hands in the back pockets of my dead sister's jeans, not bothering to deny my position—my status—to the necromancer. Because I also wore the instruments of assassination around my neck, and there was no denying the responsibility that had come along with my claiming of them. Unintended or not.

Mory tucked her knitting away in her bag. Then she bumped her shoulder against mine in an unusual display of camaraderie. "Let's go ruin Liam's night. Then eat something."

I barked out an involuntary laugh, having no idea what the necromancer held against the detective. Except, of course, the simple fact that he was a sorcerer. It made sense that Mory carried the same prejudice as I did. She had certainly learned to not trust sorcerers at the same time I had—including Mot Blackwell himself.

Without pestering her with questions, I wandered across the grass with the tiny necromancer at my side, silently contemplating that I was pretty certain that Mory had a thing for Benjamin Garrick. Because for a necromancer, there couldn't possibly be a worse romantic choice. For countless reasons. And everyone had to pick wrong at least once or twice until they figured out who the right choice was. Didn't they?

Browns Socialhouse was a restaurant that specialized in elevated pub fare on the corner of West Fourth Avenue and Vine Street, just west of and across the street from the bakery. I was a rather big fan of their teriyaki chicken dragon bowl, for obvious reasons. And Kandy often dragged me there on a Thursday or Friday to watch whatever sport she was currently—and most often raucously—following.

The pub was at capacity when we arrived, reminding me that we were about to be late for dinner ourselves. Still, the two rows of tables lined up on the tiny sidewalk patio along Vine Street were empty. Even with heat lamps set above them, it was too chilly to dine outside in December in Vancouver.

I didn't bother shouldering my way through the guests waiting to be seated in the tiny vestibule beyond the glass front door. I could see Liam through the windows, watching hockey—Canucks versus Flames, it looked like—on a massive TV over the bar. He had a half-full pint glass of what appeared to be a golden lager in hand. The woman seated to his right, watching the game as well, was darker-haired than the sorcerer but lighter skinned. She wasn't, however, magical. Or if she was, any taste of that magic was hidden underneath Liam Talbot's creamy-peanut-buttery power.

Mory peered around my shoulder, snorted inexplicably, and then wandered back to climb into the back seat of Gran's car. We'd scored a parking spot out front of the Starbucks on the same side of the street.

Kandy laughed under her breath, eyeing the sorcerer and his apparent date. "So the eldest Talbot is a bit of a player." She turned her back on the window. "Good to know."

"One date doesn't make a player," I said.

"True, dowser." Kandy flashed her teeth in my direction. "Not terribly observant. But true."

I huffed out a laugh, then texted Liam.

We're outside. Waiting.

Blunt, and just on the edge of pissy. But then, I generally preferred to be snarky when dealing with sorcerers. All except Henry Calhoun, that was.

"So when is the marshal making another appearance?" I asked, trying to kill time.

Kandy shrugged belligerently. "I don't have Henry's schedule in my head."

Inside, Liam tugged his phone out of his pocket, glanced at his screen, and said something apologetic to his date. Crossing to the far edge of the sidewalk, so that I wasn't blocking the door, I glanced at Mory in the back seat of the car. "Think they're dating, then? Mory and Liam?"

"Nah. She's playing around with us." Kandy joined me, deliberately looking away from the pub as Liam made his way through the tables toward the entrance. "Or they aren't exclusive."

"He is a little old for her," I said, repeating myself from earlier. Though I knew I was being overprotective, I was apparently unable to stop myself.

Kandy snorted. "Says the woman scheduled to marry the five-hundred-year-old."

"You know all those years don't count," I said, peeved. "Warner is only like ... fifty ..."

I started to laugh. Kandy joined me as Liam pushed open the door. He was wearing a light-brown ribbed sweater and light-blue jeans. The sweater was a little loose on him, its sleeves covering the backs of his hands. The collar of a white T-shirt showed at the edge of the oversized neck. The look was deliberately, almost affectedly, casual. But there was nothing casual about Liam Talbot. His dark hair was almost too short, his jaw always freshly shaven. I would have bet that he went for a jog every time he consumed any sort of 'bad' calories.

I grinned involuntarily, imagining him needing to run home in order to burn off the cupcake I forced on him every Thursday.

Liam's step faltered. His gaze was glued to me.

Apparently, my smile was a little off-putting. Well, that was new. Okay ... newish.

Kandy chuckled darkly. But quietly, so the sorcerer might not have heard.

"Sorry to interrupt you," I said, deciding to play nice since I was actually intruding on his date. "The interlopers have made a couple of plays."

Liam glanced to both sides of us, but the sidewalk was empty for a dozen or so feet in either direction. "Tonight?" He closed the space between us.

"Yep," Kandy said. "And in Whistler yesterday."

Liam raised a concerned eyebrow.

"Your parents know," I said, lowering my voice as a group of chatty guests exited the pub. "But the elves seem to be back in Vancouver now."

Liam nodded. "Okay. Good to know. Has anyone been hurt?"

I shook my head. "No ... well, not by the elves."

Liam eyed me but didn't ask for clarification. He was smart like that.

"This evening, they attacked Jasmine—"

"The vampire?" Liam asked.

Kandy lifted her lip in a snarl. "What do you care?"

I stifled a grin.

Liam eyed Kandy warily but steadily. "I've never met her ... so I was just asking for clarification. Attacking a vampire seems like an odd opening move."

"Right ..." I briefly considered going back and filling him in on Whistler, but Kandy glanced at the time on her phone, then shifted impatiently. "There were a couple of ... interactions before that, but—"

"All easily handled by Jade," Kandy interjected. "No need for you to puff out your chest and start flashing your gun around."

Liam frowned, seemingly missing the gender-dynamics lesson the green-haired werewolf was belligerently trying to foist upon him. But with Angelica as his mother, I seriously doubted that Liam was over-protective because he thought women were weak. As far as I'd figured out, he was that way because he was accustomed to being the strongest magically—and therefore the least likely to be targeted—among his siblings.

"Point is," I said, "I wanted you to know. Two elves, one skilled in illusion and one skilled in telepathy. Well, some sort of telepathy, but not just mind reading."

Liam tilted his head to one side. "Like what?"

"Psionic manipulation. Jasmine thought so, anyhow. Transmitted through some sort of blood magic. I had a sample of the blood they used, but I lost it."

Liam glanced back and forth between Kandy and me, his shoulders and jaw suddenly tense. Then he glanced back inside the pub.

Seeing his concern, I realized that I had somehow forgotten to be as worried about the magical prowess of others as I should have been. Which was plain stupid of me. I turned to Kandy, apologetic. "I think maybe we should cancel—"

"Absolutely not!"

"I know you've been planning this for months, but ..." I trailed off. Honestly, continuing with a bachelorette party when we were possibly under attack was irresponsible. "We should be tracking the elves ... really."

"We're already pretty clear that we can't track them," Kandy said. "And we know they'll come to us. You've already quashed all their volleys ... the warrior, the illusionist, and the telepath. Easily. So if they can't get through you, they seriously can't get past all of us gathered together."

"Plus ..." Liam said thoughtfully. "You might actually draw their attention. Grouped together."

I was surrounded by insane people. Even the police officer—sorry, detective constable—thought it was a good idea to draw the elves out. "And any innocents who happen to get caught in the crossfire? At the restaurant, say? We just write them off?"

"Of course not," Liam huffed indignantly. "But you can control the environment, keep it contained."

Kandy grumbled. "I'll cancel the dinner. We'll get takeout instead and eat at your apartment. It doesn't get much more contained than that. But we're still going dancing!" She stomped off toward the car before I could respond to her plan.

Liam gazed after the green-haired werewolf, then lifted a hand in a wave when he spotted Mory in the back seat. The necromancer didn't wave back.

I looked at him pointedly. "So? Anything to report?"

He cleared his throat, shaking his head.

"What about the rash of break-ins you were looking into? The ones you said where nothing was stolen? Have they continued?"

"No. Last one was at BC Place two days ago. Which is weird, but there wasn't any magical trace when I went by to check it out."

I frowned. "BC Place...weren't there others around there as well?"

"Not enough to make a pattern."

"And how many does that take?" I asked teasingly.

"Well, uh, at least three."

"I'm joking."

He nodded but didn't smile. "All the incidents were in large spaces, though. If you are looking for some sort of connection between them. Large, empty spaces."

"And how are you checking for magic?" I asked. "Do you have...some sort of a device?"

Liam nodded, but he didn't elaborate. Adepts were fanatically close-mouthed about their personal magic.

"And it's calibrated for elf magic? How? Did you take it to the park before the residual fully faded?" That was the residual from me murdering the warrior elf. But I was certain I didn't need to add that part.

Liam looked at me, a little aghast.

Great. Apparently, I wasn't the only one prone to making assumptions. "Yeah, if the elves can hide from my dowser senses and Kandy's nose, then your device might not be picking them up either."

Liam cursed under his breath. "They're from another dimension."

"When you have a moment, maybe take your device down to Kits Pool. The illusionist put on a little show there about an hour ago. You might be able to pick up a trace of it."

He nodded, already turning back to the pub. "I'll head there now. Then I'll backtrack through the series of break-ins."

"At least finish dinner," I said as he opened the door to the pub and stepped back inside.

Liam waved his hand over his shoulder, acknowledging me but obviously intent on his new course of action. The door slowly closed behind him.

Well, his date was going to be seriously peeved. Most likely at me. I hustled over to the car, eager to be out of the way of any deadly looks. If she was a local, she might recognize me from the bakery—and I had a reputation for being fun to uphold.

Whether or not I was perpetually a magnet for magical chaos, my cupcakes should make everyone happy.

Kandy circled the block in Gran's car, dropping me off at the mouth of the alley before looping back in the opposite direction. Her plan was to stop at Mory's so the necromancer could get changed, then pick up Jasmine at Gran's before meeting up for a take-out dinner at my apartment. The green-haired werewolf had shoved her phone into Mory's hands as we pulled away from the pub, seemingly ready to dictate text messages the entire length of the drive.

Apparently, I had foiled the second stage of her intricate bachelorette party plans with my uncharacteristic caution. But my inability to easily taste, and therefore track, the elves' magic was unnerving me. At some point, their games were going to become deadly—and more and more, it felt as though I wasn't going to be able to do anything about it until there were bodies on the ground.

Just like the incident with the warrior elf in the park. And he'd been wounded before the fight started.

That was supposed to be my job now, wasn't it? Protecting my territory? That was what everyone kept insisting, anyway. And by 'everyone,' I meant Kandy and Gran.

I stepped out of the Lexus, holding the door open as I stooped and offered up a tentative request. "Sushi, maybe?"

Kandy snorted dismissively. "In December? Really?"

I stifled a laugh. The werewolf ate anything at anytime. She was just being pissy.

"Sushi Gallery has great party trays." Mory spoke up from the back seat, her face illuminated by the ghostly blue light coming off Kandy's phone. "Including veggie options for Rochelle."

Kandy sneered something under her breath—most likely a comment about the lunacy of vegetarianism. "I'll take care of it, dowser." She lifted her foot off the brake pedal.

Thusly dismissed, I shut the car door as the vehicle rolled away.

Kandy sped off down Vine, cutting right on West Third Avenue. I waited until the car was out of sight, then I turned to scan the dark alley. "Come out, come out, wherever you are."

Magic rippled near the door to the bakery, and the illusionist elf stepped into view. Her pale skin was luminous, though the stars hadn't broken through the heavy cloud cover. She didn't have so much as a blemish from having been badly burned just a couple of hours earlier. Apparently, elves healed in our dimension more quickly than I'd thought.

The elf had traded out the ruined light-blue jacket for a light-yellow one, in the same design as far as I could tell. It didn't do wonderful things for her coloring. Which was a nasty thought that I kept to myself.

I had tasted the illusionist's mossy magic the second I'd stepped out of the car, but I hadn't been sure whether I was simply picking up residual or if another trap had been laid. And with Mory in the potential line of fire, I wasn't interested in triggering anything that might have inadvertently hurt the necromancer. Though I knew Kandy would be pissed that I hadn't told her.

"You are getting more difficult to sneak up on, dragon slayer," the elf said, practically purring the words.

A chill ran down my spine at her use of my title. She knew way too much about me. And I knew far too little in return. I took two steps toward her, painfully aware of the brightly lit apartments on either side of the alley. It was dinnertime. Everyone was at home, and within easy view of whatever display the elf was about to put on.

I ran my fingers over my knife, still sheathed and invisible. Doing so stirred up the damp-forest taste of the elf's magic.

She watched me for a long moment. Then she held her hands slightly out to the sides, as if indicating that she held no weapons—and therefore meant no harm. "I let the werewolf and the death witch leave, didn't I? When I already know that to harm either of them is the best way to harm you."

My heartbeat ratcheted up. For the first time in a long while, I felt the beginnings of a true creeping fear. One-on-one, I knew I was a match for the elves. I'd proven that without a doubt. But they were coming at me in a different way, undercover and annoyingly observant. And executing a plan I had no capacity to fathom.

I was about to wade in. I was about to be out of my depth.

I might have been physically strong and mentally resilient. But I just wasn't all that clever. And there was nothing I could do about that except learn from my mistakes. Like the mistake I was certain I was about to make.

"I am Mirage," the elf said.

That threw me. I'd been expecting an attack, a renewal of threats. "Mirage?"

The elf tilted her head to the side. "It fits, doesn't it? I used one of your dictionaries."

I nodded, dropping my hand from my knife and casually moving closer still. "It fits. But why are you here, Mirage? In the back alley of my bakery?"

"I knew you'd eventually come home. And I ..." She touched her neck thoughtfully, maybe remembering the feel of Gran's magic searing her skin. "I am...bereaved by the loss of my brother."

A nasty pinpoint of pain formed in my chest, just over my heart. She meant the elf I'd killed. The murder I'd so coldheartedly flung in her face. "He'd hurt—"

She waved her hand, cutting me off. "He was doing his duty. And, I assume, you were doing yours."

I waited for her to continue. To tell me why she'd chosen to try to chat with me instead of throwing another illusion my way.

"We don't belong here," she finally said. She looked up almost mournfully at the dark, cloudy sky. "Even the rain is the wrong color."

"What should it be? Purple?"

She laughed quietly. "No. Only the seas and tributaries are purple in my world."

"So...you want to go home?"

She looked at me steadily, but she didn't respond.

I laughed ruefully. "You think I'm stupid. Ignorant of the incursions your race has continually made into earth's dimension?"

"No." The elf shifted, stuffing her hands in her pockets. Then she just as quickly removed them, showing me her palms.

She was nervous.

Now that was odd.

"I'm not here...in this alley with permission." She reached up and touched the clear gemstone embedded in her forehead. "I'm not transgressing, but...I thought if I could bring my liege an idea, a chance to go home...then ..."

My liege. So the illusionist—and presumably the warrior before her—took orders from someone. Likely the telepath, who'd also been locked away with them.

Damn Pulou. If he'd responded to my requests to meet, then I might not have been standing in the alley completely blind to the history of the trio of elves he'd stashed in Vancouver.

"Return home, then," I said. "If you can travel here, certainly you can go back?"

"Not without help." Mirage stuffed her hands in her pockets again, gazing down at her feet. Her uberstraight hair fell forward, and for a moment she looked almost human. Vulnerable.

It was totally a ploy. Just another trap. And I was going to walk right into it.

"What kind of help?" I said.

"I'm not quite certain. The working... the technology, as you would call it, is beyond my understanding. There is a device that opens a doorway."

"And without it, you can't go home?"

She nodded, but stiffly and just once.

"Anyone else getting shades of *E.T.*?" I muttered.

"Sorry?"

"Never mind. An earth movie from the early eighties."

Mirage nodded, once more lifting her face to the night sky. "Did he die well?"

She meant her brother.

"He did." I quashed another pinch of pain over the devastation I'd wrought, whether it was necessary or not.

"We were only half alive in that prison," she said. "I wasn't certain I was still alive. I could not feel... anything. Could not create anything. And I did not know if anyone else lived until my liege opened the door."

"I know the feeling."

"Do you?"

I nodded but didn't elaborate.

"You have many religions in this dimension," Mirage said.

"We do."

"What do you believe, dragon slayer? When you die, do you cease to exist?"

"No," I whispered. "I am ... magic."

She nodded sadly. "And my brother? And me, when I die at the end of your blade? Am I the same magic?"

"Yes." I struggled to keep my voice steady against a wave of mixed emotion.

"Will you meet with my liege if she will agree? Then take our request to the dragons?"

"I will."

She smiled, but not victoriously.

"And ..." I added, hardening my tone. "If I'm walking into a trap, I'll slaughter you both."

"Just like my brother."

"Yes."

"And if it is a trap, and you fail. Who will come after you?"

I closed the final two steps between us, feeling the magic of the bakery wards brush against my shoulder. "If you have to ask, you haven't been paying as close attention as I thought."

"A future I would avoid ... Jade." She reached out to me, offering to shake my hand. "If you don't see me again, I have died in my attempt to convince my liege that we should leave."

I gazed at her hand, though I didn't take it. "If that happens, shall I avenge you?"

She laughed mirthlessly. "I have been watching. Closely. I know you by your actions. Killing my liege is beyond even you. But I would never wish such a fight upon either of you. Will you come to a meeting? Will you at least hear our request?"

"A ceasefire?" I asked.

She tilted her head thoughtfully. "A temporary end of aggression, you mean?"

"Yes."

"Agreed. Though I can speak only for myself."

I reached over and grasped her hand then. Her skin was smooth, her grip strong. Her elf magic fluttered underneath my fingers like the wings of a bird trapped in a cage. "I will listen then ... Mira." I hesitantly offered up the nickname, hoping to cement our tentative bond. Hoping that the nuance—the offer of friendship—would translate, even though we came from different dimensions. The illusionist's obvious love for her brother led me to believe that she was capable of forming such a bond.

She smiled, flashing her shark-like teeth at me. "Mira. Yes. That fits this place better." She released my hand, then spun away, jogging down the alley.

As I watched, she gathered her magic and disappeared from my sight. I tasted just a hint of her moss-and-evergreen-bark power as she went.

I had most likely just negotiated and set up the terms of the trap meant for me. But at least I would know when it was coming. And that it wouldn't be directed at anyone else.

I turned to open the exterior door of the bakery, hoping that I'd have enough time before Kandy returned to change and to properly blow-dry my hair. Hoping I was wrong about Mira.

I didn't much like leaving my city, let alone the country. As a result, I could only barely imagine what it would feel like to be trapped in another dimension.

Away from everyone I loved. So even though I was certain I was being played, that yet another game had just been set in motion, I still hoped I was wrong.

But wrong in a good way for once.

Chapter Nine

As I stepped through into the bakery kitchen, feeling my blood wards slide across my skin, a huge pulse of magic erupted in the alley. I spun toward it, calling my knife into my hand. Intense golden guardian magic buffeted me as a portal blew open before me.

I loosened my hold on my knife. Even I wasn't stupid enough to want to be caught wielding a weapon by anyone who could walk through portals. The instruments of assassination hanging from my necklace were already a constant source of provocation. For the brief moment that the power of the portal ravaged the air around me, I leaned into it, gathering it greedily as if it were chocolate and I'd been bereft for months. Even years.

This potent magic and its underlying taste of strong tea and rich cream called to the power simmering in my blood—power stolen and absorbed from Shailaja, child of a guardian herself.

Then, in a breath, it was gone.

A large figure stood at the side of the alley, wielding a shortsword embellished with an obscenely large emerald gemstone. He was shadowed by the tall fence that backed the apartment building across the way. All the magic that had sprung forth snapped back, absorbed into the guardian who had just stepped through the portal he'd manifested.

Pulou.

Mercy me. The treasure keeper himself. Ankle-length fur coat and all.

He stepped forward, revealing himself in the light cast by the upper apartments on either side of the alley. His hair was grayer than I remembered it, and the lines etched across his face seemed deeper. He locked his shadowed gaze on me standing with the bakery door open at my back. His grip on his weapon tightened.

Almost involuntarily, my hand moved toward my neck, to my necklace and the instruments it held. Then I waited. Already breathless from the onslaught of the portal's magic, I became almost lightheaded as the tension between me and the treasure keeper grew tighter.

If Pulou attacked me now, I would fight. And I would die. But I would definitely try to take him with me. And then I'd haunt his prejudiced, arrogant ass ever after until the end of his days.

But before I even had time to think the gesture through—and the strategically weak position it put me in—I bowed my head, dipping into a stiff curtsy and holding it. Then I peered up at the guardian through the golden curls that had tumbled around my face.

"Treasure keeper. I would have gladly come to you."

Pulou frowned, then tucked his sword back into the pocket of his massive coat. "Wielder," he said benignly. "It was easier to make the journey myself." His British lilt—the accent the elves seemingly emulated—was a low rumble.

"Guardian," I said, straightening. "I was just on my way to dinner. It's my bachelorette party."

Pulou raised an eyebrow in amusement. "I shall not interrupt your wedding games for long. You requested an audience. There has been some annoyance that you apparently need help to deal with?"

I clenched my jaw, trying really hard to not lose my mind over him calling the elves he'd hidden away in Vancouver without anyone's knowledge a mere annoyance. "Treasure keeper." I struggled to keep my tone smooth. "Thank you for coming. I do have some questions. Would you like to step inside the bakery?"

He tilted his head, making a show of thinking about it. "Are there cupcakes?"

"Probably not. Nothing fresh, at least. But I believe we were just about to order sushi."

Pulou grimaced. "Raw fish."

"We could order some tempura." Yes, I was cajoling one of the nine most powerful beings in the world with deep-fried prawns and veggies. Because I had the feeling it was either that or give in to the need to beat him around the head until he apologized—first for locking me up, then for not telling me about the elves. "And there might be some leftover petit fours." That was a long shot. I had lost track of the second container of pastries after the earlier skirmish with Jasmine—and as such, had no idea whether the werewolves had subsequently eaten them all in retribution.

"That will have to do, then. Not created by your hand, alchemist, but I shall endure." He offered me a smile.

I returned the smile, though I showed less of my teeth. I wasn't fooled by his attempt to charm me. Seriously. A girl instinctively knew when her former mentor wanted nothing better than to kick her ass and retrieve the instruments of assassination. By force if necessary.

Still smiling, Pulou and I eyed each other like gun-slingers. Then I stepped out of the way of the bakery door.

"After you, guardian," I said as deferentially as I could. I really did need some answers.

He stepped by me, brushing me with the epic power contained within his coat—and momentarily scrambling my brain. It wasn't an intentionally aggressive move. At least I didn't think it was.

The idea of shoving my hand into his pocket and seeing what I could retrieve flitted through my mind. Thankfully, I quashed the notion before it was fully formed...though the three-foot-tall smiling ivory Buddha that had once worn my mangled katana like a crown would have totally rocked my apartment entranceway...

In his coat, Pulou was so massive that he filled the exterior door frame to frame. He stepped through the wards without disturbing them. And even though I'd invited him in, I was still surprised that the defensive magic hadn't even whispered with his passing. Perhaps that was a side effect of the treasure keeper's ability to create portals? Though that didn't explain why Suanmi had been able to pass through my wards just as easily.

I opened my mouth to ask about it. Then I remembered that my former mentor was probably as close as I was ever going to get to having a real nemesis. So I closed my mouth on the question, and followed him through into my haven.

The bakery kitchen was pristine. Nary a hint of the tussle that had occurred between Audrey, Jasmine, and me remained. I whispered thanks to Blossom under my breath while Pulou lumbered over to and entered my office.

I followed, pissily slapping on the interior light. Then I was forced to circle to the other side of the desk in order to stand in the tiny room with him. He was that large. Or maybe it was his magic that took up so much space. He hadn't bothered to dampen it at all, as Suanmi had when she came to the bakery, and as my father usually did when he casually walked the streets of Vancouver.

Pulou partially closed the door, revealing the magically layered safe behind it. Without speaking, he passed his hand across the top and down the front, clearly sensing the magic of the wards. But he didn't try to open it. "It holds the dragon slayer?" he asked. He meant my katana.

"Yes. Along with some coins, the pen, and other trinkets."

He nodded, turning to look at me—and making a thorough examination of my necklace. "But you wear the instruments."

"Yes." When he didn't respond for an uncomfortably long moment, I found myself needing to explain. "They are a part of me, and will not tolerate being apart."

He grunted. Unhappily, I thought.

"And the elves you kept in the prison here?" I asked. I wanted to change the focus, and to hopefully remind the treasure keeper that he wasn't without flaw himself when it came to the hoarding of dangerous magical objects. And dangerous magical beings. "What should I know about them?"

"A trio was all that remained of that particular incursion. They surrendered." Then, answering my unasked question. "It would have been murder to have killed them after that point."

"Why not send them back?"

"I had no ability to do so."

"Why not find someone who could?"

He glowered at me. "Why not release beings who'd tried to invade the world under my protection? So that they could attempt to do so again, forewarned of what would be waiting for them on the other side?"

"They want to go back now."

He raised an eyebrow. "You've conversed with them?"

"One. I killed another. A male who was already wounded in some fashion. And I believe the third is their leader. The elf who can construct powerful illusions refers to the telepath as her liege."

He nodded thoughtfully. "Yes, I remember this. The final two protecting a third. I had not thought much of it." He gave me a look, as if anticipating my chastising him. "It had been a lengthy fight, across many continents. 'Twas before your father wielded the sword."

"And the fight ended here? Which is why you built the prison?"

"No. We finally vanquished them somewhere in the Mediterranean. But the cells were already in place, courtesy of the former treasure keeper. And the people who occupied the land were nomadic. Plus, they practiced a different kind of magic. Incompatible. So there was no chance of exposure."

"The First Nations peoples?"

He shook his head sadly. "Most of that magic has disappeared from the world now. We are all the lesser for it."

His tone was so mournful that I almost opened my mouth to tell him about the reemergence of the skinwalkers. But instead, I hoarded that piece of information away, silently and vindictively spiteful. Yes, this was what my grudge had reduced me to.

"Why not take them to Antarctica?" I said.

He gave me a quelling look. Possibly in response to my sneering tone. "The items that decorate your neck answer that question for you, wielder."

Right. If the elves had ever managed to break out within the treasure keeper's chamber, they would have had access to every magical artifact and weapon it housed. Of course, they would then have had to get off the continent without freezing, and without attracting the treasure keeper's attention. But in the scenario I was running in my head, Pulou would likely have already been dead if his prisoners were walking free.

"You've run out of questions already?"

"No. I was thinking."

"That's unlike you." Pulou smiled, pretending he was teasing.

I gritted my teeth. "Do you have a way to help them get home or not? Do you know of someone who can open …"—I waved my hand, searching for the correct term—"… dimensional gates?"

"Sorcerers and witches can reach into the demon realm, but not without grave consequences."

I squashed my need to snarl *Tell me something I don't know!* and simply nodded to encourage him to continue. See? I could be a grown-up. For short, short periods of time.

"The elves themselves are the only ones who have the knowledge you seek."

"A working, Mira called it. Then she called it technology."

"Mira?"

"The illusionist elf."

"You've named her such? She is not a friend to add to your ... eclectic collection, Jade."

Well, that was just a snooty way of calling all of us 'misfits.' And only Kandy got away with that, mostly because she included herself in the assessment. I jutted out my chin, ignoring the fact that Pulou sounded exactly like I had when I'd warned Mory away from the shadow leech.

The treasure keeper sighed. Heavily. "A working ..." Then he dug into his pocket, pulling something out from within the endless depths of its magic.

I flinched, forcing myself to not respond by reaching for my knife.

Pulou hesitated, noting my reaction with narrowed eyes.

Yes, I had instinctively thought he was going to attack me.

"I would not be so careless, wielder," he said mildly. "To try to take you within the center of your power. I assumed you would be more at ease here."

I huffed out a sigh, relaxing my hands. "How about ... you wouldn't attack me because we're allies?"

"When you prove we are, then I will add that addendum. But for now, you are simply an asset ... and the child of a guardian."

Unable to come up with a response that didn't involve yet again wanting to pull my knife, I glanced down at the object in his hands. It was a half circle of layered metal about ten inches in diameter, somewhere between silver and gray in color. It appeared to have been sliced down the middle with something wickedly sharp. I would have classified it as a magical artifact—except it held no magic. Nothing I could feel or taste.

I slipped around to the other side of the desk, attempting to get a closer look at the half circle. When I did, I saw that it was actually comprised of a series of metal pieces, or components, slotted together. A number of gemstones were attached to it, but I didn't recognize any of them. They might have been rare ... or they might have been from the elves' dimension. Most of them looked damaged, cracked and missing shards.

"Elf technology?" I asked.

"Indeed."

"But it's broken?"

"Sliced in half by the warrior's sword." He didn't mean my father.

"This is part of a dimensional gate? Similar to a portal, but opening between worlds?"

"I believe so."

"Could you get it working again?"

"Not without the other half. And even then ... no."

"What about ..." I looked up to meet his dark-brown gaze. "An alchemist?"

"Even if you had the second piece, the operation of the device would likely kill you, Jade. The force it takes to tear through dimensions would swallow you. Burn you up."

I glared belligerently.

His tone softened. "Trust me, alchemist. I have seen it with my own eyes. The warrior walked into the sphere of this device's magic and ... was never the same afterward."

"But ... Warner, Haoxin, and my father have been dealing with other incursions for months."

Pulou shook his head. "Minor pathways opened from the other side. This device was at the center of an attempt at a full invasion, and was set up on our side. It likely took them years to gather enough energy to open it. All the while fleeing from the warrior's pursuit."

"They know how to remain hidden effectively, that's for sure." I looked at the piece of broken tech in Pulou's hand glumly. "So...these minor pathways are...like what? Weak spots?"

"Thin spots, yes."

"So, if you know where they are, we could...I don't know...negotiate with the elves? Promise to get them back to the other side through one of those spots...if...um, well, if another elf opens it from their dimension ..." I trailed off, already knowing that the idea would go nowhere because it had nowhere to go.

Pulou began to stuff the piece of elf tech back into his pocket.

"Wait...can I have that?"

"Can you have a piece of a dimensional gate? For what? Your trinket collection?"

I huffed—again—but this time indignantly. "It's broken, right? I can't feel any magic from it at all. Plus the other half is missing, correct?"

"It's likely that the second half is simply buried among my treasure. Items do...on occasion...get misplaced."

I chuckled snarkily at this admission of being less than perfect.

Pulou narrowed his eyes and frowned.

Reminding myself of my goals—getting rid of the elves as peacefully as possible—I curtailed my sneering. "So...let me use it as a bargaining piece."

"You want to bargain...with elves."

"Listen, they've been in your prison a hell of a long time...like what? Five hundred years?"

Pulou's glower deepened, but he didn't correct me.

"They want to go home. We just...we say that we have the second piece."

"You're going to lie to them."

"Okay, not lie. Just a show of good faith. They want to talk with you. I arrange a meeting, say we're trying to figure out a way to get them back. Flash the useless piece of tech as proof. They agree to meet. And we figure out the second part after."

"The second part."

"Yeah."

"Where we take them to one of the thin spots and wait for another elf to attempt an incursion."

"Listen, it's diplomacy, right? We negotiate a ceasefire on this end, then we send back the two elves to negotiate a ceasefire on their end. You already said that you didn't even try to send them back originally because they knew what was waiting for them over here. We can use that to our advantage now. So…we let them take that info back…that the guardians are insurmountable…and maybe we stop the incursions altogether. Countries do this sort of thing all the time."

"Not terribly successfully."

"In some cases. But in other cases, peace works."

"Are you planning on baking them cupcakes and hosting peace talks, alchemist?" the treasure keeper asked with amusement.

Seriously, I preferred it when he was pissed off at me. "Can I have the broken tech or not?"

Pulou shrugged. Then he handed over the half circle of metal. Even in my hands, it still felt completely inert.

"You negotiate the meeting," Pulou said. "If you are successful, send Blossom with the time and location. The warrior and I will do the rest."

"But …"

He raised his hand. "Trust your elders, Jade. The opportunity for peace talks with the elves is long past. Now, where is this tempura you promised?"

He swept from my office without another word. I shoved the elf tech into my satchel and was pleased to feel the space within it enlarge to accommodate the device. As an engagement gift, Gran had finally added the expansion charm to the bag that I had repeatedly requested.

I pulled out my phone to text Kandy. *The treasure keeper has made a request for prawn tempura.*

Grinning in anticipation of Kandy losing it over Pulou joining us for my bachelorette dinner—and me therefore forcing her hand over picking up sushi—I followed the guardian out of the office.

After dragging Pulou into my apartment upstairs, then distracting him with an award-winning Porcelana chocolate bar from Amedei because I couldn't find the second container of pastries, I retreated to the bathroom. Quickly scrunching some product through my still-damp hair, I fished my hair dryer and its diffusor attachment out of the drawer.

I was willing to part with the rare, expensive chocolate—with its harmonious notes of rich cocoa powder, honey, and red fruit—only because I still had two other bars, purchased with a gift certificate I'd won through a silent auction held by my small-business association. After the incident with Bitsy in the butcher's shop down the street, I'd been slightly worried that I'd be ostracized from the group. But I had cut a cheque for the meat the unfortunate werewolf had consumed, and Dave hadn't said a word about the incident since. Not even the fact that the damage to his stainless steel cupboards had miraculously disappeared overnight.

Thanks to Blossom, of course.

Thinking about the shiny new state of my bakery kitchen downstairs, I found myself wondering whether the brownie actually chose to 'serve' me because I made the best messes. I mean, in addition to how much she loved being able to sneak up on me.

A text message flashed on the screen of my phone.

>*Gotcha, babe. Doubled the order.*

Trust Kandy to be completely unfazed that a guardian dragon was coming to dinner. Though with elves running amok, it was probably only a matter of time before Haoxin or my father showed up. Vancouver was technically Haoxin's territory, and Yazi functioned as the executioner of the guardians. And I had no doubt that he'd be fulfilling that role unless I was successful with my hastily planned negotiations.

Though as I thought back on my conversation with Pulou in the office, it seemed obvious that the guardians didn't have a surefire way of finding the elves either. Except maybe if the far seer got involved? Though even then, I wasn't certain that his visions came with detailed directions to enemy hideouts.

A nagging thought occurred to me—as they often did when I was wielding my hair dryer. So leaving my hair still partly damp, I wandered back down the hall to check on Pulou.

He was standing before the TV, holding the chocolate bar in one hand while he navigated the menu of my Apple TV. He selected Netflix, then scrolled down to *Downton Abbey*.

All righty, then.

"Um, treasure keeper?"

He grunted.

"You don't have more prison cells in Vancouver…or the immediate area, do you? More stashed elves, or demons for that matter, that no one knows about, but should probably be checked out? Because of, you know …"

Pulou didn't bother looking my way. "No."

"Ah, good. Good."

The treasure keeper bit into the chocolate.

And chewed.

Chewed.

He was chewing a twenty-five-dollar bar of chocolate.

Seriously, I almost reached for my knife. I almost launched myself across the room to snatch the precious bar from his ignorant, ham-fisted hands…

I got myself under control, slowly turning away. Then, because we were already communicating so very well, I asked another question. "That's what the summons was about…three months ago. The elves. Right? Not, like, some apology? You know, for not letting me know I'd been exonerated by the Guardian Council …"

Pulou gave me a look that would have withered the bravest of souls. Then he took another bite of the chocolate. And apparently, that was all the answer I was going to get.

"You're supposed to suck it," I said peevishly.

He looked affronted. "Pardon me?"

"I said…suck it." Then I grinned. "The chocolate. What did you think I meant?"

He narrowed his eyes at me, then glanced down at the bar.

With an added spring in my step that came only from getting in the last word, I hustled back to the bathroom to finish drying my hair and to dash on some makeup. When I was done, I stood staring at my closet, having absolutely no idea what to wear for my bachelorette party.

I felt the wards shift, admitting Kandy, Mory, and Rochelle into the bakery downstairs. They had found the oracle, apparently. Along with sushi, I hoped.

I yanked on a newer pair of dark-wash jeans, cursing slightly when I had to give them a firm tug to get them over my thighs. A bra, a tank top, and a deep-green silk blouse that narrowed at the waist but flared prettily over my hips completed my outfit.

I wandered out into the living area to find the treasure keeper overseeing the unpacking of the takeout onto my kitchen island. Mory was pulling plates out of the cupboards, and Rochelle was filling a glass pitcher that I didn't even know I owned with water.

I paused, momentarily thrown by the scene set out before me. No one but me looked the slightest bit fazed by the addition to our group. Since the far seer was Rochelle's mentor—and rumor had it that she'd stood before the entire Guardian Council on my behalf—I could mostly justify her seemingly relaxed reaction. But seriously, the fur coat and the amount of space Pulou took up should at least have had the necromancer eyeing him. I couldn't have been the only one who could see the danger simmering underneath the surface of the guardian? The brutal, exacting judgement that could twist and snap without hesitation?

Then I realized that Pulou had dampened his magic so much that I couldn't even catch a diluted hint of tea or cream at all.

Apparently, it was just me he wanted to continually keep on edge. Ah, to once again be ignorant of the capricious ways of the powerful and manipulative. Those were the days...

"This is way better," Kandy said, completely ignoring me as I stood in the hall in all my staring, slack-mouthed glory. She had commandeered the remote and was in the process of putting on the first episode of *Peaky Blinders*. "Bloodier."

Pulou grunted noncommittally. He'd found the tempura prawns and was in the process of eating directly out of the styrofoam container.

Kandy turned finally, eyed me head to toe critically, then jabbed a finger toward my bedroom. "You're missing your T-shirt, dowser." She pointed at her chest. She was wearing her orange *I Do Bite* T-shirt. Then she pointed at Rochelle.

The oracle was wearing a black T-shirt with some white printing, but its message was hidden underneath a half-zipped, charcoal-gray sweater hoodie. The hoodie swamped Rochelle's shoulders and was loose around her lower hips, but it fit snugly across her middle.

"Oracle," Kandy growled.

Rochelle sighed, setting the pitcher down. She'd been filling glasses with water. She unzipped the hoodie, tugging it open to display her rounded belly and the words emblazoned across her chest: *I see you when you're sleeping, awake, and about to die.*

Kandy cackled madly.

Rochelle shook her head, zipped her hoodie closed again, and turned back to the sink.

"Now you, necromancer!" Kandy commanded.

Mory popped what appeared to be a soy-sauce-soaked piece of California roll in her mouth, then pulled off her bright red poncho, sending all the beads knotted in the multicolored fringe clacking together. Her red T-shirt was printed in deep black: *I knit so I don't rip out your soul and send it straight to hell.*

Kandy fell back on the couch, laughing madly.

Pulou started to chuckle, then guffaw. But more at Kandy's antics than the shirt itself, I thought.

Mory shook her head as she slung her poncho over the back of one of the stools at the kitchen island, then picked up a plate. "This entire container is veggie," she said, pointing Rochelle toward a series of rolls.

"Looks good." The oracle set the pitcher beside the six water glasses she'd filled, then passed the necromancer and Pulou paper-wrapped chopsticks.

"T-shirt, dowser," Kandy said, still wiping tears of laughter from her cheeks as she climbed over the back of the couch and bellied up to the kitchen island.

I spun on my heel, heading into my bedroom to quickly swap my silk blouse for the bright-green T-shirt Kandy had made for me a few months before. Thankfully, it was clean. And I was fairly certain that Blossom was actually ironing my T-shirts. Doubly thankfully, the sentiment printed across it in bold white lettering wasn't wedding related. *Never mind the cupcakes. I can totally kick your ass.* Nothing with the word 'Bridezilla' in it.

Back in the kitchen—as if there were nothing odd about one of the nine guardians of the magical world crashing my bachelorette dinner—we gathered around the kitchen island and filled our plates with tasty bits of sushi.

As I claimed three ebi nigiri and a slice of salmon sashimi, I spoke quietly to Kandy. "Audrey? Lara?"

"At the airport." Kandy stuffed a roll that appeared to be filled with shaved beef in her mouth. Trust the werewolf to have found red meat at a sushi restaurant.

"They're actually leaving? Before the wedding?"

Kandy side-eyed Pulou, but the guardian was peering at the vegetable tempura as if it might have been poisonous, completely ignoring us. Which meant he was hearing every word, though it seemed unlikely that he'd be overly concerned about wedding drama or possible Adept infighting. Guardians were as prejudiced as any other Adepts—and given that he was over five hundred years old, Pulou was maybe even more so.

"It's not you, dowser," Kandy finally said. "They'll try to get back for the wedding. Pack business. Desmond can't leave Portland with Audrey out of town."

I nodded, letting the topic go. If Audrey wanted to be in a snit, I couldn't do anything about it. The next time the pack needed a dowser, they would call, whether or not my 'friend of the pack' status had been revoked. And Jasmine had a lifetime to heal any unintentional breach of Adept etiquette, assuming she cared to do so.

"Try one of these," Mory said, eyeing Pulou's plate. He had it piled high with teriyaki chicken and tempura. She nudged a prawn tempura roll toward him. "Except for the veggie bits, it isn't raw."

He took the end roll—with the largest piece of prawn. Then he made sure it didn't touch anything else on his plate.

I stifled a smirk, because I really didn't want to find the guardian amusing. He was too much of an ass-hole for me to want to forgive him over a single shared meal—at least not without him apologizing first.

Our plates filled with food, we gathered in the living room and ate too much. And as we did, we listened to Pulou marvel at hidden razor blades, racy sex scenes, and 'brilliant' motorcars while we watched episode one of *Peaky Binders*.

Jasmine slipped into the living room from the bakery stairwell, then proceeded to silently stalk around the back of the couch toward the kitchen. Obviously, the golden-haired vampire was attempting to not draw the attention of the fur-coat-swathed guardian who had eaten almost all the prawn tempura by himself. I could have told her not to bother. Pulou had likely known she was in the building the second she stepped through the wards, as I had.

Rochelle was curled up on the far chair, texting. Kandy had been practically force-feeding her for the previous thirty minutes, insisting that she 'eat some meat for the baby's sake,' and that no shifter could grow properly on rice and veggies. The oracle stonewalled the werewolf by simply nibbling on what she wanted and ignoring everything else. I squashed my own urge to mother Rochelle. Kandy had it more than under control. The oracle actually looked healthier than I'd ever seen her. And not just because I personally thought a touch of plumpness was becoming.

Mory was crammed next to Pulou, who was taking up the entire middle section of my well-loved leather couch. Kandy was perched on the back of the couch, her feet on the seat cushion to Pulou's right, but she gave no acknowledgement of the golden-haired vampire as she crossed behind her.

"Jasmine," I said quietly from my perch on a kitchen-island stool.

"Your grandmother kicked me out," she said, casting a concerned sideways glance at the back of Pulou's head. The guardian's gaze remained riveted to the TV.

"Kicked you out?"

Jasmine shrugged sadly. "Pearl insisted on dropping me off because she had dinner plans. She was getting annoyed by Kandy texting."

"Dinner plans? With, ah, a...date?" My mind boggled at the idea of my grandmother being involved with...anyone.

Jasmine gave me a look. "Witch thing, I think. Not a sex thing."

"Delightful, vampire. Thanks for that image."

"Heads up, baby girl." Kandy chucked a dark-brown T-shirt at Jasmine.

The golden-haired vampire caught the edge of the shirt, but still got a face full of fabric. She spread it out shoulder to shoulder in either hand, assessing what was printed across the chest in bright white. *Beware. Vampire in training.*

Jasmine sighed. "Do I have to?"

Kandy started chortling.

I jabbed my thumb toward my own chest. "Yep."

"But the T-shirts look so cute on you, dowser—"

"Stop sucking up, vampire. And put it on!" Kandy pointed emphatically toward the hallway behind and to our right.

Jasmine cast another concerned gaze at the back of Pulou's head, then slipped away down the hall. If she were planning on cloistering herself away in my bedroom until Kandy made her come out, it wouldn't have surprised me.

Pulou suddenly straightened up, tilting his head as if listening to something. Mory stole a California roll off his neglected plate—right before a portal blew open in the doorway to my second bedroom.

"What?" Kandy cried around a mouthful of food. "I thought you were staying for dancing?"

Jesus. Please, no.

Pulou chuckled, passing the rest of his food to Mory. She looked pleased, apparently too lazy to get off the couch and take the two steps to the kitchen island to refill her own plate. "Alas, no, my darling wolf." As he stood, his fur coat almost knocked over the drinks scattered across the coffee table. "You will have to make do without me."

He sauntered toward the portal, turning back to grin at Kandy. "But I understand you requested the presence of my replacement." His grin faded as he glanced across to where I was still perched on a stool near the island. "Wielder. As discussed."

"Gotcha, treasure keeper."

He narrowed his eyes at me.

I grinned.

Pulou grumbled something under his breath. Then he turned and walked through the portal.

"My God," Jasmine whispered, suddenly appearing beside me. She was shielding her eyes as she attempted to stare at the golden dragon magic. "That's … that's …"

Kandy scoffed. "That ain't nothing, baby girl. Wait until Jade drags you through one. Then you can really freak out."

Jasmine looked at me with saucer-wide, bright-blue eyes.

"I'm not going to drag you through the portal," I said.

Mory, completely nonplussed, grabbed the remote and turned the volume up on the TV. I wasn't sure when she might have seen a portal up close, let alone met a guardian … except, of course, for that time Sienna unleashed a horde of demons on the beach in Tofino. Though if that had been the case, it would have been Qiuniu who the necromancer met. And from my personal experience, there weren't any two guardians so vastly different from each other—both in power and in personal philosophy—as Pulou and the healer.

Rochelle untucked her legs from the chair she'd commandeered. She got up a little awkwardly, then crossed around the island and poured herself another glass of water.

The portal hadn't closed.

What had Pulou said? Something about a replacement.

Please don't be Suanmi. Please don't be Suanmi. "Um, Kandy?"

"Yes, oh dowser of mine?"

"You didn't invite—"

Haoxin, the petite blond guardian of North America, wandered through the portal into my living room. She was dressed in skinny-legged skintight jeans, envy-worthy high-heeled ankle boots, and a silk peasant blouse that narrowed at her upper waist to perfectly show off her curves.

The portal snapped shut behind her.

"Guardian!" Kandy crowed.

"Yes." Haoxin smiled pleasantly, taking in the room with a single glance that assessed and calculated every bit of power, exit, and edible item within it. "You were expecting me?"

The question was for me. I remembered to stand—and the fact that greeting any and all guardians formally was expected. Of course, Haoxin's and my relationship was rather complicated by the fact that I wore the prophesied item of her death around my neck. "Guardian. You are very welcome."

Jasmine slipped in behind me. Not exactly cowering, but definitely avoiding drawing attention.

Kandy yanked a heathered blue T-shirt out of her backpack. Yes, the purple dinosaur pack had made a re-appearance. My BFF held the T-shirt aloft, spinning to show off the white printing emblazoned across it. *Fueled by coffee. And epic mystical powers.*

Haoxin laughed, utterly delighted. Then she proceeded to shuck her blouse and tug the T-shirt on right in the middle of the living room. She was wearing a pretty cornflower-blue bra with white daisies on the straps.

Kandy grinned. Okay, she leered. Then she glanced over and wagged her eyebrows at Jasmine, who looked utterly affronted.

"So?" Haoxin spun to show off the T-shirt, which fit her perfectly.

"Nice," Kandy said.

"Good." The guardian brushed her hands together matter-of-factly. "Now, the treasure keeper suggested there was sushi and dancing still on the schedule? But I suppose introductions are necessary."

I opened my mouth to formally introduce Rochelle, since I wasn't quite certain of the proper ranking between the oracle, Jasmine, and Mory. But then it occurred to me that given Rochelle's relationship with the far seer, there was probably a chance that she and Haoxin had already met.

"Nah," Kandy said, saving me the trouble. "Food is getting cold. And warm."

Haoxin abruptly appeared beside me, giving me a wink as she reached for a plate on the corner of the island. "Well, we can't have that, can we?"

"No...ah, guardian." I cleared my throat, still thrown by her presence in my living room. Our last meeting hadn't been exactly friendly. "You bless us with your—"

Haoxin laughed as she dipped sushi rolls in soy sauce, then carefully arranged them on her plate. "Don't worry, Jade. I'm not here to tussle. I mean, I'm sad there aren't any cupcakes. You know, the ones you promised to woo me with. But I understand you're a little busy with getting married. And with the elves."

She popped a negitoro roll in her mouth before I could respond or pepper her with questions—questions that would likely have just rehashed the conversations she and Warner had already had about elves. And, specifically, about the elves in Vancouver. Then she pinched a pile of ginger between her chopsticks and wandered over to commandeer the center seat on the couch.

"Hello," the guardian said, addressing Mory. "Who are you then?"

"Mory. Necromancer," Mory said. Then, straightening her shoulders, she spoke more seriously. "The wielder's necromancer."

Oh, Jesus. It was catching.

Kandy leaned backward over the back of the couch and offered me one of her patented nonsmiles.

I shook my head at her.

"And what exactly are we watching?" Haoxin asked.

Mory paused the show, then proceeded to launch into a detailed explanation of the plot, characters, and everything the guardian had missed so far. Haoxin listened to every word as if she were being told something of great importance, nodding as she carefully placed a single slice of ginger on each piece of her sushi before she ate it.

My phone vibrated in my pocket. I pulled it out, reading the text message from Liam.

>*Picked up a trace at the pool. Will scan from the first break-in to the last and report back.*

I glanced over at Kandy.

My BFF shook her head at me—emphatically *no*.

I sighed, applying my thumbs to my screen keyboard.

Keep me updated.

>Definitely.

And Liam? Anything more than a trace, you back off and wait for me.

>I'm not an idiot, Jade.

I let the conversation end without ripping the sorcerer's head off. He might not have needed the reminder to avoid running blindly toward trouble, but I certainly always did. But then, I was an idiot.

Kandy was staring daggers at me. I tucked my phone back in my pocket and showed her my empty hands. Only then did she nod, satisfied.

Chapter Ten

Kandy actually insisted on blindfolding me. Though if I'd been so inclined, I could have probably figured out our location by paying attention to the minimal number of turns my werewolf BFF took to drive us to our destination. After guessing that we were either in Yaletown or Chinatown, I didn't worry about it any further.

Kandy and Mory guided me down a set of stairs, through a light brush of magic that tasted of my mother's strawberry-and-grassy witch power, and an exterior door that sounded like it was metal. Once we were through what I assumed were sound-dampening wards, I could hear music. It grew louder as my giggling captors continued leading me along a short hallway and into a room that felt large. Even without the pop song blaring over speakers strategically placed all around us, I would have guessed that we were in a club of some sort. The occasional staccato flashes of light that filtered through the blindfold simply confirmed it.

Laughing, Kandy removed the scarf she'd cinched over my eyes. My first glimpse of her, she was grinning madly as she executed a series of impressive pirouettes with her arms flung wide, spinning into and showing off the space around her. The main room of the club was windowless, suggesting that we were at least partially underground. It was also entirely black, including its slick-looking concrete floor, matte walls, and the steel beams and ductwork that crisscrossed the ceiling. Except for a few tables and chairs that had been pushed to the edges, the place was practically empty. Overhead spotlights were intermixed with typical dance-floor lighting—strobes, disco ball, and such. A low stage built out of risers—again, painted matte black—stood against the far wall between the clearly marked washroom signs.

"The place is ours for the evening," Kandy crowed. "It doesn't usually open Sunday nights, and the staff that came with the rental were easily persuaded with a little charmed cash to take the evening off. Add in a little more magic, courtesy of your mother, to keep the nonmagicals at bay. And voila!"

I grinned, probably more relieved than I should have been. But I had been more than a bit worried that we'd been heading to a strip club of some sort. Plus, the idea of being around too many vulnerable humans while being hunted by elves—ceasefire or no ceasefire—was ridiculously irresponsible. It was bad enough that Kandy and I were already dragging Mory, Rochelle, and Jasmine around with us.

We had all managed to cram into Kandy's SUV—but only barely. And I'm pretty certain Haoxin hadn't had access to a seat belt. The guardian had also produced a magnum of obscenely expensive champagne from somewhere, then was peeved when she couldn't persuade anyone else to swig it directly from the bottle. Apparently, she wasn't concerned about being pulled over for drinking and driving, even if she was in the back seat and this was a bachelorette party.

Kandy dashed forward, tugging me farther onto the dance floor and already swaying her hips to the music. The stage area was set up for a live DJ, but the music currently playing was canned. Maroon 5's *What Lovers Do* was a staple from my sparring playlist—and made me suspect that Kandy had created a mix just for the occasion, even though she claimed to loathe my taste in cheesy twenty-first-century pop.

Mory and Rochelle brushed by Kandy and me, heading over to set up camp in the grouping of tables. Jasmine hovered between us and the two younger Adepts, as if not certain whether she should follow them or stay with Kandy, Haoxin, and me. Though she was almost as skilled as her cousin Wisteria at acting unaffected, I could tell the guardian dragon in our midst unnerved the newly remade vampire.

Then, as one of the spotlights launched into an automated sweep of the dance floor, I spotted a huge cake on the right front corner of the stage. No ... not a cake. It was tier upon tier of cupcakes. I made a beeline toward it, dragging a chortling Kandy with me to examine this delectable mountain of frosting and cake.

But one step away from getting my hands on the sure-to-be delectable desserts, I stopped short.

The cupcakes were ... well ... obscenely decorated was the nice way of putting it.

"What the ..." Haoxin muttered. The guardian stepped up next to me, picking up and examining a cupcake that I would have sworn was topped with a vagina constructed out of chocolate and strawberry icing.

The ... um ... vaginal cupcake had been nestled between other samples decorated with icing-sculpted full lips, and ... well ... rosy-nippled breasts in a variety of skin tones.

The middle tier was dedicated to the male anatomy. Again, with every possible skin color represented. And on the top...actually, without a closer look and better lighting, I wasn't exactly certain what I was staring at. Toes?

I gave Kandy a look. "Dancing and obscene cupcakes?"

She shrugged. "You said no strippers."

"And...you wouldn't happen to have a thing for feet, would you?"

"Me? You're the one with the shoe obsession!"

"What are the cupcakes on the top tier supposed to be?"

Kandy glanced at the cupcakes in question. "Those are plain iced, dowser. Geez, get your mind out of the gutter."

I had no idea whether she was lying or not.

Haoxin started laughing. Then she delicately swapped out the vagina cupcake she was holding, selecting a ...well, selecting what appeared to be a mocha-iced penis instead.

I desperately attempted to avoid thinking about any male, who might also be a guardian, who might have had smooth, darkly tanned skin, and magic that tasted like coffee and chocolate...

Haoxin caught me watching her. "Do I eat the cake or the icing first?" she asked, feigning innocence while carefully peeling the paper off the cupcake.

Kandy eyed Haoxin's selection with approval. "Bryn does good work."

"You roped Bryn into this?" I cried. "While she was in the middle of opening a bakery?"

"It didn't make sense for her to join us right in the middle of the Whistler opening, but she wanted to contribute." Kandy's casual shrug was offset by her wicked grin. "What did you think was in the boxes in the back of the SUV?"

"I didn't even notice."

"I would have arranged them differently," Jasmine said, still making an obvious effort to keep me between her and Haoxin. "Mixing together lips and nips makes sense, but I would have had pricks intermingle with pussy."

Kandy sniffed dismissively. "Sure you would, vampire. But I don't mix."

Haoxin began choking on the rather large bite she'd taken of her cupcake.

Taylor Swift took over the speakers with *Look What You Made Me Do*.

My phone buzzed. I retrieved it from my back pocket, finding a text message from Liam.

>*I picked up minor trace elements at the first location. Slight enough to simply be an error reading. Second location had a definite spike. An elf likely broke in and did something magical. Still no indication of what or why. As far as I can tell they haven't returned. Heading to the third location now.*

Thank you. Keep me posted please.

"Jade," Kandy said pissily. "It's your party."

Nodding absentmindedly, I tucked my phone away. I reached for a cupcake—and then hesitated over which one to take. Normally, I'd grab whichever one had more chocolate without thinking twice about it. But I honestly wasn't completely sure how I felt about eating—

"Hello?" a deep male voice called out from what sounded like the entrance to the club behind us. I could barely hear it over the pulse of the music. "Is this the right place?"

I spun on Kandy again. "You said no strippers!"

She shrugged, grinning. Again. "I don't think you'll complain if these guys decide to take their clothing off."

The door that led to the street swung open, and Warner, Kett, Drake, and Beau invaded the room. You know, if they were actually capable of conducting a full-scale invasion while appearing to be half drunk.

Warner's gaze zeroed in on me, becoming smoldering. His hair was perfectly mussed, a slight shadow of stubble edged his jaw, and he was dressed in dark jeans and a black lightweight sweater that barely made the stretch across his broad shoulders.

Mine. All mine.

And then I was halfway across the room, in his arms and being kissed fiercely. He tasted of smoke and chocolate and … peat? Whiskey?

My dragon grabbed my arm, lifting it over my head and spinning me around so fast that the room kept moving even after he'd checked my movement with a hand on my hip.

Laughing, he threw his head back and bellowed over the music, "We're crashing your party."

"Are you drunk?"

"I most definitely am." Warner cinched me against his chest, then dragged me a couple of steps to the right. He clapped his free hand on Kett's shoulder. "The vampire has connections."

The executioner, who was clothed in his typical light-gray-cashmere-and-jeans combo, stumbled underneath the weight of the friendly blow. Not because he couldn't handle it, but because the red of his magic ringing his ice-blue eyes made me fairly certain he was completely buzzed as well. "The Isle of Islay." Kett smiled contentedly, as if he'd actually provided some sort of clarification.

Of course and as always, I had no idea what the executioner was talking about.

"I'm the designated driver," Drake abruptly announced, overcompensating in volume to be heard over the music. Then, without further explanation, he wandered toward the tables, tugging off his leather jacket to reveal a short-sleeve printed black T-shirt that he'd paired with black-washed jeans and sneakers. He greeted Mory and Rochelle boisterously. Beau, also in dark-blue jeans and a long-sleeved henley, had already settled in next to his wife, who was gazing at him adoringly.

"Driver?" I echoed, concerned. "Does Drake even know how to drive a car?"

"He does now," Warner murmured. He wrapped his hand around my waist and tugged me against him so he could sway both of us to the music. "We're here to dance, aren't we?"

"Yes, um, but ..." I glanced over at Drake worriedly. "Kandy had Bryn decorate cupcakes with genitalia."

"I'm certain they will be delicious."

"Warner!" I slapped him on the shoulder. "Stop being drunk for a moment, and listen to me. The fire breather is not going to be cool with you and Kett getting drunk with Drake, then me feeding him penis cupcakes."

Warner just blinked at me, still grinning. Clearly, he wasn't grasping the problem.

I sighed.

Beside us, Kett held out his hand toward Jasmine, who was hovering a few steps away. She practically teleported forward in order to take it. He brushed a kiss against her forehead. "All is well, my child?"

She nodded.

"Go play with the wolf, then." He pushed Jasmine gently back toward the dance floor, where Kandy was already dancing.

The golden-haired vampire grinned as she practically skipped away.

Haoxin had finished her cupcake—and had a second one decorated with a red slash of lips across chocolate icing already in hand. She sauntered toward us, pausing a couple of steps away and eyeing Kett.

A chill ran up my spine. I hadn't even thought...I mean, Kandy had arranged the guest list, and I had noticed how uncomfortable Jasmine was around Haoxin. But not until seeing her standing next to Kett did I really remember that guardian dragons and vampires didn't mix. Like, not at all.

I pushed away from Warner. He let me go, begrudgingly.

"Introductions, dowser?" the guardian demanded haughtily.

I cleared my throat. Which seemed the better choice than bodily shoving myself between her and Kett. "Haoxin, guardian of North America, please allow me to present Kettil, the executioner and elder of the Conclave, sire of Jasmine."

A slow smile curled across the petite guardian's face. "Reckless and adventurous."

"Excuse me?"

"That is my secondary title, dowser. If the executioner gets to use two, then so should I."

Yeah, I still had no idea what 'reckless and adventurous' meant in dragon speak. But knowing as much as I did about the power the guardians wielded—with each of the nine fulfilling different obligations and embodying different magic—I knew that being the guardian

representing reckless adventure couldn't be anything other than terrifying.

Haoxin slowly offered her hand, palm down, to Kett.

My vampire BFF swept forward, taking the guardian's hand and pressing a kiss to it.

"Executioner, the healer was supposed to make an appearance ..." Haoxin glanced over at Warner.

"Qiuniu was called away, guardian," he said, answering her not-quite-spoken question.

"After he joined you in deeply imbibing the sorcerers' elixir?" she asked frostily.

A large grin spread across Warner's face. "Indeed, guardian."

Haoxin sniffed, obviously excessively put out. Then she turned her attention back to Kett. "You may lead me to the dance floor, Kettil. We shall show the children how it is properly done."

Kett laughed quietly, offering his arm to Haoxin. She took his elbow. And thus entwined, they practically floated over the polished floor toward Jasmine and Kandy.

I stared after them, not completely following the sequence of events. All I could figure was that Haoxin had expected the healer, but knowing that he wasn't showing, she decided that the executioner of the Conclave was a solid substitution. Never minding that Kett was literally the complete opposite of the guardian of South America in looks and in magic.

Shaking my head, I turned to Warner. "The sorcerers' elixir?"

"Scotch. Potent, tasty scotch."

I put two and two together and came up completely pissy. "You went ... all the way to Scotland? For magical scotch?"

"Yes." He playfully slurred the word. "There was a specific process that needed to be conducted in person."

"A process? Like what? You had to pass a test to prove your worthiness?"

Warner laughed. "Well … a test of taste buds, and magical absorption."

I gave him my best not-at-all-impressed look. "You mean there was a tasting room."

"Yes. A brilliant invention of the twenty-first century."

I didn't bother disabusing him of the timeline of how long tasting rooms had been a thing. "And if we're attacked by elves while dancing?" I said instead, not completely certain why I was being all pissy and edgy … though I was definitely worried about the potential fallout of dragging the younger Adepts to a dance club filled with obscene cupcakes.

Warner brushed my curls away from my face, then lingeringly caressed around the back of my ear and down my neck. "What's wrong? What's happened?"

I shook my head. Nothing had really happened. Nothing that Kandy, Jasmine, or I hadn't already texted in our updates to Kett. But something was definitely happening, or about to happen. "Actually, I've inadvertently negotiated a sort of ceasefire with the elves. And I have a bargaining piece from the treasure keeper."

Warner grunted, acknowledging me but not wanting to interrupt. I gazed up at him for a moment, seeing the gold of his dragon magic glimmering in his eyes. I registered his relaxed body language as he let me look at him, then smiled slightly as he ran his fingers across my shoulder and down my arm.

I threaded my fingers through his, lifting up on my tiptoes so I could brush a kiss against his ear. Then I whispered, "I think…I think I just want to get on with it all."

He wrapped his hand around my waist, pulling me closer and swaying slightly to the music.

"I…I have this weird feeling …" I pressed a kiss to Warner's cheek, then brushed my lips against his, heedless of my lip gloss. "An idea hovering just out of reach …" I shook my head, unable to fully articulate what I meant. "Maybe this has just taken too long…the wedding and the elves…I don't know. I'm restless. I'm worried. I'm…worried that maybe we waited too long."

"There is no 'too long' for us, Jade. There is no rush."

"There was no reason to delay, either. But I let Gran insist on things. Properly printed invitations and napkins and…now the elves …"

"Four days," he murmured, slowly moving me closer and closer to the middle of the dance floor.

I heard the dulcet tones of Ed Sheeran, singing the incredibly danceable *The Shape of You*—and I was a goner. I was in Warner's arms and I couldn't resist dancing any longer, no matter how many things felt as though they were hanging over me, weighing me down.

Rochelle and Beau had joined Kandy and Jasmine. Haoxin and Kett were spiraling around and around the room, leaving streams of magic in their wake. The taste of peppermint intermingled with that of chocolate, bitter and sweet, and with apple, and with spicy dragon power. No one was bothering to dampen their magic. It was my bachelorette party, after all. If dancing was on the menu, then magic was as well.

Tucked into the delectable pocket of tasty energy slowly building in the center of the room, and with the strength of Warner's arms around me, I felt my shoulders finally relax.

"I don't need a ceremony to tell me I belong to you, Jade," Warner whispered against my ear.

I wrapped my hands around his neck, rocking my hips against his. He chuckled, sliding his hand up my back, then leading me in a swirling, spinning dance that was more about riding the power surging around us than matching the beat of the music. I gathered that power, all that energy freely given by my friends. I gathered it around us, luxuriating in it, greedily hoarding it in my necklace and knife, even as I channeled it into Warner's knife.

The sentinel—my sentinel—chose to appear in sweater and jeans courtesy of his chameleon magic, wanting to blend into the contemporary world. But to me, his manifested clothing only ever barely concealed the warrior in dragon leathers. I could always feel the power of the blade that he wore in the built-in sheath on his thigh. A weapon I'd inadvertently created in desperation and terror, tainted by blood magic and the death of a sorcerer. But tamed by Warner.

The songs changed. Then changed again.

We danced. And danced.

At some point, I caught a glimpse of the younger Adepts. They'd left the dance floor and gathered around the tables together. One of them, most likely Drake, had relocated the diminishing stack of cupcakes so it sat between them. Drake, Mory, and Beau appeared to be systematically mowing through the obscene desserts, laughing and shouting. Rochelle seemed content to simply oversee her companions' extreme indulgence.

Kett passed Warner a silver flask as he and Haoxin danced past us. Warner uncapped it with a flick of his thumb, offering it to me—only to have the guardian of North America snatch it back as she and Kett spun around to our other side.

I laughed, not a bit bothered by missing a sip of my own. I was riding my own magical high. I didn't need any sorcerer-fermented barley juice to feel a buzz. The room was brimming with tasty and potent dragon, vampire, shapeshifter, necromancer, and oracle magic. And I was—

An elf was standing a few feet from the entrance door, watching us. I caught sight of her just before Warner spun me away.

"Elf," I hissed.

Warner stopped dancing. The room continued to spin, tip, and swirl around me as I pivoted back toward the door, my knife already in hand.

No elf.

I scanned the room quickly, but with the floor, walls, and ceiling all in black and the random bright lights overhead, my vision was totally compromised.

"Where?" Warner whispered.

Kandy brushed against my right shoulder, still feigning that she was dancing. She had tucked Jasmine behind her. Kett and Haoxin continued to twirl blithely around us, executing the steps of some ballroom dance flawlessly. But by the set of their shoulders, they'd picked up on something. Probably me picking up on something else.

But maybe I was seeing things...

Magic shifted—just a fleeting glimmer, quickly dissipating. Then Mirage appeared a few steps away from me. She was still wearing her yellow jacket and jeans, lifting her hand to the jacket's zipper. "I thought I could—"

Warner lunged, grabbing her by the throat so swiftly that she was unable to finish her sentence. "You dare, elf!"

Choking, Mira struggled. Her eyes widened as she realized she could neither breathe nor break away. Her magic shifted across her skin, the fine scales reflecting patches of black to mimic the walls. Then they showed a warmer skin tone, presumably matching Warner's. Seeing that finally confirmed how Mira moved around so easily without being seen. It had previously only been a guess that the elves might possess a chameleonlike ability similar to Warner's, but I hadn't seen any direct evidence of that ability before.

Haoxin and Kett executed a final twist, broke apart, and came to a stop behind the elf, boxing her in. Kandy and Jasmine stood to either side of Warner and me. I could feel Drake, Beau, Mory, and Rochelle stepping up behind us.

"Warner," I whispered, touching his outstretched arm lightly.

He loosened his hold.

Mira stumbled, bending over to cough, then to wheeze. She had gotten her zipper partway down, and I could see the top of the logo on the T-shirt she wore underneath.

Baby blue with pink printing.

She was wearing a Cake in a Cup T-shirt.

I felt like a complete asshole.

I knew what it was like to be an outsider. To not know how to fit in. I'd spent three months living in the guardian nexus, and during much of that time, the only person who'd spoken to me was Drake.

"I'm sorry," Mira croaked. "I didn't mean to startle you."

Warner scoffed. "We aren't interested in your games, elf."

"No?" Mira straightened, her hand still pressed to her neck. "You looked like you were playing some game...or maybe having sex? Or, no...it's called fore-play in this world, isn't it? I just didn't know that you did it in large groups." She glanced toward the younger Adepts arrayed behind us. "Or with cupcakes."

Kandy laughed harshly, as if a moment of mirth had been pulled from her against her will.

Warner didn't take his fierce gaze off the illusionist. "Coming in here was a suicide mission."

Mira met his gaze, then flicked her eyes to me.

"We were dancing," I said, painfully aware—again—how foreign and strange everything in this dimension must seem to Mira.

"Ah, yes. A dancing game." She said it as though she'd only read the word before, not heard it out loud. "I could feel the magic." She touched the zipper of her coat again, hesitating. "But...I was wrong to approach. I've ruined your mating game."

Damn it. She'd put on the T-shirt because we all wore printed T-shirts every day in the bakery. Because she wanted to fit in...

Or because she was completely playing me.

But if that were true, it would indicate that elves were well versed in human psychology. And it just seemed unlikely that hundreds of years in a guardian prison and three months in Vancouver would have been enough time to work out the intricacies of human emotions.

"I told you dancing was a prelude to mating," Drake said, cutting through the pop-music-scored tension that had swallowed the conversation.

I had no idea who he was talking to, though. Probably me.

"Shut your yap, fledgling," Kandy muttered.

Completely ignoring the werewolf, Drake shouldered up behind me. Then he thrust his hand past me toward Mira. "I'm Drake."

She flinched, then stared at his hand.

"I've never met an elf before," Drake said, completely earnest.

Yeah, I wasn't the only one easily beguiled by pretty magic.

Haoxin sighed the sigh of the long suffering. "You have absolutely no idea what power this one wields, fledgling. Yet you offer to touch her, to shake her hand."

"She's the illusionist, isn't she? Jasmine has kept us informed by text message."

Mira's eyes had widened at Haoxin's words. She nodded as if she'd come to some understanding. Then she stepped forward, placing her hand in Drake's. "I am Mira. So named by Jade."

Kandy glanced toward me. I dipped my chin, acknowledging the assertion without taking my attention from the elf.

The illusionist released Drake's hand, then offered her hand to Warner. He didn't take it, so she dropped it to her side again, looking back to me. "I thought to join you. To play with you. Your game. Since you don't like mine." She grinned, displaying her sharp teeth.

"This is ridiculous," Warner snarled. "Her friend in the park tried to kill Kandy."

"Hey!" Kandy cried indignantly. "Maybe I would have had it under control if you hadn't butted your fat head in."

"I believe that was my neck, wolf."

I raised my hands to the sides, cutting off their bickering. "I have an offer from the treasure keeper."

Haoxin stepped to the side, clearing her sight line so she could meet my gaze directly. "Do you?"

She sounded intrigued. And I suddenly wasn't certain whether that was a good thing, given her secondary title. Plus the champagne and the so-called sorcerers' elixir she'd been drinking.

A grin slowly spread across Mira's face. She leaned slightly forward to whisper, "You know what your dancing game looks like to me, Jade?"

Despite my best intentions to be adult about the negotiations I'd promised the treasure keeper I was more than capable of undertaking, an answering smile spread across my face. "Sword fighting?"

Mira laughed, tossing her head back.

"Elves aren't known for their ability to distinguish war from peace," Warner growled. "Or friend from foe."

"No?" Mira took a step to the side, then a step back, swaying her hips to the music still pounding through the speakers overhead. "I understand dancing. Jade has taught me—"

And then Mira's hand suddenly shot to her head. She staggered, pressing against the gemstone embedded in her forehead as if it pained her. She looked over her shoulder, back toward the club entrance.

"Come with me, Jade." Some sort of stress had replaced the elf's playful tone. "Come make your offer to my liege."

She glanced back at me when I didn't immediately answer, reluctantly taking her gaze from the door. "Please."

"No." Warner and Kandy spoke in unison.

But it was Haoxin's gaze I caught over Mira's shoulder.

The illusionist's offer was most likely a trap. I could be leading everyone, my friends, into danger. I already knew the telepathic elf wasn't to be trifled with—and neither was Mira, whether she truly wished to get back home or not.

But … if we were going to blithely walk into a trap, we were stronger together. Formidable, even. Two elves—hell, even a dozen elves—couldn't get past Haoxin, Warner, Kett, Kandy, and me. In fact, I was pretty certain that Warner and Haoxin could face off against the elves just by themselves. At least as long as the sentinel wasn't trying to save Kandy's neck. The guardians had been doing just that for months, cleaning up the mess Shailaja had made when she compromised Pulou.

In response to my unvoiced question, the guardian of North America nodded. Telling me to proceed and that she would back me, all in one simple gesture.

I took a step forward, feverishly thinking about where and when to suggest we meet—

Rochelle's hand fell on my shoulder. "Jade … wait …" The oracle's tart-apple magic boiled across my back and up my neck.

Oh, God. No.

"We must go now," Mira said, taking a couple of steps back toward the entrance. "They're coming, Jade … and … and I can't stand against her."

Mira didn't have to explain who she meant. And though I was slightly concerned about her indication that multiple people—multiple elves?—were on their way, I needed to deal with one disaster at a time.

First, the oracle.

I slowly pivoted to face Rochelle, ignoring an almost desperate need to tear away from her grasp. Warner and Kandy tightened the space on either side of me, covering my back but not completely blocking me from Mira.

"Jasmine!" Kett snapped. "The music. Please."

I didn't see how or if the golden-haired vampire responded. Because all I could see were Rochelle's eyes and the white power simmering within them, spilling out over her cheeks.

The oracle reached up, placing the fingertips of each hand lightly under my eyes. "Jade," she murmured. "Something…something is pending. White mist is stretching all around you, obscuring everything else …"

"We must go now," Mira cried, taking a few more steps toward the door.

The music stopped playing. An almost-deafening silence flooded the room.

I had to force the words from my mouth. "What do you see, oracle?"

"You. Here. In this room," Rochelle whispered. "You. Jade. The beginning of the end. It's you. You are the weapon."

Jesus. But tell me something I didn't know. "I'm listening. Tell me…tell me …" Tell me what? What not to do? How the hell would Rochelle be able to process that in the moment? The vision was obviously just in the process of manifesting. That wasn't how her gift worked. "Beau?"

"She'll need to draw," Beau said gruffly. "Then we'll know…then we'll begin to understand, at least."

"No," Rochelle said, shaking her head emphatically. But it was like she couldn't further articulate whatever she was protesting.

The taste of Mira's magic splashed around the edges of the room. As I turned to see that the illusionist elf was now standing by the door to the street, I inadvertently knocked Rochelle's hands away with the quick twist of my head.

Mira wasn't alone anymore.

A dozen other elves—each at least a head higher than the six-foot-tall illusionist—stood arrayed around her. While Mira was in jacket and jeans, the newcomers were arrayed in white-shelled armor. And bristling with weapons.

"Time to play, Jade." Mira's tone had turned bright with false cheer, indicating, to me at least, that the elves showing up hadn't been her idea.

Haoxin stepped up, taking Kandy's spot beside me. "I was informed that there were three elves originally imprisoned here. And that you eliminated one, dragon slayer."

"Yes."

"Yet a dozen stand before us."

"Mira," Kandy whispered. She'd stepped back to make way for Haoxin, standing just behind my right shoulder.

I nodded, agreeing with Kandy's unvoiced observation. "I felt her magic a moment before the elves appeared."

"So," Kandy asked. "How many are real?"

"Let's find out," Warner murmured to my left. Then his sweater and jeans disappeared, replaced by dragon leathers. He unsheathed his blade. I felt its deadly, eager magic dance across the bare skin of my hand, wrist, and forearm.

Then I remembered who was standing with us. They were tucked behind the dragons and the other powerful enforcers, and more than ready to follow us into whatever battle was looming. But Mory...Rochelle...even Beau and Jasmine might not have been up for what the elves could deal out. If they weren't just an illusion.

"Is there a secondary exit?" I asked, not taking my eyes from the newcomers.

Haoxin and Warner were also diligently assessing the power of the elves, all of which remained stationary before us. As if awaiting orders—but from who, I didn't know. Not Mira. So then the telepath, Mira's so-called liege, was still hiding herself?

"Also, I need my satchel," I said. Kandy had blindfolded me before I could grab the bag from my apartment.

"There's another exit behind the stage. It leads to the alley, but it's a dead end," Kandy said. "The SUV is parked on the main street, so the front door is actually safer passage. If it's the fledglings you're worried about."

I nodded.

From behind me, Jasmine reached over my head, wordlessly settling my satchel across my shoulders. I wasn't certain where she'd gotten it, or if she'd had it the entire time. And I couldn't even blame my lack of observation on sorcerer's scotch. I wasn't even buzzed from the magic I'd been dancing in only minutes before.

"Thank you." I lifted the satchel's flap, angling my hip toward Haoxin as I lifted the broken piece of tech from the interior depths, just enough to show it to the guardian. "Shall we try to continue with negotiations first?" I met her intensely blue gaze. "At least until we get some of our companions behind wards?"

Haoxin smirked. "How will they ever learn if you coddle them, Jade?"

"This isn't their lesson, guardian. They have their own strengths and abilities. They are far too valuable to risk to a brawl."

The guardian eyed me for a moment—a moment I spent silently pleading that she understood the need for caution just as much as the need for strength. Then she nodded, taking two steps forward.

The elves keyed in on Haoxin. Otherwise, they were still as statues. Well, statues that glistened with magic and emitted a low hum of menace.

Though that last part might have just been my imagination.

"I am Haoxin." Completely contrary to her petite stature, her declaration was carried forward and around us with a heady wash of dragon power. "Guardian of North America."

The warriors swiveled their heads to look at Mira in unison. The illusionist didn't appear overly pleased to realize there was a guardian on the dance floor, but she didn't otherwise respond.

"This is my territory," Haoxin purred delightedly. "Cross blades with me and die. There will be no respite. No cushy prison. No simple banishment from this dimension." The guardian's tone turned icy, punctuating each word. "I will eviscerate each one of you."

Mira glanced at me. The warriors kept their gazes on the illusionist.

I waited. Silence stretched tautly through the room. If Haoxin wanted to take the lead, she was welcome to it. Though after that declaration of destruction, I didn't know how much actual negotiation was likely to be accomplished under her leadership.

The petite guardian nodded at me curtly.

I stepped forward, holding the broken piece of elf tech aloft. "A conversation was requested. An offer has yet to be made. Take me to the one who makes the decisions, and no one needs to die here today."

Mira smiled tightly. Then, without a word of response, her magic folded back to her and she practically melted through the ranks of the warriors. Amid the folding of the illusionist's magic, the elves funneled backward, following her out through the door. Then, as

I tracked the mossy taste of Mira's magic, I felt the elves quickly exit the building.

I glanced at Haoxin as I tucked the tech back into my satchel. "I'm not quite sure that was a yes."

She laughed. "They do like to keep their options open." Then she strode off after the elves.

Warner immediately closed the space between us, reaching up and smoothing a lock of my hair through his forefinger and middle finger without speaking. His attention was already half on the coming confrontation.

"Take care of your neck, please," I murmured, unable to let him go without at least saying something. Even though he was more than capable and had much more experience fighting elves—alongside Haoxin specifically—than any of us.

"The only one getting near me is you, Jade."

"Promise."

"Promise. Multiple times."

I grinned. And just like that, we weren't talking about him accidentally getting his neck broken again. "Well, you have been away for a couple of days."

Warner swept me forward into a fierce kiss flavored with his black-forest-cake magic. Then just as quickly, he was striding after Haoxin. His power shifted around him, triggering his chameleon abilities, and he had disappeared within the black-shrouded room before he even exited.

Shaking off the sense of dread that was threatening my ability to react rationally, I turned to the others.

Rochelle was rubbing her forehead, clearly still disorientated. But when I met her gaze questioningly, her magic had abated to a shimmer around her pale gray eyes. She shook her head, distressed. "Something is happening. But…the mist usually resolves into a clear picture and it hasn't…yet."

Okay. So all I could do was execute the first part of the plan—or what I saw as the first part, at least. "Beau, you'll get Rochelle to Gran's. Or the bakery if that's easier. Behind wards."

Kandy tossed her keys toward Beau, and the werecat caught them without effort. The green of shapeshifter magic was blazing in both their eyes.

"Our place would be better," Beau said. "Rochelle is all set up to draw there."

"It's much farther away."

"I won't risk the oracle's welfare," Beau said stiffly.

Apparently, I was stepping on all sorts of toes. And the night was still young. I nodded, then added, "Jasmine, you'll go with them."

"No." The golden-haired vampire jutted her chin out indignantly. "I'm not some fledgling—"

"Kett," I said.

"You will guard the oracle, Jasmine. She is more important than either you or I will ever be."

"Geez, old man," I groused. "Being nicer wouldn't hurt."

The executioner gave me a cool look. "Being nicer apparently means standing around chatting while the guardian and the sentinel get to have all the fun."

"Haoxin and Warner are less than twenty feet away," I said snottily. "Securing the passage for the others."

Kett raised an eyebrow at me, smirking.

I shook my head. To my side, I could feel Drake forcing himself to stand still. The fledgling guardian was waiting for orders, like a good soldier. "Drake, Mory is under your protection. You'll get her to Gran's."

"Jade ..." the necromancer started to protest.

I shook my head at her, just once. And my look was apparently beyond reproach, because Mory shut her mouth and stepped up beside Drake.

"And then?" Drake asked morosely. It was obvious he wanted to join the epic elf brawl possibly about to break out on the streets of Vancouver—and that he already knew that wasn't going to happen.

"Then, if you haven't heard from any of us within twenty-four hours, you'll get my father."

He nodded, disappointed. But I knew that he understood that keeping Mory safe was far more important. "The healer and the warrior have been called away," he said.

"They'll come if needed," I said grimly. "But we won't count on it."

I glanced at each of them in turn, trying to stress how serious the situation was without belaboring the point. Then I looked at Rochelle in particular. "Oracle … shall we proceed?"

Her eyes were still rimmed with her oracle magic, but again she just shook her head. "I'm sorry. Until there is something more to see, I can't help."

I nodded curtly, but honestly I liked it better that way, preferring to make my own choices in the moment instead of worrying about each step ahead of time. "Kandy, Kett, and I will get you to the vehicles."

I turned toward the entrance, expecting them to follow. They did.

With Kandy, Kett, Drake, and me arrayed around our more vulnerable companions, we traversed the hall and the stairs, making it onto the sidewalk without an elf sighting. Even without a blindfold, I still didn't have a solid idea of where we were in the city. Based on the direction of the parked cars, noses all facing left, we were on a one-way street, surrounded by apartment tower after apartment tower. Some were still under construction. Large cranes strung with Christmas lights, and one decked out with an actual Christmas tree, loomed overhead. The center of the sidewalk was cobblestones—but new, not reclaimed. Putting that all together, my best guess was that we were somewhere on the outskirts of Yaletown, knowing how that section of the city seemed to constantly shift and grow.

It was raining lightly. Dark. Near midnight. But the city was still brightly lit. The streets and sidewalks were thankfully empty on a Sunday night, but I could hear fairly steady traffic nearby, and I knew they wouldn't remain so indefinitely. We were close to a main thoroughfare through the city, then. One of the bridges, most likely Cambie Street.

"I'll drive," Mory hissed, thrusting her hand palm up toward Drake. They were both standing at the driver's-side door of a white BMW SUV. Kett's vehicle.

"I have the keys," Drake said, completely unruffled by the pissy necromancer, who didn't even come up to his shoulder.

I took two steps and plucked the keys from Drake's hand, gave them to Mory, and opened the door to the SUV. I shielded the necromancer—who was busy sticking her tongue out at Drake—from view of the street with my body.

Drake snorted, laughing. "I can better defend you while not driving anyway."

"Yes, you can." I shut the door while Mory was still fiddling with adjusting the seat. "Thank you, Drake."

He nodded, grinning at me easily while he jogged around to climb into the passenger seat. "You owe me a fight, dowser."

"Hopefully it won't come to that."

Kandy skulked up beside me, slipping into the back seat of the SUV as a temporary escort. She moved so quietly that Mory didn't actually see her until she reached up to adjust the rearview mirror. The werewolf earned herself a death glare from the necromancer, but if my BFF noticed, she didn't react. Then Mory pulled away from the curb, carefully navigating the narrow street as she sped away. Paid parking spots lined both sides of the street, but after 10 P.M. the meter didn't need to be plugged until morning.

Haoxin appeared beside me. Kett glanced over at her, completely unruffled, but Jasmine flinched. I could feel Warner's magic in the shadows about halfway up the block.

"The elves?" I asked Haoxin.

"Waiting for us in the alley." She gestured across the street and to our left.

In the next parallel parking spot over, Rochelle stumbled as she was climbing into the back seat of Kandy's black SUV. Twisting her ankle at the edge of the curb, she protectively pressed her hands to her belly.

And for the sickening moment that it took for me to surge forward, I thought something might have been wrong with the baby. But as Beau caught his wife's elbow and her white oracle magic flooded her eyes, I understood that the gesture was probably instinctual.

"Beau," I urged quietly. "Now. You need to go."

"No," Rochelle gasped. "Jade. Jade. Jade. It's Jade again. Mist. Endless white mist, trapping her, holding her. But I can't see! Something is going to happen. But I can't see it. I can't see it."

Jasmine snatched the keys from Beau, stepping forward and climbing into the driver's seat. Beau gathered Rochelle in his arms, attempting to load her into the SUV even as she struggled against him.

Struggling to reach me?

I closed the space between us.

Rochelle's fingers brushed my cheek. Her eyes cleared of her oracle magic. And for a moment, she just looked at me, blinking in confusion.

"Tell me what you see, oracle." It was my name Rochelle kept repeating. And I told myself I could handle anything that might happen to me. Just…

I just couldn't handle losing anyone else.

Rochelle shook her head. "I'm sorry. I can't see you clearly, but…I feel…you feel …" The white of her oracle magic flooded her eyes, and she arched upward in Beau's arms, breaking contact with me.

"Beau?" I asked, uneasy.

"It'll come," the werecat said calmly. "Things will resolve, and then Rochelle will be able to draw."

But given Rochelle's confusion, I was fairly certain that I didn't have time to wait around for the vision, aka my pending future, to resolve into whatever shape it was going to take.

"Beware of the stones, Jade," Rochelle whispered tensely. "The gemstone."

Fear coiled in my belly—triggered by the terror laced through the normally placid oracle's tone.

"I hear you," I said, keeping calm. "I remember the sketch. Text me if you get anything more."

"I will," Beau said, climbing into the SUV with his wife in his arms.

"No!" Rochelle cried. "This isn't that."

Kett slipped around and into the front passenger seat of the SUV, shutting the door behind him in the same motion. "Go, Jasmine."

The vehicle lurched into motion. I stepped back, closing the back passenger door and watching as Jasmine drove off.

In the back seat, Rochelle twisted out of Beau's grasp and began pounding at the side window. I could see more than hear her screaming my name. As the SUV sped off, the oracle was pressed to the glass, her magic streaming from her eyes, her mouth hanging open in terror.

Kandy appeared at the far corner of the street, jogging back from wherever she'd jumped out of the SUV carrying Mory and Drake. Presumably before they'd crossed the Cambie Street bridge.

The SUV driven by Jasmine turned the corner, taking the oracle from my sight. I stood on the sidewalk, chilled to the bone.

"And if she's seen something relevant?" Haoxin asked. Her tone was level, nonjudgemental. But I heard it as chastising anyway.

"I won't risk her, or the others, because Pulou chose to imprison elves here without letting anyone know. And then, when he was compromised, he didn't even bother to mention there might be ramifications."

"The ramifications of almost being killed, you mean. By the centipedes that you now hold."

I turned to Haoxin. She was easily four inches shorter than me and much, much tinier. But she could seriously kick my ass. Still. Even despite the weapons that decorated my neck. But now wasn't the time for that conversation. "I'm not going to attack you, Haoxin. I'm not going to use the instruments. In fact, I was the one who saved Pulou from that assassination attempt."

Haoxin regarded me dispassionately. "You are perhaps the only one who could have saved him, dragon slayer. But one day you might decide differently."

"Yeah? Well, today I'm living in the now. Today I'm protecting those who matter, like in the present. Not in some farfetched future in which you envision me going insane, killing all the guardians, and stealing all their magic."

"Problem?" Kandy asked in a soft, only slightly threatening growl.

Haoxin's gaze flicked to the green-haired werewolf standing at my shoulder. Then she glanced down, possibly to the cuffs Kandy wore. "No problem, wolf. The dowser was simply telling me how it is...in her present. While I was simply reminding her that the centuries of knowledge that a guardian carries, along with the choices he or she makes...choices that are the best they can be in the time of their occurrence...cannot be assessed by today's ramifications."

"Well, that's totally clear. Eh, dowser?" Kandy asked mockingly.

"Yeah. As mud." I tore my gaze from Haoxin's. There were elves to deal with, after all. "All dragons take their lessons from Chi Wen seriously."

The petite guardian snorted. But she let the subject drop.

And yeah, maybe she was right, and benching Rochelle had been a mistake. But I would rather die in the now than see the oracle or her child harmed in the near future. And if that was too shortsighted for a guardian, she could deal with the damn elves on her own.

I opened my mouth to say as much. But then I decided my time was better spent texting Gran than bandying words with a dragon who was at least a century older than me. Kandy had presumably updated everyone who needed to be updated, but I wanted to make sure. I tugged my phone out of my pocket.

And only then did I realize that I'd missed a series of text messages while dancing. All from Liam.

>*Something is going on at BC Place. Elf magic, maybe dormant? At a series of spots around the perimeter. No sighting of actual elves. And I have no idea what the magic means or does.*

>*Jade?*

>*Jade?*

Against the noise and the movement in the club, I hadn't even felt the phone buzz.

Sorry. I'm here. Are you still at BC Place?

"Liam?" Kandy asked.

"Yes." I shifted the phone forward so she and Haoxin could read the texts at the same time.

The guardian swiped her finger lightly across my screen, reading the thread from the beginning. "BC Place? A stadium, yes?"

"Yep." Kandy pointed slightly to our right. "At the edge of False Creek, right beside Rogers Arena."

"Ah, yes. I remember."

Kett stepped out of the shadows a few feet away. "I escorted the vehicle over the bridge. Jasmine will text when they're behind wards. Beau is insisting on going all the way into Southlands."

"Thank you." My phone buzzed.

All four of us leaned in to read the message from Liam.

>*I'm still here. What do you want me to do?*

"Where the freaking hell are we?" I asked Kandy.

"Abbott. Closer to Hastings than Pender."

"Abbott ..." Seriously, I'd lived in Vancouver my entire life and I still didn't know exactly where the hell we were. "Gastown?"

"Very edge."

"How close are we to BC Place?"

She pointed up and slightly to our right again. "About three city blocks, the way the crow flies."

I nodded, texting.

Stay close, but don't enter the building. Don't draw attention. Do you have your gun?

>*Of course.*

"Gun?" Haoxin asked.

"Sorcerer," Kandy said, as if that would cover the actually quite complex answer to that question. But Haoxin nodded thoughtfully, so maybe it did.

We're near. But so are the elves. Possibly dozens of them.

>*Okay.*

The simple acceptance in Liam's response chilled me. I didn't like how everything was lining up...the game playing, the tests, whatever the elves were doing around BC Place, the oracle's frantic visions. I had done something wrong, taken some wrong step these last few days. Either that or I was about to do something terrible. Terrible enough to make an oracle scream my name.

"Please," I murmured. "Please God, don't...let me get anyone killed."

Kandy pressed against my shoulder, silent but supportive.

I returned my attention to texting Liam. I wanted to tell him to go home, to hide behind the wards on his parents' house. Except he wasn't some fledgling that I could force protection on. He was valuable as backup and a player the elves hadn't engaged yet.

Hole up. Kandy will find you when it's okay to move. Don't shoot her.

I angled my phone toward Kandy. She nodded.

>*And the elves?*

I paused again briefly, desperately trying to piece together all the pieces of the puzzle. But I had no idea of what the big picture was going to turn out to be.

If they come at you, shoot to kill. Through the gemstones on their foreheads.

>*Okay.*

I tucked my phone in my satchel rather than my pocket. Less chance of it getting broken that way. I glanced up and down the sidewalk. Haoxin had lifted her face to the mist, seeming perfectly content to wait for me to get my shit sorted out. I could feel Warner in the deep shadows across the street, presumably making certain that the elves stayed where the guardian said they were gathered.

"Listen," I whispered to my two best friends. "If something happens to me—"

"Jade," Kandy growled. Kett was silent.

"Please." I could still see Rochelle pressed against the SUV window and screaming my name in my mind's eye. "You know we're walking into some sort of trap."

"Even a dozen elves have no chance against us," Kett said coolly.

"Listen to me." My tone was harsher, shakier than I'd intended. "Please."

Kett wrapped his fingers around my wrist. His cool touch grounded me.

"We three have done this dance before ..." My voice cracked. "My life isn't more important than yours."

Kandy hissed harshly.

I continued, needing to just get out what I had to say. "If I'm going to fall…if that is what the oracle sees…and someone else can be saved. You save them."

"Absolutely not," Kett said.

"The oracle—"

"I couldn't care less what Rochelle sees for you, Jade. If I allowed my choices to be dictated by others, I'd have succumbed to oblivion centuries ago." And with that pronouncement, the executioner of the Conclave released my wrist. Turning his back on me stiffly, he crossed to stand by Haoxin.

I looked at Kandy, raising my voice so Kett could still hear me. "I'm not explaining myself very well. I can't stop whatever the oracle sees, not even if she managed to fully articulate the vision. I can't stop fate. I can't fight destiny."

Kandy shrugged nonchalantly, walking backward toward Kett. "No one thinks you can, dowser. But it's our territory to defend, isn't it? Our choices to make. Not just yours. What will be, will be."

Then the green-haired werewolf turned her back on me as well, leaving me alone on the wet sidewalk while she joined Kett and Haoxin.

I took a shuddering breath, wrapping one hand around my necklace and one hand around the hilt of my knife. I allowed the magic that resided in both to settle me. I closed my eyes and let my power curl out and around me, released from the confines of the artifacts so I could call upon it in an instant.

The taste of Warner's black-forest-cake magic was pulled into the mix, filling my senses and tickling my taste buds.

I opened my eyes.

My soon-to-be husband was standing before me, resplendent in dragon leathers, and with the gold of his magic flecked through his fierce blue-green gaze.

I grinned at him. Regardless of my attempt to be an adult and make adult choices, I couldn't deny the anticipation of the fight waiting for us around the corner. At some point, caution always got flung to the side. The pieces would be picked up and mended in the aftermath. That was how things always unfolded. That was how it always ended.

"Ready to kick some ass, my love?"

"Always."

He chuckled. And together, we followed Haoxin across the street and into the mouth of the alley.

Chapter Eleven

The elves were waiting for us in the alley, as Haoxin had said they would be. The warriors were once again arrayed around Mira. I could taste her illusion magic stretching across the width of the alley and up the exterior walls of the towering apartment buildings on either side. But unless Kandy was right about the warriors being the fabrication—a show of force and nothing more—I couldn't see what other reality the illusionist was possibly projecting. Unless she was hiding something else.

I stood about twenty-five feet back from the group of elves, with Haoxin on my left, Warner on my right, and Kandy and Kett tucked up behind us.

"How drunk are you two?"

Warner shrugged. "Drunk enough to make it interesting."

"Nothing like a buzz to get you through that whole not-my-usual-type thing, eh, sentinel?" Kandy laughed. "Been there, done that."

Kett chuckled darkly.

Delightful. The oracle had me quaking in my pretty boots while everyone else was cracking wise. But then, it was my name she'd been shouting, not theirs.

"Beware of the stones," I murmured, reminding myself of the one clear warning Rochelle had been able to offer up. It was something she'd already warned me about, in the sketch from three months before. The charcoal drawing of me holding one of the gemstones that were embedded in each of the elves' foreheads. I still had no idea what the vision foretold. Unless it somehow connected to the other warning that had been issued to me earlier that night...

I turned to Haoxin, casting my voice as low as possible. "Pulou warned me not to try to fix the elf tech. That even if I managed to figure out how it was broken, the operation of it would kill me. It had injured the former warrior when he disabled it. Enough that he was...that the damage never healed properly."

Haoxin met my eye, then nodded curtly.

With everyone informed of all the meager info I had to offer, I stepped slightly forward, drawing the attention of all the elves. I raised my left hand, vaguely stretching my arm in the direction of the bakery. Though I still wasn't completely sure where we were in the city, I could feel the magic of my wards in the distance. I called for my katana. Magic whispered through the rain, which had increased from misting to sprinkling.

The weapon, still sheathed, appeared in my hand. I still hadn't tested my range outside Vancouver. But yeah, since absorbing Shailaja's magic, I could now call forth any and all artifacts tied to me by blood, even through confinement wards not of my own making. That power was seemingly some combination of my own alchemy abilities and the capacity to open or manipulate portal magic that had belonged to the treasure keeper's daughter.

A delighted grin spread across Mira's face, and she bobbed on the balls of her feet lightly with anticipation.

A disconcerted murmur ran through the warriors who backed her.

"I request an audience with your liege." I addressed myself to Mira, but scanned each of the warrior elves in turn, trying to be stern but most likely managing only to project pissiness. I didn't mind the rain in general, but standing around in it while waiting for destiny to catch up with me was seriously annoying.

Yeah, my attention span was so short that I could stay terrified of what Rochelle had seen coming for only so long.

Mira dipped her chin formally. "I will take you to her." By the illusionist's grin, I assumed she'd shaken off whatever had been worrying her on the dance floor. So clearly, I wasn't the only one who preferred to live in the moment.

"We will follow," I said. Then, though it pained me to do so, I offered my katana to Haoxin.

The guardian laughed. But then instead of taking my blade, she reached up over her left shoulder and unsheathed one of her own, seemingly out of thin air. Her guardian magic shimmered across her back. She wore an invisible sheath—its magic so harmonious with her own that I'd missed it completely. Even when she'd practically done a strip tease earlier to put on her T-shirt. That was some useful sleight of hand.

So it wasn't just the elves' magic that could foil my dowser senses. Annoying, but good to know.

"Do you think I'd dance with the executioner of the Conclave unarmed, dragon slayer?" Haoxin said.

Kett chuckled from behind my shoulder.

She flashed him a saucy grin.

Though the guardian was easily four inches shorter than me, her katana was that much longer than mine. Haoxin casually tossed her weapon from her left hand to her right, then back again. Guardian magic splashed across the alley, expanding and contracting in a way I'd never felt before. Which reminded me—yet again—that I still had no idea what Haoxin's specific guardian ability was.

But I was fairly certain I was about to find out.

Twisting my satchel so that it hung forward, I settled my katana over my back, leaving it sheathed for the moment. I preferred to fight with my knife, and would really get only one good draw of the sword with it over my back. But wearing the katana at my hip in combination with the knife and the satchel was awkward. Glancing to my right, I offered Warner a smile.

He grinned back, completely at ease.

But that wasn't particularly odd. Even if they were all real, a dozen elves were no match for the five of us. I had a feeling Haoxin could probably have quelled this miniature uprising by herself, if I'd been inclined to walk away from the fight.

And I certainly wasn't.

I called my jade knife into my right hand, holding it slightly behind me and offering it silently to Kett.

He laughed again—the sound full of anticipation. "My hands will be just fine. Thank you, Jade."

Now it was Haoxin's turn to chuckle delightedly.

What was wrong with all of us? Each more eager than the rest to test our strength? To challenge our mortality? I was supposed to be negotiating a peaceful resolution, but we were all certain it would come to a brawl. Including the treasure keeper, who didn't think I was capable of being diplomatic in the first place.

I really wouldn't have minded proving him wrong.

Problem was, being diplomatic just might not have been in my nature anymore.

Mira pivoted, turning back into the huddle of the warriors. More magic churned around her, rippling out and lapping the edges of the alley.

I moved, giving chase. The others surged forward with me as one dreadful force. The pavement under our feet trembled in the wake of our combined power.

The warriors spun away, chasing after Mira.

Seemingly fleeing before us.

But even I knew this was just part of whatever trap they were about to spring. And still I ran for it. Gleefully. Eagerly.

As I stepped into the tunnel of illusionist magic and still saw nothing but the alley and the buildings around us, I realized that Mira must have been masking herself and the elves from the buildings above. Which meant that she would likely provide cover for the five of us, as long as we were close enough to her.

Well, that was a bonus. Because Gran would have been seriously peeved otherwise that we had thrown down with elves in the streets of Vancouver without distraction and barrier spells in place.

I ran, knowing that those with me could match me stride for stride. Knowing that for a brief while, I didn't have to worry about pulling punches or being nice.

At the intersection of the next street—West Pender, perhaps?—the warrior elves on the far right and left of the group ahead of us peeled off in either direction.

"Kandy," I barked, taking command without even thinking about it. "Kett."

Warner, Haoxin, and I crossed the three lanes plus bike lane in a half-dozen strides. Kandy veered right, and Kett winged off to the left, both pursuing the elves who'd split off from the main group. I was fairly certain that if they'd wanted to go after Mory or Rochelle, they would have done so already. But whatever the elves had planned, Kandy and Kett would certainly show them the error of their ways. I trusted in that. I had to trust that my BFFs could hold their own.

Still maintaining about a twenty-foot lead and with Mira in the middle, the elves leaped over the cars parked at the far curb without touching down.

Haoxin, Warner, and I followed. My landing was the only one to make any sound on the rain-slick sidewalk.

The elves zigzagged through a series of short side alleys, avoiding the main streets. They obviously knew this section of the city far better than I did. But then, they had been plotting and planning whatever game they were playing for three months.

Three elves broke off to our right, leaving the rest of the group and Mira running ahead.

Warner cursed under his breath, then veered after the three, getting close enough to skewer the straggler in the back with his knife. Magic rippled, tasting faintly of bark.

And in the moment before I turned the opposite corner with Haoxin at my side, I saw Warner slash through that magic a second time. The elf disappeared. I had created the blade Warner wielded to cut through any magic, and apparently that included elven illusions manifested by Mira.

Kandy had been right. Not all the warrior elves were real. So perhaps Mira was the only one we were really pursuing. Which meant that drawing the others away was just another attempt to get me on my own.

I cut the corner, losing sight of Warner.

A hulking elf, easily topping seven feet tall, appeared before me. With no warning, he smashed a kick directly to my chest. I flew back, crashing into and badly denting an industrial-sized garbage bin.

The elf disappeared a second before Haoxin's blade would have taken off his head.

"Teleporter!" The guardian laughed, completely delighted as she whirled back to check on me.

I blinked up at the clouded night sky, trying to absorb some of the pain radiating across my chest. The buildings to either side of us were under construction. Concrete floors and steel beams slowly came into sharper focus. The alley otherwise appeared empty.

I rolled up, literally peeling myself out of the crushed metal of the bin. Crouched over my hands and feet, I paused to cough up blood. My heart felt as if it had been punctured by every one of my shattered ribs. My necklace felt as though it had been embedded in me. But there was no way I'd be trying to get to my feet under those circumstances. Right? Right?

"Dragon slayer?"

"I'm fine."

The hulking elf appeared again, attempting to decapitate Haoxin. And she...moved...somehow...without moving her feet. Maybe it was just a super quick shift of her shoulders and I'd missed it...

The elf avoided Haoxin's return blow, disappearing then reappearing a few feet away and slightly to the right.

I staggered to my feet. My ribs crunched and shifted. The elf had a monster of a kick—and he most certainly wasn't an illusion. Which clearly raised the question of where the hell the other elves had come from. I didn't think Pulou had lied. No matter how much of an asshole he was, protecting the world from such things was his primary function. But somehow, the treasure keeper had a bigger elf problem than even he knew.

Haoxin and the teleporter traded a few more blows. The length of time between strikes and the elf appearing and disappearing was getting shorter and shorter. Haoxin was steadily closing in on him, perhaps assessing and learning his attack patterns. Branson, the dragon sword master who had trained me, was always going on about such things, about analyzing your opponent's footwork...

Wait...was Haoxin...taller? And moving in an odd, almost boneless way ...?

I shook my head. I must have cracked it pretty seriously, though most of the damage felt contained to my chest.

The elf miscalculated. Apparently thinking I was still too injured, he appeared closer to me than to Haoxin. I lunged forward, calling my knife into my hand in the same motion—then stabbed him in the back. My blade slid through his white-shell armor without resistance.

But instead of him simply spinning to knock me away, the warrior's pine-scented magic flooded across the knife, the hilt, and my hand. For a long moment, I had to struggle to keep hold of my weapon.

He was trying to teleport. And to take my blade and my freaking hand with him.

I slammed a kick to the back of his knee. He fell forward, and I yanked my knife free.

The elf disappeared.

"Well," I said, still holding my ribs with my left arm. "The teleporter appears to be real."

Haoxin cried out, laughing. "You may fight by my side any time or place, dragon slayer!"

Then she took off ahead of me down the street.

Right.

Back to the running.

The elf's blood on my blade solidified, then began to flake off.

God, I really did hate the running.

I lost track of Haoxin, but my ribs mostly healed, leaving just a residual ache that would hopefully ease further as I moved. Once I realized I wasn't going to catch up to the guardian—and began to worry that she'd darted off in another direction after the teleporter—I paused, stepping back under the wide eaves of a dark restaurant on the corner of two one-way streets.

Momentarily shielded from the rain, I reached out with my dowser senses, immediately catching a taste of Warner's black-forest-cake magic to indicate he was just a couple of blocks behind me. I caught only a fleeting hint of Haoxin's smoky-tomato-and-basil dragon magic, but since all the guardians could mask their power, I wasn't surprised.

Kandy's bittersweet chocolate was farther away. Maybe stationary to the south? I really needed to train just using my senses, having been focused on wielding the instruments for almost two years. I could easily pick up Kett's cool peppermint heading steadily my way.

Then, so dim that it could have been a memory, I caught Mira's moss-and-bark illusionist magic. I stepped back out into the rain the second I tasted it, just in case it faded as abruptly as I'd picked it up.

My phone buzzed in my satchel, forestalling my dashing off into the night. Which might have been a good thing, actually. My chest really was still killing me.

I was afraid to look at my necklace, because it still felt as though the sharp edges of the instruments of assassination—the centipedes, specifically—might have been lodged in my breastbone.

I tucked back against the building again, not interested in turning any more corners while distracted. Usually it took a few attempts for me to learn a lesson, but apparently getting kicked in the chest once by a teleporter was enough for that one to lock in.

The text was from Kandy.

>*The misfits are behind wards. Beau took Rochelle home. Mory is at Pearl's.*

And Liam? Are you near BC Place?

>*No. Opposite direction.*

Okay, so I was seriously turned around. The buildings in and around Yaletown seemed to appear out of nowhere, practically springing up and reshaping the streets of the area daily. If I could taste Kandy's magic behind me—moving toward me again—then that put me only a block away from BC Place and Liam myself.

>*Want me to find VPD?*

No. What happened to your elf?

>*Either he was an illusion or he got away.*

I'm near Mira, but have lost Haoxin. Find me?

>*Will do.*

Oh. And one of the damn elves can teleport.

>*Bring it, baby.*

I laughed under my breath, then had to pause to press a hand to my aching ribs. And as I did, an out-of-place shadow shifted over top of the metal housing of the exterior light at my right shoulder.

"Hey, Freddie," I murmured, keeping my gaze on the street. A car drove past slowly, looking for parking. "Anything to report?"

The shadow leech settled its wings down its back, regarding me with slitted red eyes. Then it chittered. Rather loudly.

I gave Freddie a look. The leech appeared in as solid a form as I'd ever seen it, talons tipping its wings, rounded mouth full of needle-like teeth. But I could taste only its regular crispy-cinnamon-toast magic, so I didn't think it had been feeding on anything it shouldn't have been. At least not in volume.

"Something has you riled up," I murmured. "Is it me?"

Freddie's shadowed magical aura compressed inward, solidifying the leech's body further. It shuddered, its scales lifting and rolling.

I felt pretty sure that was a no.

"Want to come with me, Freddie? You never know, I might find you something tasty to eat."

The shadow leech stretched forward, practically oozing through the empty air between us. I reached out to it, offering it my hand. Becoming more shadow than solid form, it balled into my palm, then slithered up my arm onto my shoulder. Tiny claws pinched my T-shirt. Kandy would be seriously peeved if they left holes in the fabric.

"Don't poop on me, leech."

Freddie chittered quietly, but I could hear the indignant inflection.

"Don't tell me you don't poop." I tucked my phone into my satchel, readjusting it and my katana in preparation for more damn running. "I've seen what you eat. Magical toots."

Man, I cracked myself up. Though apparently, the demon on my shoulder wasn't amused.

Stepping around the corner in the direction I'd tasted Mira's magic, I took a moment to scan the immediate area. I could see the towering white pylons of BC Place between buildings, about two blocks away. Whenever I thought of the stadium, I usually pictured its old Teflon dome—despite it having been deflated and replaced with a retractable roof about seven years before. Seriously, I needed to patrol this part of the city more often.

Sensing a hint of Mira's magic shimmering between buildings up ahead, I started to jog. Freddie's claws momentarily tightened on my shoulder, but the leech managed to hang on without issue.

As I ran, I felt the overwhelming sense that the entire area I was in might have been completely new. White steel and tinted windows soared above me. A huge building ahead of me and a half block over stood out above the others surrounding it. Even in the dark, it appeared to be constructed out of copper panels, windows and all.

Glancing right, I passed a tiny neat square of a park. One of the green spaces that seemed to appear with each new building. I was pretty sure that adding outdoor spaces, and even small playgrounds, was a city requirement for developers now. The street was lined with parked cars but empty of other traffic. Many of the apartments overhead were brightly lit, though.

I could still feel Warner's tasty magic, maybe a block to my right now.

I paused at the edge of the illusion I'd spotted. The space between the buildings appeared empty. But I reached out, coaxing the illusionist magic into my hand and tearing it away from the white steel and glass. The space rippled, then seemed to fold in on itself.

Mira and another elf appeared, standing in the middle of a paved roundabout. Even in the dark, its asphalt appeared so new that it might never have been driven over before. The elves appeared posed, as if they'd been waiting for me to tear through the illusion.

The new elf was dramatically thin. Almost emaciated—by my standards, at least. Her hair and skin were paler than Mira's. She stood maybe an inch taller, arrayed in the same flexible armor that the warriors had been wearing, as well as a dark-green cloak that was so ridiculously long it pooled around her booted feet.

Not a warrior, then. Unless the cloak was an illusion, it would completely hinder any attempt on her part to engage in a fight and have any chance of winning.

Mira and the cloaked elf were backed by a huge, startlingly shiny chrome bear. For a moment, I thought it was some sort of magical construct. Then I saw a baby chrome bear and a gray cobblestone surround half hidden behind Mira, and I realized it was a statue. Presumably one of the many the city made an effort to commission and display.

The copper-sided building loomed to the elves' right. The white steel behemoth rose to their left. But the area was dark. It felt empty, so new that it hadn't been occupied yet. The building to my far right was still under construction. No wonder I was turned around.

I stepped between the buildings and onto the paved roundabout, closing the space between myself and the elves. I had to force myself to swallow a sarcastic crack about the cloak. I was the joker with the demon on my shoulder, after all. Plus, I was supposed to be trying to negotiate—even if getting kicked in the chest had really put a dampener on my eagerness to chat.

I couldn't get a read on Mira's expression. Stoic, maybe.

Metal, teeming with foreign magic, edged the cloaked elf's gemstone, radiating out of it and curling into her hairline…like a crown. It was just a guess. But had I gotten an actual taste of it, I would have bet that the metal framing the elf's gemstone—maybe even holding it in place—was the same metal that the throne and the dais had been constructed of in the first illusion Mira had shown me.

"You didn't say she was a mute idiot," the cloaked elf said with a sneer. Her English was heavily accented, especially on the word that followed 'idiot.' It was something I couldn't quite catch the sound of. Mira's Elvish name, or her title, perhaps.

Mira's shoulders stiffened, but she didn't respond. But as I contemplated her expression again—similar to the stoic readiness the warriors had displayed in the dance club—I wondered for a moment if she actually could respond.

"I'm not the interloper here," I said, keeping calm. But just barely. The cloaked elf seriously gave me the creeps. "It's you who should have formally announced your presence and stated your business."

The elf—Mira's so-called liege—laughed. Or at least I thought it was a laugh.

A chill ran up my spine. Feeling out of place and therefore slightly lost—surrounded by concrete and steel and glass, devoid of life or magic—I instinctively reached out with my dowser senses. I sought the comforting, grounding magic of my companions. Warner was still about a block away, near Haoxin. Kett was close as well, though in the opposite direction.

Freddie chittered, aggressively fluffing its wings on my shoulder. The cloaked elf frowned, her gaze flicking all around me. She could apparently hear but not see Freddie. I remembered, though, that the elf in the park had at least felt it when the shadow leech attacked him, so perhaps Freddie was only shielded because it was perched on my shoulder. Similar to the way I could carry the instruments of assassination around my neck without anyone being the wiser.

I smiled. Apparently two could play the let's-rattle-each-other-until-one-of-us-pulls-a knife game.

"The name I have chosen for myself is Regina," the cloaked elf announced haughtily. "It comes from your region's dictionary."

Ah, Jesus. Regina. And she chose it herself. Paired with the freaking cloak and the crown, it was ripe, ripe material. But I wasn't going to laugh. Or make fun of her. I was there to negotiate. Apparently, I just had to keep reminding myself of that.

"I am Jade Godfrey. I'm authorized to negotiate with you on behalf of the treasure keeper."

"Negotiate?" Regina raised her chin, regarding me disdainfully. As if I were garbage, actually.

I quashed the impulse to slap the look off her face.

And in that breath, that opening, she tried to grab hold of me with her magic. The damp and woodsy power pulsed across me, besieging the center of my forehead with what felt like a hailstorm of jagged rocks. The taste of saltwater and decomposing wood flooded my mouth.

Freddie's magic contracted, and the leech disappeared.

I slashed through the thundering magic with my knife, easily severing the connection the elf was attempting to establish.

Regina stumbled.

Mira gasped.

It had just been half a step. But even as I ignored my need to spit the taste of salt from my mouth, I couldn't help but smirk. "Underestimating me is a bad idea," I said evenly. "Had you asked, I would have suggested skipping the part of the conversation where you test me."

"I see," Regina said, agreeably enough. "Yes." She glanced over at Mira. "As you said."

"My liege," the illusionist elf murmured.

A shadow shifted around the ear of the larger of the chrome bears. Freddie. The shadow leech was lining up directly behind the prey who had just revealed herself to be fair game by attacking me. Oh, for the luxury of having my priorities so clearly laid out.

"The others have returned," Regina announced, speaking to no one in particular.

For a split second, I assumed that she meant my others, my friends. But when I reached out for Warner's, Kandy's, and Kett's magic, I could feel that they were closer to each other—but not any nearer to me.

Three elves appeared behind Mira—two wounded warriors half carried over the shoulders of the hulking teleporter, who stumbled as he released his companions. All three looked more than a little battered around the edges. One of the wounded was missing whole hunks of his armor, and bore a number of raw, seeping claw marks across his throat. The armor of the second elf was marred with dozens of slash marks, likely from a knife. It was an easy guess that the teleporter's timely rescue was the only reason the other two warrior elves had survived whoever they'd faced off against. Kett and Warner, based on their wounds. The teleporter, I had stabbed myself.

Anger flitted across Regina's face, but she quickly quashed the emotion.

"Were you expecting more?" I asked, hazarding another guess. "And for them to be…less worse for wear?"

No one answered me.

"All righty, then." I fished the piece of elf tech out of my satchel.

Regina instantly zeroed in on the artifact, taking a half step forward before she checked herself.

I flipped the tech up into the air, showing it off. But it still felt like just a deadened hunk of metal to me. No magic, no pretty residual. "Let's get on with these so-called negotiations. Get the formalities out of the way, before you refuse to leave and I have to kick your ass."

"Yes," Regina said. "I understand Mira wishes to leave. That she asked you to convince us to return to our dimension."

Mira glanced at her liege, her expression showing sudden concern. Maybe even confusion.

The other three elves spaced themselves evenly behind Regina. The teleporter was standing close enough that I knew he'd be able to lay a hand on his liege's shoulder and disappear almost in the same instant. His picking up the wounded warriors suggested that he could teleport just as effectively with someone else as he could on his own.

"What's your other choice?" I asked. "To die here? On foreign soil? Your magic is so incompatible with this dimension that it turns to a fine crystal and simply dissipates in the wind. You will come to nothing here. Be nothing."

The warriors looked a little disconcerted at this information. Apparently, it was news to them.

"This piece is broken," I said, holding up the elf tech. I wanted to be as truthful as possible. "But if you agree to meet with the treasure keeper, we will find a way to get you home."

Regina laughed, sending more creepy vibes my way. "My allies brought me a present when they answered my call to gather. Having watched you and the witches bumbling around blindly for months, it was clear that your conquest would be easy. And through you comes the key to keeping the guardians at bay. Such ripe territory makes for ... straightforward alliances. And a gladly bended knee." She glanced imperiously over her shoulder toward the teleporter.

He nodded, though he didn't seem terribly pleased about it.

"They brought me this little treat to cement our relationship." She reached into her cloak, pulling out a piece of elf tech that she must have tied to the back of her armor.

It appeared to be the other half of the dimensional portal Pulou had entrusted to me. My stomach churned at the sight, but I ignored my reaction. The tech in Regina's hand was just another hunk of broken metal.

"So I shall simply take that piece from you. Then I will force you to fix the dimensional gate, bringing forth my full army. Once we lay claim to this land, our magic will supplant all others. And then it will be you who crumbles into nothing. You are a skilled alchemist, aren't you?"

"Right." I tucked the piece of tech back into my satchel, then drew my katana from its sheath with a smooth motion. "Little problem with that plan, Reggie." I snapped my teeth on the impromptu nickname, grinning.

Anger flickered across the elf's face as she spoke haughtily. "And what is that?"

I didn't bother answering. Not with words, anyway. I simply lunged forward, slamming a kick to the knee of the first elf who tried to block me from getting to Reggie. Already injured, he went down easily.

Before he'd even hit the ground, I was moving forward, jumping up into a downward slash primed to take Reggie's head.

She and the teleporter disappeared. But not before I saw a look of confusion cross her face.

Yeah, I moved quickly.

I'd told her not to underestimate me, hadn't I?

Fix her dimensional gate, and unleash her elvish army into Vancouver? Please.

Mira met my blade with a crystal sword she'd manifested on the fly. I sliced through it easily. She cried out, stumbling back and hunkering down next to the chrome bear as if I'd severed her arm.

Freddie got into the brawl with gusto. The leech appeared and plastered itself to the elves in unpredictable fashion, then disappeared before they could react to it siphoning their magic.

The third warrior was suddenly in my face. He was too close to engage with my katana, so I dropped the sword even as I called my jade knife into my hand.

The elf twisted away, stepping just out of my reach. My knife sliced through his armor instead of skewering him in the heart, and the severed section crumbled into a fine white powder. Armor made from blood? Well, that was new.

Before I could press my advantage, Mira pushed off the belly of the chrome bear and dove toward me.

Thinking she was going for my legs, I danced out of the way.

But she flew past me, intent on reaching my katana.

"Don't!" I cried.

Too late. Mira closed her hand around the hilt of my sword, rolling forward onto her feet and spinning back to face me triumphantly. Then the magic embedded in the blade, which couldn't be held by anyone but me, seared her hand. She stifled a scream as she dropped the weapon.

The third elf made another attempt to grab me.

Not knife me.

Grab me.

I slammed the heel of my hand up underneath his chin. He stumbled back and I took out his good leg. Bone crunched. He fell. Freddie was on him before he hit the pavement.

The elves were trying to…hold me? Kidnap me? That was a stupid, stupid idea. How the hell did they think they could keep me confined?

I cast a glance over at the two fallen warrior elves, neither of whom seemed inclined to engage me further. Not yet, anyway. Leaving them to Freddie's not-so-delightful ministrations, I stalked over to Mira. Pulling my sheath off over my shoulder, I retrieved my katana, sheathing it but keeping the weapon in my left hand.

The illusionist was kneeling, holding her badly burned hand but looking up at me steadily. She twisted her lips. "I should have known."

"What?" I asked, holding my hand out to her. "That the blade would burn you?"

She hesitated for a second. Then she accepted my hand, allowing me to help her onto her feet. "No, that—"

Regina and the teleporter suddenly appeared right behind the illusionist.

I pulled my jade knife, reaching to knock Mira away.

A pale knife appeared through her chest, skewering her from behind.

Mira gasped. Her arms fell slack. She swayed forward.

I grabbed for her shoulders, trying to hold her upright. But Regina twisted, then withdrew the blade with a sharp yank.

Mira listed backward with the motion. Thick white blood bubbled at the edges of her lips.

"My liege ..." Mira whispered. "Please, please. I'm ... loyal ..."

"I know. You've given everything you could. You cannot give any more than I have already required of you."

Mira stumbled, falling between us.

One of the downed warriors moaned. A low, almost inaudible sound of pain.

But I had eyes only for Reggie. She smirked at me, retribution and satisfaction etched across her face.

"It's not always about who is physically the strongest, alchemist," she said.

"Yeah," I said, slashing my knife toward her throat. "I've already learned that particular lesson, asshole. Endurance wins every time."

But the roundabout was empty.

Either the teleporter could move people without touching them, or ...

Magic rippled across the pavement underneath my feet, turning it to black sand. The sound of a pounding surf rose behind me. As I pivoted, I saw a deep purple sea lit by two moons.

Mira was at my feet, lying on her back but gazing out at the water.

I knelt beside the illusionist.

"Mira." I touched her shoulder lightly. "I'm sorry. But I need to see ..."

"I'm dying," she whispered.

A sharp pinpoint of pain exploded in my chest. I tried to push the feeling away. I didn't know Mira well enough to mourn her, to get caught up in this moment and let it distract me. I had a city to protect. People to protect, who did matter to me. Except...

"You promised me something, Jade," Mira whispered.

I had. Almost flippantly, I had made her a promise.

"Revenge." I touched her shoulder again. "If I couldn't get you home."

She turned her head, painfully slowly, to look at me. Her eyes were a glassy, milky green. "Tell me again... how my brother died. We came here, born to serve. Born to survive ..." Her hand twitched. She was trying to run her fingers through the black sand she'd manifested. "But it doesn't feel right here... the magic doesn't ..." She lapsed into a lyrical language full of vowel sounds that I couldn't understand.

I didn't know what she was trying to say. I didn't know what she wanted to hear from me. I wiped my cheek, realizing only then that despite my resolve, I was crying. I should have been tearing through the illusion and carving Reggie's heart out. But I was afraid that if I destroyed Mira's last bit of magic, I would kill her.

She touched her chin to the back of the hand I was still resting on her shoulder. "Tell me of my brother, please. And I will pretend it is him holding me here for this moment. In our favorite place ..."

Desperately trying to figure out what she wanted, I tried to remember as much as I could about the elf I had casually murdered in the park three months before. "He was tall ..."

"Yes," she murmured.

"And strong. And quick. Brave to have stayed behind to protect you, despite being injured." I paused, thinking through the conversation and the blows I'd traded with Mira's brother. "Sharp tongued."

Mira shuddered, sighing. But I was fairly certain she was trying to laugh.

"He didn't cry out. Not even allowing himself a single moment of pain."

"He died well."

"Yes … his magic tasted of the air a moment before a storm hits, paired with cedar and sap."

She whispered something that I thought might have been a name. Her brother's name.

Then the cushion of the black sand underneath my knees turned to hard pavement, and the sound of the surf faded away.

Rain joined the tears on my cheeks.

The illusion fell away.

Mira was dead.

Reggie was crouched on the other side of the illusionist, her head bowed and her gaze on the dead elf between us. The roundabout was otherwise empty. The warriors were out of sight—presumably having headed out to try to hold off my companions. But I didn't need help to deal with an elf who didn't know any better than to wear a cloak that dragged around her ankles.

"I'm not a murderer," I said. "But if you have a version of hell in your world, if it's even accessible from here, I'm going to enjoy carving out your heart and sending you there."

Reggie met my gaze. Then she nodded. "We shall see."

Her magic hit me full force, a torrent of power that instantly began to suffocate me. And in the moment it took for me to fight through that magic, trying to thunder and rage its way through my skin and into my bones, Reggie reached down.

She ripped the gemstone out of Mira's forehead.

She pressed it against my own.

Lightning lashed through me, burying its roots deep within my brain. I screamed as I tried to wrench away from Reggie's hold. She climbed on top of me, pinning my arms even as the hurricane of her magic streamed through the gemstone cutting into my skin.

Driven by the onslaught, the thunderstorm, the gem burrowed into my forehead.

A shadow appeared before me. Freddie was attacking Reggie, latching onto her face. She tore him off with her free hand, somehow managing to pin him to the ground with a crystal knife only inches from my face.

I screamed, but in frustration. Using the sharp focus the anger brought me, I reached out with my alchemy and wrenched the knife out of Freddie. The blade exploded into a fine crystal powder.

"Go, Freddie," I cried, getting my feet underneath me in an attempt to buck Reggie off my chest. "To Mory. Take care of Mory."

The shadow leech disappeared.

I turned my full attention to Reggie, reaching out with my unleashed alchemy and trying to take hold of her magic even as she tried to invade my mind. My power battered against hers, as hers battered against mine. But I was the stronger—

Rough hands yanked my legs straight, pinning each to the ground. I couldn't move. I couldn't physically shake Reggie off me.

The telepath began to mutter, chanting. And with each utterance, another tendril of magic was coaxed from the gemstone, then painstakingly anchored in my brain. Another. Another.

I tried to counter the magic with my own, tried to close off the pathways being carved through my mind, but I would shut down one only to miss two others. My sense of self, my sense of my magic, my abilities, began to wane … swallowed … supplanted …

Unable to bear the pain any longer, my mind shut down. It closed itself off, taking my consciousness with it.

Chapter Twelve

*C*old...rain sprinkled my cheeks...my neck...my aching forehead.

I opened my sore, dry eyes, looking up at a dark, cloudy sky through sticky eyelashes. I was lying on hard pavement. I could feel the smooth edge of a concrete curb underneath the fingers of my left hand. I tried to lick the raindrops off my lips, but my tongue felt as though it were glued into my mouth.

A tall, pale woman stood over me. She bared sharp, pointed teeth. "Rise and do your duty."

I opened my mouth to answer... but then ... I didn't speak. *Couldn't speak?*

"Rise," the woman hissed. No. The elf...she was an elf.

A hurricane swept through my mind, thundering a wave of pain through my skull, my neck, down through my limbs. I arched up, twisted away, trying to get away from the pounding pressure. Words were torn from my throat.

"Yes...my...liege ..."

The pain abated. Achingly. Slowly.

Panting and shaking, I found my feet. But unable to stand, I crouched by my lady's side. She touched my head. Another command ran through me. Unspoken this time. Telling me to heel.

I stayed where I was. I did what I was told. I didn't want to invite the hurricane back.

The pavement was wet with rain. A huge shiny steel bear and a cub were at my back. More elves stood arrayed to either side. Their blood armor was a smear of white against the darkness surrounding them ... me ... us. But they were hurt, favoring wounds.

One elf was dead. Lying only a few feet away. Her ... magic ... was crumbling. Falling into tiny flakes to be washed away by the rain ... minuscule flakes of ... nothing.

My chest felt heavy at this sight, then tight. I bowed my head so I didn't have to see the pretty elf crumble. I pressed my palms to the ground, spreading my fingers. Something red dripped onto the back of my hand, mixing with the rain, sliding across my skin ...

Was I bleeding? From my forehead? And why didn't my skin glow, as the others' did?

The lingering pain in my head was distracting. I didn't want to try to think.

Footsteps approached.

Four separate sets. Magic rumbled underneath my hands. The energy traveling through the pavement was different for each of the newcomers. There was something I was supposed to know about the power approaching. But I still couldn't quite ... figure out what it was—

My liege brushed her fingers against my head, as if checking that I was there, that I was ready. Ah, the newcomers were enemies of my lady.

I looked up. My wet hair was tangled around my face, obscuring my vision.

The newcomers had paused about a dozen feet away.

At the center forefront stood a tiny blond woman. She was the most dangerous. Though what I based that assessment on, I didn't know. Instinct. And the long blade that brimmed with power in her left hand.

At the woman's side stood a tall, broad-shouldered, dark-blond male. He was staring at me, not deferentially at my liege as he should have been. He held a knife that teemed with power, urging me ... *to do what?*

To the right, but slightly behind the first two, stood a green-haired woman wearing thick golden cuffs that brimmed with magic. And a pale-faced, pale-blond man, who held no weapons of power.

All four of the strangers stared at me.

Shocked. Concerned. Fearful.

Why?

"Jade?" the green-haired woman whispered, pushing her way in front of the other three.

My lady laughed.

The sound scurried down the back of my neck and through my limbs. I shuddered to rid myself of the feeling, pressing my hands to the pavement on which I was crouched. The asphalt cracked. I'd pressed too hard.

"Not anymore," my liege crowed.

Energy—epic amounts of power—boiled around the four strangers. I could practically feel the thickening of the air between and around us.

No. That was magic. Their magic unleashed. And it didn't ... hurt, didn't try to hold me at bay or command me. That was important ... there was something important about that feeling.

"Dragon slayer," my lady said, tapping me sharply on the head. "I need them alive."

"What have you done?" the broad-shouldered male snarled.

"Take them."

The hurricane rampaged through my mind. Again. It spurred me forward, it demanded … obedience …

No.

Forced. It forced my obedience.

I lunged, knowing that the pain would abate once I fulfilled the command.

One of the weapons held on the chain around my neck gleefully desired the utter destruction of the tiny but dangerous blond, so I let it loose with a flick of my wrist. It spun toward her with a flash of silver.

Dashing forward on the rain-slick pavement, I slammed my fist up underneath the green-haired woman's chin. Knocking her out of the fight before she'd even seen me move.

Avoiding an arcing blow coming from my left, I spun away, reaching up and pulling the necklace I wore over my head off in the same motion. I snapped the chain out to its full length as I turned to face the broad-shouldered man. With the side of my hand, I knocked away the knife he held raised against me. Then I stepped closer, lassoing him with the chain.

The tiny blond fell, cracking the pavement in a wide radius all around her. The centipede I'd unleashed upon her writhed across her chest and up toward her neck.

The green-haired woman flew backward, slamming against the concrete foundations of the building to the left. Then she tumbled, falling insensible to the ground.

The male I held fast with the necklace struggled against my hold, attempting to speak even as I choked him. The skin of his neck reddened. His hands were burning as he tried to rip the chain from his neck. He fell to his knees. I tugged him back against me, holding him fast.

The pale, weaponless blond watched his companions fall without reacting, without taking his gaze from me. His eyes were bright red.

"I said alive," my liege said.

A tornado backing her command flashed through my mind. I immediately loosened my grip on the chain, returning it to my neck. The broad-shouldered man collapsed forward, making no attempt to break his fall.

Stepping over him, I retrieved the centipede, returning it to my necklace before it could enter the tiny blond's brain through her ear. She moaned but didn't otherwise move.

Calling my sword to me, I stalked toward the pale man. A vampire, I now saw.

He didn't move, simply continuing to regard me. Again, if he carried a weapon, I couldn't sense it. But I could see his magic glistening in every cell of his body, and I knew without any doubt that the best thing I had to counter him was my katana. My sword was a murderer, a slayer. Like me.

But that wasn't what my lady had commanded. She wanted, she needed, the newcomers alive for some reason.

It was difficult to speak, to form words. But I didn't know how else to communicate, to explain why I would dare to hesitate to fulfill her commands. "This one I would have to kill to subdue."

"No matter," my liege said.

The other elves shifted around us, circling back behind the vampire, then fanning out. But the pretty elf still lay on the wet ground only a few feet from me. She was almost half washed away. I tried to angle my head so I couldn't see her, but in order to still keep my attention on the vampire, I couldn't turn far enough.

Five elves in blood armor loosely circled the vampire. Three appeared badly wounded. Their skin was as pale as his, but tinted green. I glanced down at the hand I had wrapped around the hilt of my sword. My skin wasn't as pale as either of them.

Wasn't I an elf?

The vampire closed his eyes, though he didn't appear to be in pain. "Jasmine," he said. He wasn't speaking to the elves ... or to me. "Jasmine. Heed me now."

Power was laced through his words. But it wasn't directed toward me or my liege, so I didn't feel the need to react.

A golden-haired woman, another vampire to judge by her magic, stumbled out from behind the building I'd thrown the green-haired woman against. She moved jerkily, as if she'd been pulled forth by his command.

As I was commanded by my liege?

As I was controlled?

"Go to Pearl," the vampire said, speaking to the woman he controlled without looking away from me. "Pearl must know that Jade has been compromised. Watch over the others. Go now." The power in those last two words practically knocked the second vampire back. She stumbled away.

"Take her," my lady said, but the command wasn't for me.

An elf warrior slipped by us, pursuing the golden-haired vampire. His departure lowered the elves' number to four plus my liege ... though why that was important, I wasn't certain. I hoped the female vampire was swift on her feet. Though why I would care about that, I also didn't know.

"She answers to you," I said, addressing the vampire. "The golden-haired one, who you called Jasmine."

"Yes," he said. "She is mine. As I am yours."

Then he knelt before me, placing his hands on his head.

Confused, I raised my sword. I didn't understand why he would kneel to embrace death. But I was ready to deal that death on my lady's command.

"Take him," my lady said. Again, the magic in her words wasn't for me.

Two of the elves behind the vampire surged forward, grabbing his arms. I sheathed my sword, turning back to my liege's side.

The vampire threw off his captors without apparent effort, lunging forward to grab me. Pressing his hands to either side of my face, he pulled me toward him.

I expected him to snap my neck.

I expected him to kill me.

But I didn't call forth the knife strapped to my thigh, though I could feel it urging me to protect myself.

Because I welcomed death. Welcomed the reprieve to the relentless storm that threatened to consume my mind and control my very soul.

He kissed me.

His hold was impossibly hard, yet his lips were soft against mine. Cool magic slipped through the tempest simmering in my mind. His magic. He wielded some sort of telepathy, like my liege. But he wasn't trying to hurt me or command me.

He was trying to dampen the hurricane, to quell the tornado.

I parted my lips, breathing him in …

He tasted of peppermint.

And freedom.

"Remember, my love," he whispered. "Remember who you are."

An elf wrapped his arm around the vampire's neck, while two others got a hold on his arms and shoulders, yanking him away from me.

The vampire let me go, but the elves were struggling to drag him away. He was too strong for them to easily subdue.

I wasn't an elf.

I wasn't a vampire.

"Then...who am I?" I whispered, brushing my fingers against my lips and feeling his magic lingering there. The storm in my mind had eased, but it wasn't fully dispersed.

"Jade ..."

I could hear the truth twined into the magic he wielded. Power that allowed him access to my mind...and maybe my heart?

"Jade Godfrey."

Jade Godfrey.

Yes.

I was Jade.

And Jade didn't heel or heed...anyone.

I whirled around. Another elf shouldered past me, piling on to subdue the vampire...

Kett.

The vampire's name was Kett.

And Kett could deal with the elves.

I had only one thing I needed to do.

Already calling my jade blade into my hand, I lunged for my liege.

No.

Her name was Reggie.

She tried to block my strike, but she wasn't anywhere near fast or strong enough. I drove my knife home, hoping that her elf's heart was situated in the same place mine was.

She gasped. But instead of fighting me off, she grabbed the back of my neck with one hand and slammed the palm of her other hand to my forehead. She drove her magic and the power of the gemstone farther back into my brain.

"Stop," she commanded.

I twisted the knife, fighting the pain streaming through my head. I tried to pull back my hand, to deal another blow.

Reggie's breathing was labored, greenish white spittle forming on the edges of her lips. "Heed me, dragon slayer."

Then I couldn't move my arm any further.

I couldn't speak.

I screamed but made no sound.

"Step back," the elf said, coughing up blood.

She held me fast with the power of her mind, but she couldn't actually make me move. I could still taste Kett's peppermint magic. I clung to that taste…to the feeling of belonging…

Reggie snarled viciously. She pressed her hand to her chest, next to where the blade of my knife penetrated, coating her fingers in her own blood. She smeared that blood across my forehead, across the gemstone. The magic carried within it bit into my skin, further cementing the stone—then shooting multiple strands of magic back into my brain at once.

A squall rose in my mind. A tidal wave. It crashed down, thundering against the cool pockets of reason I was trying to protect. The peppermint magic was washed away. All that existed was a hurricane of raging, demanding power.

My liege's power. My liege's will.

My grip on my knife loosened.

"Step. Back." My liege's command forced my compliance.

I stepped back, taking my knife with me.

My liege stumbled forward, using my shoulders to hold herself upright. I allowed my weapon to fall. But instead of hitting the ground, it settled automatically into the sheath strapped to my thigh.

Crystal blades scissored around my neck from behind. "Shall I dispatch her, my liege?" an elf asked.

"No," my lady said. She pressed a hand to a wound in her chest. "I still have need of her. We have need of her."

The elf removed the blades from my neck. Reluctantly, he stepped away, moving to where the others were bending over the foes I'd vanquished.

I could see the yellow sleeve of the jacket the pretty elf had been wearing. It was damp with rain and... empty. Her magic had departed this world.

One of the elves hissed harshly. A blade she had tried to pick up clattered to the ground.

"Collect the weapons from the fallen," my liege said, commanding me once more.

I didn't move. I didn't want to move. I stared at the empty yellow sleeve...

My liege coughed. Then she coughed some more, spraying blood into the palm of her hand. It was almost the same color as her skin. She stepped up to me, pressing fingers slick with that sticky, thick blood to the gemstone in my forehead. "Collect the weapons."

Lightning strikes of agony backed her command. I turned and did her bidding. The pain abated to an ever-churning surf in my mind.

The vampire had fallen to the other elves. But he was without weapons, so I paid him no heed. The sword of the blond I slung over my shoulder, alongside my own.

"I'll have to cut off her hands," an elf said, drawing my attention. He was standing by the green-haired woman. His blade was set next to the golden cuffs she wore.

My liege waved her hand dismissively. "No matter. She is the least powerful among them. We can do without her."

"No!" I cried.

My liege narrowed her eyes at me. She was hunched over, favoring the wound in her chest.

"I...I can remove the cuffs," I said. Not certain why maiming, potentially killing the green-haired woman grieved me.

My liege nodded curtly.

The hulking elf stepped away. He snarled quietly as I passed by him to kneel by the unconscious woman. I had to use my magic to coax the gold cuffs from her wrists. Once removed, I placed them in my bag.

I stood, crossing to and bending over the broad-shouldered man. His chest was rising and falling steadily, and the burns on his neck were already healing. I took his blade, but then paused. The magic of the weapon danced in my grip.

His magic? Or...

Wasn't his magic supposed to taste like...something...

My liege shifted into my line of vision, watching me. The other elves were picking up the fallen, who I'd divested of weapons. They were having trouble lifting the tiny blond.

I glanced down at the blade in my hand again. It felt as though it might also belong to me. But why would the broad-shouldered man be wielding my weapon?

I looked at his face. Was it familiar? Perhaps I'd fought him before. Perhaps he'd taken the weapon from me?

I shook my head, unable to answer the riddle. I tucked the blade into my bag.

My liege was speaking, but not English. Or perhaps she hadn't been speaking English at all? I lifted my hand, brushing my fingers against the gemstone in my forehead. Pain ricocheted through my skull, but not like the earlier hurricane…

This felt like a wound. An open wound.

I glanced at the other elves. The gemstones in their foreheads looked… natural.

"She's going to fix the dimensional gate." My liege was speaking to the tall, hulking elf who'd wanted to slit my throat and cut off the woman's hands. "And when those who are ours have walked through, then you may have her head."

They turned to look at me. I remained crouched by the broad-shouldered man, watching them.

"Hand your weapons to the traveler, dragon slayer," my liege said. "Then you will carry this one." She nudged the tiny blond with the toe of her foot.

I straightened, looking her in the eye. "Hand over my weapons?"

My liege looked concerned for a moment. Perhaps I shouldn't have questioned her orders, but I didn't hand over my weapons to anyone. Did I? I was, after all, the wielder of—

"No matter," my liege said, backing her words with a forceful push of magic. "Take the guardian. You may deposit the weapons in the cache if that makes you feel easier."

I nodded, stepping over and lifting the extraordinarily heavy blond over my shoulder. The hulking elf—the traveler—bared his teeth at me, crossing back to lift the broad-shouldered man. He couldn't get him fully off the ground.

I laughed. Then I followed my liege past the chrome bear and between the buildings.

No one retrieved the yellow jacket the pretty elf had worn. I felt bad about leaving it behind, but I didn't get to decide these things.

A dark-haired man was watching me from a niche in the rounded wall of the stadium. The place my liege had selected as her command center. I wasn't certain why she called it that, but the tiny blond was heavy, and I was just so…weary. So I followed her and didn't ask any questions.

I could feel the man's magic. But it was nothing compared to the power of those the elves carried, so he was no threat to them…to me…to us. He was just a man. A lone sorcerer.

He raised and pointed a weapon that glistened with his magic at me. Targeting me specifically. With some sort of…gun. The gesture should have felt threatening. But the weapon could not harm me. How I knew that to be true, I wasn't certain.

I shifted the burden on my shoulder, not bothering to alert the other elves to the man's presence. Together, the elves and I crossed through the large doors of the huge stadium. Traveler barked out a word I didn't understand, and magic slammed shut behind us, sealing the doors.

I turned, looking for the dark-haired man through the glassed entranceway. A thick wall of magic stood between us now. He lowered his gun, looking ... dismayed? Concerned? Terrified?

Then he turned and ran away, swallowed by the dark night.

That was good. A good choice.

He was safer away from the elves.

Though ... wasn't I an elf?

Why wouldn't he have been safe from me?

I stood staring through the crystalline bars that secured the tiny window. A city sprawled out beyond the magic that coated the walls, the windows and bars. A neatly made cot stood to my right, with an empty built-in bookcase beyond that. Tightly woven beige berber carpet ran underneath my feet.

It was deep into the evening. I was supposed to be sleeping. I'd been ordered to sleep on the cot in the tiny magically fortified office. Hours ago. After I'd begun to fumble and drop minuscule but important pieces of metal, accidentally cracking one of the gems that adorned the machine. But I wasn't the only one who'd needed to rest, whose magic had been drained. So much so that I'd begun to feel ... her ... her thoughts, then her concern about the feedback moving through the connection we shared.

The connection that had been forced upon me?

The window was too small for me to escape through.

Though if that was the case, it was odd that it was also barred.

I reached for my knife, but it wasn't on my hip.

Didn't I have a knife that could cut through magic?

But if I did...why would I need it? Why would I need to fit through the window at all?

Movement. Outside. A flash of red, drawing my attention to street level. A girl wearing a bright red poncho was staring up at the building.

No. She was young, tiny. But not a girl.

I frowned, pain spreading across my forehead. I was still wounded there, still healing. But from what injury, I couldn't remember.

I squinted. The young woman was carrying something. Something small...something domed-shaped, with four legs. An animal of some sort? I couldn't make it out in the dark.

She shouldn't have been standing out in the open, exposed. But some part of me...warmed at seeing her there.

Didn't I know her?

I raised my hand, waving.

The young woman looked away, talking to someone over her shoulder. She gestured with the animal she held. *A turtle?* People didn't usually carry turtles around, did they? That felt like a fact I should know.

I dropped my hand back to my side. The young woman couldn't see me. She couldn't see me through the magic that encased the building. Maybe no one could.

No one but me. I saw through magic.

A dark-haired man stepped up behind her. The sorcerer from outside the stadium. With the gun. He drew her back into the shadows of the building across the street.

I was glad that she had someone to protect her. But I felt...bereft at losing sight of her. As if without her, I had no idea who I was or what I was doing.

I reached up, wrapping my hands around the bars. Magic seared into my skin, but I held fast. Then I started to pull. The thick crystal creaked, shifted.

I could pull these bars off the window. I could rip through the magic. Then the young woman in the red poncho who'd been looking up at the building—*looking for me?*—would be able to see me.

I could escape.

Heavy-duty locks clanked and clicked behind me. The magic that sealed the door to the hall shifted. The door opened.

"Come," a pale-skinned elf in white blood armor said behind me. "Our liege says it is time for you to go back to work."

I turned and looked at him.

He took a step back into the hall. His hand was raised, ready to trigger the magic that sealed the door.

Scared of me?

Good.

Good? Why would that be good?

I tore my hands away from the bars. Some of my skin stayed behind. I glanced down at my palms and fingers. They were burned. Badly.

I didn't much feel like going wherever the elf wanted me to go. Or doing whatever it was that I was supposed to do. I hadn't felt like sleeping either, though that was what I'd been ordered to do right before the door had been closed and locked behind me.

I didn't want to go, but I didn't want to stay.

What was it that I wanted, then?

My hands healed as I watched. Dark-red burns easing into deep pink, fading into a lighter—

The elf left, locking the door again with magic and metal.

Time passed.

I might have slept, standing there looking down at my hands. My skin was the wrong color. Pink, and not finely scaled like the elves' skin. That was an important thought, an important distinction. There was a reason for the differences between me and the elves...

Magic shifted again. My liege appeared in the doorway. "It's time for you to complete your work, dragon slayer. To open our path."

She looked tired, withered...weak.

Wounded.

"I don't think so...Reggie."

Magic crashed into me, but I could hold it at bay. I could hold it, even counter it with my own magic, my natural resistance...

Everywhere but through the gemstone embedded in my forehead.

I, too, was wounded.

I tried to raise my hand, to cover the spot that was vulnerable to the elf's psychic assault, but the hurricane rose in my mind. The storm of her magic battered my resolve. Pain streaked through every nerve ending, every cell of my body.

Despite the agony, I clung fiercely to the idea of...the idea of...the young woman in the bright-red knit poncho...looking for me. I was needed...I was necessary...I was...I was...

My liege pressed her fingers to my forehead. She was snarling something, intoning a spell...a curse...but the words didn't matter. Magic drilled deeper into my brain, blowing through my resistance.

I didn't want to upset my lady. She shouldn't have been angry. All I wanted to do was to please her. I'd go wherever she wanted. I would do whatever she asked.

I fell to my knees before her.

I wanted to kneel.

I wanted to obey her.

Didn't I?

Acknowledgements

With thanks to:

My story & line editor
Scott Fitzgerald Gray

My proofreader
Pauline Nolet

My beta readers
Terry Daigle, Angela Flannery, Gael Fleming,
Desi Hartzel, and Heather Lewis.

**For their continual encouragement,
feedback, & general advice**
SFWA
The Office
The Retreat

For the Vancouver weather update:
Karen Lam & Kelly Sarmiento

For the clothespin game
Amanda Shackelford Elliott

For the paper-and-ribbon bouquet idea
Vicky Deeble

For naming *Chill in a Cup*
Erin Wilson

For naming *Tingle in a Cup*
Linda Randall

Meghan Ciana Doidge is an award-winning writer based out of Salt Spring Island, British Columbia, Canada. She has a penchant for bloody love stories, superheroes, and the supernatural. She also has a thing for chocolate, potatoes, and cashmere yarn.

Novels
After the Virus
Spirit Binder
Time Walker
Cupcakes, Trinkets, and Other Deadly Magic (Dowser 1)
Trinkets, Treasures, and Other Bloody Magic (Dowser 2)
Treasures, Demons, and Other Black Magic (Dowser 3)
I See Me (Oracle 1)
Shadows, Maps, and Other Ancient Magic (Dowser 4)
Maps, Artifacts, and Other Arcane Magic (Dowser 5)
I See You (Oracle 2)
Artifacts, Dragons, and Other Lethal Magic (Dowser 6)
I See Us (Oracle 3)
Catching Echoes (Reconstructionist 1)
Tangled Echoes (Reconstructionist 2)
Unleashing Echoes (Reconstructionist 3)
Champagne, Misfits, and Other Shady Magic (Dowser 7)
Misfits, Gemstones, and Other Shattered Magic (Dowser 8)

Novellas/Shorts
Love Lies Bleeding
The Graveyard Kiss (Reconstructionist 0.5)
Dawn Bytes (Reconstructionist 1.5)
An Uncut Key (Reconstructionist 2.5)

For recipes, giveaways, news, and glimpses of upcoming stories, please connect with Meghan on her:

Personal blog, www.madebymeghan.ca
Twitter, @mcdoidge
Facebook, Meghan Ciana Doidge
Email, info@madebymeghan.ca

Please also consider leaving an honest review at your point of sale outlet.

DOWSER SERIES • BOOK 1

CUPCAKES,
TRINKETS,
and other
DEADLY MAGIC

MEGHAN CIANA DOIDGE

DOWSER SERIES • BOOK 2

TRINKETS,
TREASURES,
and other
BLOODY MAGIC

MEGHAN CIANA DOIDGE

DOWSER SERIES • BOOK 3

TREASURES,
DEMONS,
and other
BLACK MAGIC

MEGHAN CIANA DOIDGE

DOWSER SERIES • BOOK 4

SHADOWS,
MAPS,
and other
ANCIENT MAGIC

MEGHAN CIANA DOIDGE

DOWSER SERIES • BOOK 5

MAPS,
ARTIFACTS,
and other
ARCANE MAGIC

MEGHAN CIANA DOIDGE

DOWSER SERIES • BOOK 6

ARTIFACTS,
DRAGONS,
and other
LETHAL MAGIC

MEGHAN CIANA DOIDGE

ORACLE SERIES • BOOK 1

I SEE ME

MEGHAN CIANA DOIDGE

ORACLE SERIES • BOOK 2

I SEE YOU

MEGHAN CIANA DOIDGE

ORACLE SERIES • BOOK 3

I SEE US

MEGHAN CIANA DOIDGE

RECONSTRUCTIONIST SERIES • BOOK 1

Catching
Echoes

MEGHAN CIANA DOIDGE

RECONSTRUCTIONIST SERIES • BOOK 2

Tangled
Echoes

MEGHAN CIANA DOIDGE

RECONSTRUCTIONIST SERIES • BOOK 3

Unleashing
Echoes

MEGHAN CIANA DOIDGE

9 781927 850770